The Fantasies of
Josep

CW00435260

Also by Josephine Scott:

Time of Her Life

The Fantasies of Josephine Scott

Stories of Submission

Josephine Scott

First published in 1993 by
Nexus
332 Ladbroke Grove
London W10 5AH
All stories and novellas except *Freezeframe*
copyright © Josephine Scott

Reprinted 1994

Freezeframe © *Cul d'Or*

All stories and novellas first appeared in *Janus*, *New Janus* or *Derrière*, except: *With Friends Like That*, *Trial By Jury* and *On Course at Cornfield* first appeared in *Fessée*; *Freezeframe* first appeared in *Cul d'Or*

Typeset by TW Typesetting, Plymouth, Devon
Printed and bound in Great Britain by
Cox & Wyman Ltd, Reading, Berkshire

ISBN 0 352 32889 4

This book is sold subject to the condition that it shall not, by way of trade or otherwise, be lent, resold, hired out or otherwise circulated without the publisher's prior written consent in any form of binding or cover other than that in which it is published and without a similar condition including this condition being imposed on the subsequent purchaser

This book is a work of fiction.
In real life, make sure you practise safe sex.

This book is a work of fiction.
In real life, make sure you practise safe sex.

Contents

Foreplay   1

Stories

1 Fantasy   3
2 You Chose the Punishment   7
3 The Editor's Decision Is Final   13
4 Editorial Comment   19
5 Initiation   25
6 Being Prepared   45
7 Party Games   47
8 With Friends Like That . . .   51
9 Fire and Ice   59
10 World's Greatest Lover   69
11 A Note for Benny   87
12 Reminiscences   97
13 Teacher's Pet   107
14 Dommie   117
15 Girl Talk   133
16 Trial by Jury   143
17 The Master   159

Novellas

18 On Course at Cornfield   171
19 Freezeframe   209

Afterglow   237

Contents

Foreplay

These stories have seen the light over the years in many different CP magazines under different names. This is the first time they have been brought together in one volume for the delectation of my readers. Here is your chance to read stories you may have missed and rediscover stories you read a while ago.

There are going to be people who, having also read my Comment columns in various magazines, will say I have betrayed my own principles, having said that women should not be shown getting punished and growing to like it. I would remind those who think that way that when I began this type of writing it was the only type of story to be found and, consequently, the only type of story I could sell. At a time when making money was as essential as honing writing skills, I went along with it.

I have started the collection with such stories, and moved on to show women actively seeking out the discipline they need. Some stories straddle the boundary line ('Fire and Ice' is one), and then they do become the sort of stories I would prefer to read now.

In effect these stories show the slow development of an SM writer from early fantasy writing, through real experiences, to the confident submissive/slave I am now. They also reflect the changes in SM writing generally. My intention is to present a wide variety of stories catering for all tastes, from the 'vengeance' lovers through to those who like women to be proudly independent yet submissive. I've touched on the school scenario in one of the novellas, but kept it to adults, as my views on the school scene are well known!

As nine out of ten erotica readers are male, I dedicate this book to all of you who believe a woman's place is under your thumb and who think that all indiscretions should be met with swift and painful retribution. These stories were written for you and are really for you. I hope you enjoy them.

Josephine Scott

1

Fantasy

As a weaver of words, a teller of tales, a fabricator of fantasies, I fabricated the following fantasy for you.

Come up to the bedroom with me, step into my fantasy.

I was wrong. I admit I was wrong, I shouldn't have done it or indeed said that to you.

Will my humble apology be enough to satisfy you?

Will you forgive me? Is there half a chance you will let me off from any punishment? Will you turn a blind eye this time?

Do you know how disappointed I will be if you do?

I stand before you, my stomach a veritable plague of war-dancing butterflies, quivering with excitement and apprehension. I can't help but smile at you.

You should know me better than to treat it as contempt for the punishment coming to me. Don't you realise it's a nervous smile, anticipating the spanking to come? Can't you see the thrill I'm feeling? There is no escape, sentence has been passed for my misdoings.

I lie across your knees with my hands on the floor to support myself. My slippers have come off and my toes bury themselves in the carpet. It's rough, scratchy. I stare at my hands through my hair, which is tickling my nose and I want to rub it.

It seems an age lying there, nervous and apprehensive, before you slowly and carefully turn back my skirt and slip; you begin to take down my tights and knickers and I, fool that I am, move my body to help you. Now my knickers are half way down my thighs, well out of your way, and the air is cool on my bare bottom. If you look carefully you will see the marks from my last caning. They're faint now, but they're there; I know they're there, I check every day.

Your hands are gentle, caressing, sensual, erotic. You're deliberately keeping me waiting. What will you use? Nothing has been said.

Your hand? Right now it's gentle, but I know only too well how hard it can smack, covering me in finger-marking redness, leaving me stinging and smarting.

My slipper which I've lost? Rubber-soled, easy to hold, hard on my bottom!

But within reach is the wooden hairbrush that you delight in using, which covers my cheeks in neat, oblong, red marks until they blend and I am all one burning redness. I don't like that, its unrelenting solidness is painful, but then so is everything you use.

Each slap hurts and I tell myself I've deserved every stinging smack but it's not easy to lie here and take it. Did you expect me not to whimper or cry?

All right, I was struggling, who wouldn't? This spanking hurts! You don't have to hold my hands that tight! Please, I need my hands to support myself; I'm just a limp body lying over your knees like this. I promise I won't try to stop you again . . .

Through my veil of tears I can see my red, sore bottom in the mirror, it feels hot to touch and it hurts. I'm sorry, I promise you I'm sorry –

No more! Haven't I had enough?

I can't take any more, believe me, I can't!

Please, it's enough for now, I'm sorry. I've already said I'm sorry, what more do you want?

I am lying face down on the bed. My sobbing has

ceased, my bottom is glowing hot. I dare not touch it or move; it hurts!

I am waiting.

What would you like to do to me now?

2

You Chose the Punishment

This is the first story I ever wrote in this genre, and the first ever to sell. It was the start of my erotic wrting career and the beginning of my friendship with the assistant editor at Janus, a friendship I treasured until it was ended by the death of my friend. Re-reading it today I am surprised at the submissive overtones, as it was written before I truly understood the meaning of the word or the nature of a submissive woman.

I am shaking. This is silly, I'm only going to get a spanking, aren't I? But he's been so long upstairs, what *is* he doing? A spanking won't hurt. Well it will, of course it will, but it's better than weeks of short housekeeping, isn't it? Get my punishment over and done with, that's what I thought. But what is Peter doing? What will he use? Just his hand? My hairbrush has a wide back. My slipper? It's rubber soled and very hard! Oh I wish I'd never agreed to this after all. I feel funny butter-flies in my stomach and I want to go to the bathroom but I dare not move. He said wait and wait I must. He's in a bad enough mood without my doing anything else.

I am sitting here flustered, my face is red, my hands are sweating, I feel very, very silly. Yet I am strangely interested, or I wouldn't have agreed.

Will he want me to undress or just take off my knickers? I feel myself blushing at the thought of putting myself across his knees anyway. It's such a silly thing to do, isn't it? I mean, I'm a grown woman, not a child. Lots of women get spanked, Peter told me once, but that doesn't help me right now. I wonder if they have this stomach-churning fear before they get a spanking? What *is* Peter doing upstairs?

'Josie,' he calls. Now I do feel sick.

'Coming.'

Ten stairs, might as well be a hundred. It seems to take an age to reach the bedroom door.

He is standing by the bed looking solemn, still angry. Panic begins to increase my heartbeat and something like a surge goes through me. But he is being kind, after a fashion.

'Better go to the loo first,' he says, and grateful for any respite, I rush to the bathroom. 'Don't be too long,' he commands in a warning tone.

I hurry.

Back in the bedroom is the real shock. A hard cushion is in the middle of the bed and he has brought a three-foot bamboo cane from the shed. My stomach turns completely over.

'Come in, Josie,' Peter says sweetly.

'I thought . . . Oh you said . . . I thought . . .'

'Thought what, Josie?'

'I thought I was going to get a spanking.' I am now blushing furiously.

'Why? And why don't you start taking your clothes off while we talk?'

I fumble with my buttons. 'You said corporal punishment.'

Peter laughs. 'That can mean anything.'

'Oh I see.' My apprehension is growing as I undress, so why aren't I saying no, and going downstairs? Why

8

am I removing my clothes like this, impatient, flustering, and feeling strange? 'No one undresses in the middle of the day, do they?'

'Don't be smart, Josie.'

I'm instantly contrite. 'Sorry Peter.'

'That's all right.'

'How – how many?' I am now down to my bra and pants and I am shaking.

'Six at least.'

'Six!'

'Come on, you're wasting time.'

I take off the last of my clothes.

'Lie on the bed, with the cushion under your stomach please.'

I crawl on the bed and lie down. With my bottom stuck up in the air I feel foolish, cold and very, very vulnerable. 'Peter . . .'

'Yes, Josie?'

'Can't we talk about this?'

'No, we can't. You've been very slack lately: the food has been bad; the house has not been cleaned properly and you are not bothering with yourself. Agreed?'

'Yes,' I mumble. I have no defence.

'So, you had the choice between corporal punishment or docking of your housekeeping. You chose the punishment.'

'I thought . . .'

'I know what you thought. Over my knee, a few hard smacks and it's all over. Right?'

I don't answer.

'Right, Josie?'

'Yes.' Suddenly the cane is cold across my bottom. I cringe.

'Please keep still, Josie, I wouldn't want to hit you anywhere else, that might hurt.'

The cane is lifted off me.

9

'One.'

'Ooooowwww!' A burning line. 'No, Peter, no!'

'Two.'

Just below the other line. It hurts!

'Three.'

I bury my head in the bed. 'Please, Peter, I'm sorry!' I can't resist moving and trying to rub myself. A sharp tap with the cane makes me squeal.

'Keep still, Josie, there are only three more to go.'

Only three more, he says. I hurt!

'Please, Peter, no more, I'm sorry, I'll behave.'

I have often heard of 'six of the best'. How do the kids take it? It hurts! The cane is on me again; it's cold. How can it be so cold when it burns so much?

'Four.'

The tears are flowing. Peter takes no notice of me at all.

'Five.'

Oh soon it will be over and I really will be good. I don't want this again.

'Six.'

And it's all over. It's stinging, six separate lines, burning, stinging.

'Oh Peter, it hurts!'

'It was meant to, silly, it's supposed to be punishment after all. It's supposed to hurt or there's no point, is there?'

Gentle hands on my burning bottom, cold cream.

'Oh Peter.'

The hands are gentle, easing, soothing, wandering, probing, interesting. The first indications that I am becoming aroused.

Peter laughs. 'The books all said it worked and it does.'

The fingers are inside me and I'm fully aroused. With his free hand Peter pulls his trousers off and with a swift movement has penetrated me. Together we reach a crashing climax. He rolls away and looks at me, smiling.

'Want to choose a punishment again?' he asks, and we laugh.

'I'll have to see. Right now I still hurt!

3

The Editor's Decision Is Final

This, unlike most of the others, is a true story. The friendship developed into a real, close heart-to-heart relationship with a man who understood. This is the story of our first encounter.

A word of advice for all female would-be contributors to CP magazines – when you send in your submission, don't whatever you do, hint at anything at all. A precise letter such as the following should be sent:

'Dear Sir, please find enclosed my story entitled "Why I'm not Sitting Comfortably at the Moment" which I trust will meet with your approval. SAE enclosed. Yours faithfully.' And write absolutely nothing else.

You see, I made the mistake of admitting, in one letter to a magazine, that I'd never been birched, or at that time, tawsed, and was only writing about what I had experienced.

An *immediate* reply, so immediate it burned up the postal service to get to me, offered 'action' if I cared to visit the editorial offices. (You should know that I had already had a telephone call from the mailing department of the magazine offering me a free session, which I turned down. The phone went in the middle of dinner, my husband and daughter sitting wide-eyed while I contrived to keep a straight face and rejected the words over the phone, 'Would you like to come and visit? I could give you a good spanking, wouldn't cost you.' I should hope not!)

What was different about this letter? For one thing it was from the assistant editor, not some guy in the mailing room. This man had a name, a personality, and a proper position. And he talked as if he understood.

Even so, I thought I'd better clarify things a bit, you know, find out what he had in mind, what I could expect.

The following are just a few extracts from the letters I received; letters which sent quivers and quavers into my quim. You'll see it wasn't at all clear *what* I could expect if I went.

'Twelve good strokes of the cane would be a good start – and maybe a good finish for you.'

'You might find yourself across my knees for a bare bottom spanking just to warm up, followed by six or eight with the cane, bent over my desk, and finally a dozen or so with the birch.'

'How about I give you one stroke of the cane for every misplaced comma or apostrophe?'

I got permission from my partner, who was less than enthusiastic but agreed because the whole prospect turned me on, and I went.

Actually we went as a family, the three of us on the London coach, but we split up at the Underground, where I hopped on a train for the nearest stop to the CP magazine offices, whilst he went off to sample the delights of the Thames with a young child in tow.

Quaking with trepidation, I found the worst bit was actually going into the office. Halfway up the last flight of stairs I stopped and stared at the door. All I had to do was walk up a few more steps and I would be there. That would have been the moment to turn and run, if I was going to turn and run. (I find I've said this many times in the course of my writing, but, as most submissives will

14

tell you, the inclination to turn and run is always there even though we never do.)

The handle of the door held my gaze. As soon as I touched it I would have committed myself – to what? There were butterflies; sexy, dancing butterflies in my stomach. There was a pounding of the heart, harder than normal, a surge of adrenalin and excitement, so I took a deep breath, settled my bag a little more firmly on my shoulder and walked up the last few steps and through the door before my resolve could weaken. I stopped, and looked at the two men in the room. They both said hello from behind their individual desks, and then one came over to me. This then was the man I had come to meet.

'You made it then.'

'Yes, I made it,' I replied, and wondered if he knew how close I had been to running away.

'Come and sit down.'

With a cup of coffee in my hand and people to talk to I felt better. The typesetter came in, someone dropped by with some pictures, discussions went on about the cover – did the lettering on the model's bottom show up clearly enough? The editor said no, the assistant thought they'd get away with it – I felt myself relaxing. Everyone was nice, and it was going to be all right. I could even forget why I was there, for a while, if I didn't look around me.

'Lunch?'

'Why not?'

I was surprisingly hungry despite the butterflies which fluttered about in my stomach when I made the mistake of looking round the room. It wasn't the girlie calendars or the half pasted-up pages that bothered me. It was the 'black corner' full of ghastly looking canes, birches, and so forth. I tried not to think about it.

Lunch was a good opportunity to talk and the conversation flowed freely, considering we had only just met.

The chemistry seemed right, or at least, he smiled in a friendly fashion and I don't think they were false smiles.

Back at the office we were suddenly alone, the understanding colleague had diplomatically disappeared. My 'friend' locked the door and pulled the curtains as I watched from the comfort of a big swivel chair.

'Come on.' It was time to stand up. 'Where do you want to go?'

'Are you asking me?' I stood in the middle of the floor, uncertain. What *did* I want?

'Yes,' he said looking surprised. 'I always ask.'

'Then don't, not with me. Just tell me what you want.'

'Right, bend over the desk then, please.'

My insides had turned to jelly. Completely. Cold anticipation, hot quivering quim. Not sure even then what I was doing, feeling sexy and yet scared. Doing as I was told without question. Well, almost.

Firm hands pushed me down and I folded my arms to rest my head on them. Funny how a desk is just the right height for someone to bend over, isn't it? The manufacturers must have known.

'Look,' he said, and the cane appeared through the crook of my arm.

'I'm not looking!' I was trying not to think about it. He had obviously decided what I was to get although I still didn't know. He turned back my clothes, slowly, savouring it no doubt, while my knees trembled. My new black tights were lowered and then my pale green panties.

'Oh very nice.'

'Really?' It made me feel good, restored a little of my confidence, although it didn't stop the butterflies. The moment of pain came ever nearer.

A hand slid over my cheeks, feeling their softness, appreciating the whiteness? I don't know. All I know is, it felt nice.

'Now we'll see if you mark, shall we?'

16

A very hard slap made me yelp. It was much harder than I had anticipated! It glowed, a solid round patch of red.

'A complete hand print, you do mark easily, don't you?' And he placed another one, right on top! I could feel my bottom protesting, hurting, but one-sided: one cool cheek, one hot. I pressed against the edge of the desk trying to escape what was to come.

'We'll do something about this side now,' he said, and gave me two more hard slaps before he started spanking me all over. From the top of my bottom near the spine where the skin is pulled tight, to the undercurve which is particularly tender, he spanked me, and I cried out as the pain increased. I let myself flop forward onto the desk, let the spanking carry on as if it wasn't anything to do with me. Only the sound penetrated my conscious thought; my subconscious absorbed the spanking, wondering why I didn't think it would hurt this much.

'That looks nice,' he said, and before I could even begin to anticipate it, the cane was gone from under my arm, was whistling through the air, and was landing with devastating sharpness on the tender skin. It caught me almost by surprise, and I simply yelled out. It burned like nothing else, and I gripped the far side of the desk, determined to take it. Then came another stroke, slightly further down this time and I almost stood up but just held on by sheer willpower. Would it be six? He still hadn't said. The third stroke cut across the tender join of bottom and thighs, the tip caught my thigh and brought me to the brink of tears, and the fourth one, which seemed to go wild, was definitely all I could take.

I stood up, clutching my bottom, begging, 'No more, I can't take any more.' And he lowered the cane. 'I'm not used to it,' I apologised, which was the truth. I'd never been caned like that.

'I do cane rather hard,' he agreed, putting it away in the corner, much to my relief.

I rushed off to the ladies where, with the aid of a small hand mirror, I tried to inspect the weals. They looked horrific! They were already going black and red, and they seemed to be everywhere, not like the neat lines I had anticipated.

Back in the office, with the lines still hurting, I sat on the couch and let the pain settle down to a glow. When the editor came back, I showed him the lines, and heard him tutting.

'Not one of your better efforts,' he told my friend, and I wondered why.

With knickers back in place, and a feeling of warm satisfaction spreading to all known parts of the human body, I left the office, promising to be back one day.

I went back to my family, then back home on the coach, trying not to wriggle.

It's a good job my friend didn't carry out any of the promises made in the letters – I wouldn't have been able to take them then, that's for sure. He said he was entitled to change his mind anyway. An editor's decision is always final, a contributor has little to say in the matter.

I'm glad the other editors I work for are not all into CP or life could become extremely painful, methinks, but interesting, all the same . . .

4

Editorial Comment

This fantasy was specially written for the editor featured in the preceding true story. After my visit I got to imagining how easy it would be for him to find a series of willing ladies and he was so pleased with it he pinned cash to the return envelope, paid out of his own pocket not out of magazine funds!

Bill Kennard smoothed down his wavy black hair and straightened his tie. Then he pressed the button on the intercom for his secretary.

'Send Miss Daniels in,' he said curtly, knowing she would hear it.

'Yes, Mr Kennard.'

The door opened slowly and a young woman crept into his office, her long brown hair falling forward as she tried not to look into his eyes.

'Come and sit down,' he said, friendly but abrupt.

'Good afternoon, Mr Kennard,' she said meekly.

'Now,' he reached for the file on his desk, 'your stories have been way off standard lately, haven't they?'

'Yes, I know.'

He watched her closely, saw her wriggling a little in the chair, and grinned secretly. Had she anticipated or been told his remedy for lagging authors? A good spanking, over the knee, writhing body held firmly in one

19

arm, reddening cheeks for his eyes to feast on, there was nothing like it! Or, as in this case, a few sharp strokes of his trusty cane.

'But why? You used to send me such good stories!'

'I don't know, I don't seem to have had any inspiration to write anything lately.'

'Are you getting any practical experience?'

'Yes.'

'Much?'

'No.'

'How much?'

'Well,' she shuffled uneasily on the chair, her head tilted even further forward, the long hair falling down to hide her blushes.

'Come on,' Bill Kennard coaxed her gently, 'there isn't much I haven't heard, is there? Goodness me, you write me enough!'

'Writing it and sending it to you is different from sitting here and talking about it.'

'I know that.'

There was a long silence. Bill Kennard waited patiently. However long the interview took, he would get his own way and sometimes it was good to wait. Good for his self-control (and all that).

Finally Diane Daniels raised her eyes and looked at him. 'I've had a spanking or two,' she admitted reluctantly.

'Is that all?' Bill Kennard was astonished and showed it.

'Yes.'

'Oh gracious me, no wonder the stories have fallen off. Look Diane, I can call you Diane, can't I?' She nodded. 'Look, Diane, you're writing for me, you know I need stories, real stories, to give my readers the vicarious thrill they buy the magazine for. Let's be honest about it, it's the only way I can make any money and your stories have been rather – well, dull.'

'I know.'

'Well, has anyone told you the remedy for dull contributions? *My* remedy for dull contributions?'

'Yes.'

It was obvious someone had been talking. She was beginning to go red, and a sparkle appeared in her eyes; the thought was turning her on, even if she wanted to deny it.

'Are you willing?'

'I think so.'

'Come on then.'

Bill Kennard opened the long centre drawer of his desk and took out the whippy cane he kept there. Diane stood up and walked round to the side of the desk.

'Who's been talking to you?' he asked, curious.

'That would be telling, wouldn't it?' she retorted.

'All right then, lean over.'

Diane carefully leaned across the desk, holding on to the sides with both hands. He carefully lifted the skirt out of the way and stopped to admire the black panties pulled tight over the shapely bottom.

'No tights,' he said admiringly.

'Please be gentle with me,' she pleaded. 'It's been years since I had the cane!'

'I'll be gentle; just enough to hurt for a while so you know what you're writing about. All right?'

'I don't have much choice, do I?'

'No,' he laughed.

He stepped back and held the cane against her to test the distance. 'All right, Diane,' and he brought the cane down sharply.

'Oowww!!!' She leapt up, clutching her bottom. 'No, no!'

'Oh come on, Diane, it wasn't hard.'

'Oh!' she was rubbing frantically and pleading with her dark eyes.

One day I'll have to try this myself, he thought, watching her rub her full cheeks. Find out just how much that sudden blow with the rattan really hurts. Then he thought again, why should I? I'm here to give, not take.

'Come on, only another five to go.'

'No, please!'

'It's up to you.' He walked away and opened the drawer to put the cane back. She stared at him.

'You, you won't accept any more of my stories, will you?'

'No.'

'Why not? Can't I try again?'

'Why not? Because, Diane dear, as I have been trying to tell you, they were dull. How long is it since you were caned? Must be years. I truly didn't hit you very hard, and you leapt up as though I'd really caned you. Does it hurt now?'

She stopped for a moment.

'No,' she admitted reluctantly.

'You see. How can you write me anything realistic if you've had no experience?'

'You're right, of course, you're right.'

'Well?'

'I'll take the rest.'

'Thank you, Diane. I'd hate to lose you, you've given me some good work in the past.'

With the utmost reluctance she leaned over the desk again. He lifted her skirt out of the way and stepped back.

'Only five more to go. Now you've had one and know how quickly the pain goes away, it isn't so bad, is it?'

'No, but please –'

Bill Kennard gave her five quick whacks with the cane, placing them expertly and evenly over her bottom, ignoring her shrieks and cries. She clung to the desk obviously determined to take them all. (The money for the stories was too useful to many authors to relinquish because of a little pain!) Then it was over and she was able to stand up and restore a degree of dignity. She wiped away a few tears and watched as he carefully put the cane away in the desk.

'Hurt?' he asked. She nodded. 'It'll stop. But now you know what you're writing about, don't you?'

'Yes, I do, and it's much more painful than I thought, just lines of pain.'

'You must have experience to write properly, there's no other way!'

'I'll have to try and tell my husband when I get back.' She picked up her bag. 'Can I go now?'

'Of course, I'm not stopping you.'

'Thank - thank you, Mr Kennard.'

'I can assure you the pleasure was all mine.'

'I'll - I'll see what I can do for you.'

'I'm sure you will.'

Bill Kennard watched her walk out of the door and leaned back in his chair, smiling at the memory. Nice!

Then he leaned forward and pressed the intercom button again.

'Send in Miss Green,' he ordered curtly, so she would hear him.

'Yes, Mr Kennard.'

What a wonderful way to spend a working day!

5

Initiation

As with so much of my SM writing, this comes out of one of my fantasies yet is partly taken from real life. It could happen, but don't imagine it will happen with every woman, any more than any of my other fantasies will happen with every woman. But, if she is submissive by nature – and that's something for you to find out – it will. Believe me.

It's late, the TV has long since been turned off. Supper is over, and Bob has a look which bodes ill for my poor bottom. He goes upstairs, and comes down with a blanket and the cane. His hinted, whispered promises of the day are about to come to pass and I feel the usual anticipatory thrill of apprehension and excitement go through me.

'Come on,' he invited me.

Slowly I undress, knowing he is watching me. Knowing how the day would probably end, I have dressed especially for the night: green silk dress so every move rustles; lace-trimmed black slip; lacy black bra and brief black knickers, edged with lace. I remove them all as slowly as any stripper. My breasts are full, with large nipples which spring erect as the bra comes off, my hips invite his hands, my cheeks invite the punishment that is to come.

Not only does this please Bob, but it delays the caning for a little longer too. Naked, I wait for him to look at me before lying on the blanket in front of the open fire, flat on my back, letting the flickering flames reflect on my body and warm me. Bob undresses, swiftly. He is muscular and broad, with hair running all over his chest and in a line down his back; hair which sends tingles through me if I touch and caress him. He is large everywhere he needs to be, I can cup him in one hand but he overspills my small fingers. His member is large enough to fulfil every woman's dream, and certainly fills mine, along with my body. He lays on the blanket beside me.

'Worried?'

'No.' But I am. I'm quivering inside with need and desire; need for the sharp pain which is to come, desire for it to come and fill me with the huge rush of sexy feeling which assures us both I will have a spectacular orgasm.

He is caressing and kissing my erect nipples and I allow my fingers to travel even as his hands are. His fingers are inside me, finding the magic G-spot that lies just - there. He finds my pleasure button and caresses it, while I in turn slide my thumb over the head of his cock which is weeping just slightly, and sends a shudder through him.

I know I'm moist, it's the anticipation and it is almost too much to take; the need is growing for a few quick thrusts of fingers or cock - I can feel myself getting aroused to the point that if he isn't careful I'll climax now and it'll all be over. For some reason I've never fully understood, any 'punishment' hurts a good deal more once I've reached my climax, the desire obviously cushions the pain in some way, so I try if at all possible to hold it back.

After a long kiss, during which his tongue is almost as exciting as his fingers, he smiles at me.

'Come on, Jan, let's start.'

'Start? You've been ready for ages, in fact for so long I don't think you can wait any longer, can you?'

Bob sits up and straightens his legs. I manoeuvre myself across him, pillowing my head on my arms. It's all bones, feet pressing against the floor, pelvic bones pressing on his thigh bones, elbows creating dips in the carpet, but it pales into insignificance when the spanking begins.

The only real problem is, as far as I'm concerned, my bottom is too accessible to Bob's eyes and hands, and, being over his legs, is raised just enough to help him, as if he needed any help.

'This is how I like you best.' He is smoothing and caressing my bottom; his hands are soft, sensuous, sliding between the crack, seeking out the opening, finding little nerve ends that make me quiver.

'How?'

'Totally submissive.'

'Typical man – Ow!' That comment has earned me a sharp slap. Is this an indication of what is to come?

'I've left a lovely hand print,' he says, admiration apparent in his voice. Then he starts slapping me gently and I relax in the eroticism of it. Being still, doing as I'm told, I submit to my husband's will, which is to have me lying still and in a position to spank, just lightly. The spanking tingles, arouses in its sexiness, the nakedness, the submission to another's will, the gentle, oh so gentle, build up of smarting soreness.

He doesn't increase the severity of the slaps, it's the combined effect of them on my bottom. I'm getting tender, each slap, no matter how light, counts and I start to wriggle a little, which earns me an immediate hard smack.

'Lie still!'

I do, but it's getting painful now. I must be completely red by the feel of it.

'All right, let's get up.'

I slowly climb to my feet. My bottom feels as though it's glowing.

'Over the chair,' comes the command and I walk across

the floor, and lean over the arm of the heavy armchair, the weave of the upholstery pressing into my pubis. The frame of the chair is solid and strong. Unlike me it won't give way under pressure, for which I'm grateful. I bury my head in the cushion, my toes only just touch the floor like this. Bob whistles the cane through the air a few times, the sound of it is enough to send shudders through me, along with various thrills that are hard to describe.

'You're beautifully red, beautifully ready for the cane!'

'Go easy on me.'

'Don't I always?' he says, but being very sensitive now, the first stroke of the wicked whippy cane makes me jump up clutching my poor cheeks. Bob waits patiently until I bend over again, which I do without his asking. The arm of the chair waits, the cushion waits, the cane waits.

'Don't do that again, will you,' Bob warns me, 'or you'll get more than you bargained for!'

'Bob, please go easy.'

'Sorry, I'll try and make them a bit lighter.'

But I'm sure he only said that to deceive, for the next stroke lands an inch from the other one and makes me cry out in protest.

'I'll give you time to get used to that one.'

Good of him, isn't it? As it's burning its way across my blazing bottom, me gasping with pain, the cane whistles through the air again to land with a resounding thwack!

'Three.'

'Ooooww! Enough, Bob!'

'I'll say when you've had enough.'

'Bully! OUCH!' That was a sharp whack across my thighs.

'That's enough from you, if you don't want twelve.'

'It hurts!'

'It's supposed to. Five.'

'Nooooo!'

'Don't you make a fuss every time. Six.'

And now he lets me jump up and dance around a bit, rubbing the lines, massaging some of the sting away, but then face down on the blanket is better after a caning like that. Pot of cold cream, gentle fingers creaming my oh so painful bottom, erotic fingers, probing fingers, tantalising fingers sliding into wet places . . . And to think there was a time when this would never have happened. I remember how it all started.

There had been a secretive air about Bob that I had been aware of for some time. It was driving me insane. I had no idea what he was up to, and there were the brown envelopes each month too. He kept them in the one desk drawer that locked, so I couldn't get to find out what he was doing.

Concentrate. He'll have no tea tonight if I stand here thinking. No, the toast!

'Jan, what are you doing?'

'Burned the toast.'

'So I can see – and smell!'

'Sorry, Bob, I wasn't thinking.'

'Come on, that's not like you, where's my efficient wife?'

'I'm still here, just had a moment's brainstorm, that's all.'

'I'll believe you, thousands wouldn't.'

A pat on my bottom as he walks off. Now, why did he do that? He's never done it before. Come on, do something quick, before any more toast gets burned.

Why not just ask? No, I couldn't do that! But one day he'll leave that drawer unlocked, I know he will.

I just came up here to dust, and the drawer is open! There they are, in a neat pile, all the brown envelopes that have been coming. Oh, sex magazines by the look of the cover – no, not really sex magazines, are they? I'll just take a look –

'Jan!'

'Oh Bob, you made me jump. Oh, I'm . . .'

'Looking at my books, I see.'

'No, I was –'

'Yes, you were! Interested?'

'No, I was only looking at them.'

'And I came home early and caught you prying. It *is* my desk, after all.'

'Yes, I know that, but –'

'I knew your curiosity would get the better of you, my girl!'

'That's not it,' I say, but my indignation won't stand up to his questioning, and he knows it.

'I think you should have a spanking, don't you? For going through my desk and looking at my books?'

I am backing away and he comes after me.

'Bob, I –'

'There's nothing to say, is there?'

'No, not really.'

'Aren't you just a little curious? You've read some of the books.'

'And they all say it hurts!'

'But for how long?'

'Not for long.' Actually I am curious, but admitting it is the last thing I dare do.

'A little spanking, a few smacks, come on, you've been a bad girl, haven't you?'

'All right.' I don't feel I have a real choice in the matter.

'Good.'

'But not here.'

'No, of course not here. In the bedroom.'

I follow Bob to the bedroom, full of questions. How did he get hold of the magazines? Who started him on this? It's something that hasn't been mentioned before in our relationship. But later, I'll have to ask later, right now I'm curious and afraid, a complex mixture of emotions to deal with. In the bedroom Bob sits on the ottoman.

'Come on,' he says, and pats his knees invitingly. I lay across him, awkward and nervous, feeling exceptionally silly. His bones dig into me. I want to go downstairs and pretend this isn't happening.

He pulls my skirt up out of the way and runs his hands over my bottom. I am suddenly inconsequentially pleased I am wearing pretty flowered knickers, and no tights. Then I berate myself for being stupid. What does it matter?

'You've got a nice bottom, Jan, did you know that?'

I say nothing, I'm too scared. What have I let myself in for? This is so undignified; my hands on the floor; my toes hardly touching; all my hair falling down over my face; I feel helpless.

'Ouch!' The first smack takes me completely by surprise. I'm wriggling like mad and he puts an arm round my waist.

'Now keep still, and it'll all be over so quick you won't know anything has happened.'

He starts smacking me hard, first on one cheek then the other in a rhythm that is extraordinarily painful and oddly humiliating.

'Oh Bob, it hurts, I don't like it!'

My bottom hurts, I feel silly which doesn't help, but the smacks go on. Then he stops suddenly and lets me stand up. I'm on the verge of tears.

'You've just about paid for going through my desk.'

'Bob, it hurt!'

'But not for long, you'll see.'

I rush to the bathroom to comb my hair and make myself tidy again. I am vaguely disappointed. It seemed to me from the stories that the women got sexual excitement from the spankings, and all I got was a sore bottom! But the pain has settled down to a glow and I feel very tender.

31

Downstairs Bob pats me as he goes by to the lounge.

'All right?'

I ignore him. How can I tell him I'm disappointed? He might do it again!

Later that evening, Bob turns the TV off.

'Time to talk, Jan.'

'About what?'

'About your spanking, and about the magazines, about the things I know you want to ask but won't.'

'All right, tell me about it.'

'Someone at work had a copy of a magazine and I borrowed it. I was intrigued. I've long been tempted by your bottom, my love. So I sent off my subscription. I wasn't sure how to approach you with this new feeling, so I left it to your natural curiosity. I knew you'd look for them.'

'And what would you have done if I hadn't looked? You took quite a gamble.'

'I'd have left one out for you,' he retorts, 'but I know how nosy you are!'

Well, I can't deny that!

'Did you like it?'

'No.'

'Not at all?'

'No, it hurt!'

'Now you've had one spanking we can try again, if you want. But this time we could make an erotic experience out of it, not just over my knee like that, although I must admit even that gave me a thrill.'

'No, it just hurt, I don't want to try again.'

'Read some more magazines, and think about it,' he says and then changes the subject.

During the next few days, despite my protestations, I find myself drawn to reading the magazines. But I can't bring myself to read them in front of Bob, so I go and have a quiet read when the housework's done and Bob's at work.

One night, sitting by the fire, Bob asks:

'Have you read any more of my books?'

'Yes.'

'And how do you feel about it?'

'About what?'

'Jan, don't be difficult, I want to spank you again!'

'But I haven't done anything.'

'I don't need an excuse, do I?'

'I suppose not.'

'I'll invent one if you like.'

'There's no need. I can't see how you get an erotic experience out of it though.'

'Let's think about it for a moment. Did you feel anything when I offered to spank you again?'

'A feeling, yes, a sort of –'

'The beginning of a sexy thrill?'

'Well –'

'Jan, don't play. I want to know if we can go on with this, or whether it'll be me reading the books, and you taking no part in it, or whether we work it out between us and add a new dimension to our sex lives.'

'All right, I did feel a funny sort of thrill, yes.'

'That's all right then. When you learn to associate the spanking with sex, good sex, then the thrill will get stronger, and it'll be good, for both of us.'

'Well –'

'Doubting me again? The only way to find out is to do it.'

'And that's just what I don't fancy doing!'

'Ah, Jan, come on, a big girl like you can take a spanking, I know.'

'I'm admitting nothing!'

'Try once more? Upstairs, see what we can get out of it?'

'Yes, all right.' What on earth made me agree? Must be crazy!

We lock the house up for the night and go upstairs. Bob watches me as I undress, slowly as always. I like to take my time, to entertain him, I always have done, and the fact that he is erectly ready for bed immediately afterwards shows what effect I have on him.

As before, I carefully lay across his legs. Being naked certainly adds a new dimension to all this, I feel almost sexy, and considering the sheer indignity of the position, that's crazy! He spends some time just caressing me, sliding his hands across my cheeks, round my hips, touching my stomach and going back again, down my spine, almost lazily. It feels nice but I'm aware that I'm tense and holding every muscle as tight as I can. I still feel silly though. He starts slapping carefully, almost gently and I stop tensing up.

'That's better,' he comments as I relax. He slaps a little harder, just a little, and I'm tingling. 'Going a nice shade of pink.' The slaps are getting harder now, or is it me getting tender? Either way it's beginning to sting a little. But I can take it, it doesn't bother me too much.

'Don't wriggle,' he says warningly. Was I?

'Why not?' I ask from under my hair. It's all fallen forward over my face.

'Because I said so. I want you to get used to lying still and taking a spanking.'

My bottom must be going red now, it's getting painful and it takes a supreme effort to stay still, to absorb the feelings. Quite suddenly he lands two very hard slaps right in the middle of each cheek.

'Ow! That was unfair!'

'No, they should all have been like that. Come on. Come to bed.'

A quick glance in the mirror shows the contrast between smooth white body and glowing red bottom. But the feelings that go with it are more mixed than that. I lay on the bed, face down, while he sits on the side and gently strokes me just as he had before the spanking. His fingers are sliding, touching, finding secret places to enter, to probe, to excite.

'Is it hot?' he asks, as if he didn't know! The back of his hand could tell him!

'Yes.'

'Does it hurt?'

'Not really.'

'You were very good,' he whispers.

And the seductively sexy feeling I felt increases, my legs part almost of their own volition, and he slips two fingers inside me. I writhe and move against their rigidity, revelling in the waves of excitement. I roll over and hold out my arms.

'Now,' I gasp, and Bob enters me, erect, hard. The pressure of his body pressing my red bottom into the bed adds to the feeling and I climax swiftly and violently.

'Hey, you do learn fast!'

'I didn't mean it to be quite like that.'

'But it was – and it was good!'

'Yes, it was good.'

Lying close together in the afterglow of lovemaking, I agree, it was good.

'Next we can try your slipper, and then the hairbrush.'

'Hold on, you've not consulted me about any of this.'

'Do I have to?'

'It's my bottom!'

'And our pleasure,' he says, and I can't argue with that!

It's been about a week now since I had a spanking and I'm beginning to feel restless, a new feeling for me. I refuse to mention it as I'm determined not to let Bob think I'm that interested, not yet anyway. But I have a feeling that tonight something is going to happen. Bob keeps eyeing me and he's patted my bottom twice already since he's been home. There's nothing on TV tonight we want to watch, so we'll have to see.

'You've been a naughty girl today,' he whispers as he passes me.

'Right first time!'

'What's that supposed to mean?'

'I thought we were overdue for another painful session.'

'Oh Jan, you're being very unfair, it isn't painful and I've said nothing.'

'Yes, you have, and anyway, one more pat on my bottom and I'll have had a spanking!'

'Rubbish, but as you've mentioned it –'

'You see?'

'All right, I won't deny it, I can't! Shall we try one of your slippers tonight, just to see what it does?'

'Must we?'

'Yes.'

Having been forewarned by Bob's attitude I've dressed for the occasion in my very best scarlet undies, edged in black lace, the knickers are the briefest I possess. Scarlet is appropriate for the way I think my bottom will look when it's over! Bob is sitting on the ottoman, watching me.

'Very nice,' he says approvingly. 'Bring me a slipper when you come over here.'

'Must I?'

'Any more of that and I'll *really* spank you! Now, get over here please, with a slipper.'

'Yes Bob.'

Oops! Better be careful!

'Thank you. Now, knickers off please. Nice as they are, tight as they are, I'd rather spank a bare bottom, if you don't mind.'

'Do I have any say in the matter?'

'Not really.'

I hook my thumbs in the tight knickers and slowly ease

36

them over my hips and kick them off, sensing my own rising excitement, catching a glimpse of moisture in them as I toss them aside.

'Now over, please, Jan.'

Why does this always feel so silly at first? Hands on floor one side, and very vulnerable bare bottom exposed to Bob's eyes and anything else he cares to use.

'These slippers are nice to hold, I can get a good grip on the heel and bring it down on you like – this!'

'Ow!' Oh it stings, there is a smack on the other cheek!

I like this. Bob is smacking evenly, first one side and then the other, and it's stinging and getting sore already. It's a strange feeling, not personal like a hand, it's harder, sharper, covers a larger area and stings!

'I think it's time to stop,' he observes, not a moment too soon as far as I'm concerned. 'You're getting very red.'

'It feels like it!' I slide off Bob's legs onto the floor. 'Oh oh oh oh!'

'Have a look at yourself,' he suggests.

The mirror holds a shock for me.

'Oh look at me, you're wicked. That's the reddest I've ever been!'

'Come to bed,' he says, and who can resist such an invitation after that?

'Listen,' Bob says, as he is busy brushing down his trousers with the wide-backed wooden clothes brush that hangs in the hall. 'Fancy this across your lovely bottom?'

'No.' I don't even have to think about it.

'Come on, you're being a spoilsport.'

'Am I? I call it self preservation!'

'No, Jan, really, I'll go easy.'

'Well –'

'That's good enough, it means yes.'

'No!'

'Yes, too late to say no. Tonight then?' And he swings me round and gives me a smack with the brush which stings even through my clothes.

'Hey, that hurt!' I protest.

'I promise not to do it that hard tonight,' Bob grins. 'Bye for now.'

When Bob comes home that night he tosses me an envelope.

'Have a look at the back page, it might interest you.' It's a catalogue from a sex supermarket, full of unbelievable items, but at the back is a small advertisement for canes. My stomach flips over at the thought. Bob comes down from having a wash.

'What do you think?'

'No.'

'Jan, you're always saying that.'

'I know, but a cane?'

'Why not?'

'Why?'

'Because no spanking games would or could be complete without a cane, read the magazines, Jan.'

'I have.'

'All right, forget it.'

'I will.'

'But you've not forgotten what we're going to do tonight?'

'No, I haven't.'

Surprisingly he's dropped the subject. Very unlike Bob, that is. I'd lay odds we haven't heard the last of it. For now, as he's reminded me, I have the clothes brush to think about! And why is it when something threatens, time simply flies by? It seems no time before supper is over, and it's time for the long walk upstairs. I am a quivering apprehensive mess. Bob snatches the brush as we pass the hall stand. Help!

'And what sexy undies do I have to look at tonight?'

'Nothing special.'

'Doesn't matter.'

'Just as well!'

I undress slowly, carefully, down to my all-white almost coy undies.

'Nice.'

'Is that all?'

'What did you expect?'

'I don't know.'

'Come on, Jan.'

'Aren't you impatient when you have a new implement to spank me with!'

'Why not?'

'Just like a kid with a new toy!'

'And you're willing to go along with it, and if I get any more insolence from you, my girl, I'll really spank you with this!'

'All right, all right!'

Undies are tossed to the floor and I stand before him, naked, waiting. 'How do you want me?'

'Let's have a change, you lay over the ottoman, all right?'

In some ways it's more comfortable than being over Bob's lap, the padded top of the ottoman is soft to my nude body. Bob's caresses are exciting, as always. He traces the line of my spine, ending up between my cheeks, then moves down to the moistness which is waiting for his cock – later.

'You're so nice and soft.'

'Aren't I just?'

'Conceited, too, we'll knock some of that out of you!'

'Ouch! that hurt!'

'Made a beautiful red mark, Jan.'

'Oh that hurts!'

I can't describe it, the solid impact of wood on my soft bottom is – nasty!

'I won't give you many of these.'

'Thank you for that – Ow!' That landed on the other cheek. It's the unyielding solidness of it, I think, it really is awful. But the excitement is there, I feel the thrill as I wait, fearfully, for the next slap – which hurts even more – as it comes on top of the other ones I've had. The fourth slap brings tears, I can't help it, it really does hurt. Immediately Bob drops the brush and holds me close.

'I'm sorry, Jan, we won't try that again.' He quickly wipes away my tears, and I smile.

'It hurt, Bob, but oh I'm ready for you!'

And the lovemaking is as passionate as always.

There is a large brown envelope in the hall, addressed to Bob. It's padded. I've pushed and poked and I don't know what it is! There is some other boring mail, circulars and so on, but this packet is intriguing me. I just called my friend Sonia and she's out. Madge next door is at her mother's and I'm bored. I wish I knew what was in the envelope. Isn't it silly when something can obsess you so much? If only I had something else to think about, it wouldn't bother me so much, I'm sure.

The day has been endless, but Bob is home at last, eyeing me carefully as he looks through the bills and stuff I left for him. What an infuriating person he is! At last he is slowly opening the packet. He has pulled out, and is straightening out – a cane!

'You didn't say you were getting that!'

'You would have said no.'

'Yes, I would.'

'So I ordered it anyway. As I told you, no spanking games are complete without the cane.'

I confess to being secretly thrilled but I'm not letting Bob know that!

'We'll try it tonight.'

'Must we?'

'Do you realise how many times you say that?'

'Sorry.'

Bob's hardly looked at the television screen tonight, he has his mind on other things. When we go up, I see he has laid the cane on the ottoman, ready, and I feel my stomach leap.

'Any fancy dress tonight?'

'No.'

'Shame.'

'I don't think it really matters tonight.'

'You're right, not tonight – what did you say a while back? That I was like a kid with a new toy when I had a new spanking implement?'

'And you are too, look at you!'

All his clothes are piled in an untidy heap on the floor and he is waiting for me to undress.

'Wait!' I can sense his impatience.

Finally I am undressed and my hair is brushed out. 'Where?'

'Do you want to lie on the bed?'

'Not a bad idea.'

I lie flat on the bed, watching Bob out of the corner of my eye. This will be yet another new experience. I hope it doesn't hurt as much as I think it will.

'All right? Are you ready for this?'

'Oooowwwww!'

No, I wasn't ready but it makes no difference. A searing line has burned its way across my bottom.

'Oh, look at that.' Bob's voice is full of admiration for his own handiwork.

'Bob, that hurts!'

'Canes are supposed to, my dear, it would be useless if they didn't.'

'OUCH!' He's laid that one just below the other line, which had just settled down to hurting and not burning.

Now it's started up again in sympathy with the new line, or it feels that way anyway!

'It's part of the fun seeing if I can keep them in a straight line. We don't want them overlapping, do we?'

'No, we don't – Ooww!' There are now three burning lines.

'Can you hear the noise as it comes through the air? Can you hear that swish? Listen!'

'OOOOOOWWWWW!'

'Only two more and I'll stop for the night. One. Two.'

I scramble off the bed to look; six neat lines etched in red on my bottom, and boy do they sting! A horrid smarting feeling, a burning sort of sensation and rubbing doesn't help.

'No? Yes?'

'No yes what?'

'Do you like it?'

'No I don't!'

'Hasn't it done anything for you?'

'No.' But I'm lying, and I think he knows it too! It's a different sensation, quite different from all the other spankings I've had over the last few weeks, and will take a bit of getting used to. But, now the smarting sensation has settled down to a glow, yes, I'm about ready for bed . . .

'Penny for your thoughts?'

'I was thinking about the caning I've just had and how not that long ago I would never have dreamed of letting you do such a thing to me!'

'I certainly think the warm-up spanking and then a caning is *very* effective.'

'It's very painful. I'm not sure I'd want to do that every time.'

'I didn't say we'd do it every time, just every now and then, because I'm not giving up the pure pleasure of putting you across my knee and spanking your bare bottom bright red!'

'Thank you, it's nice to know you still appreciate the simpler things of life!'

'Oh yes, my love, I think your initiation into the joys of spanking is just about complete.'

And I think it is.

6

Being Prepared

A small sideline of fantasy for you.

Imagine the following situation: You are out for an evening with the lady of your dreams, or if need be, your wife or girlfriend – and you, during the course of that evening, have managed to injure the hand you use to do that which ladies' behinds are made for.

Right? With me so far? There you are, out for the evening and you've slammed the car or restaurant door on your spanking hand.

It is cool driving along, the stars are twinkling in the deep velvet blue sky, it is too nice to go home so you pull over somewhere and take a slow walk.

And she starts playing you up.

Now remember you have an injured hand, and it could happen to any of us, could it not? So what do you do about it?

Your first reaction might be that you could cut a hazel switch and bend the lady over a convenient log or park bench to administer something closely resembling six of the best across her waiting, quivering, cheeks until you can get home and produce the rattan cane – which as we all know is the only true implement with which to administer six of the Very Best. But hazel switches sometimes need knives to cut them with, so here's my first item of emergency spanking kit, a knife.

Another good idea, and an essential part of the kit too, could be a nice wide leather belt holding up the trousers. That would make a very deep impression on the bottom of the young lady who has been cheeking you most of the evening, thinking, no doubt, that with an injured hand she would get away with it!

I'm full of ideas today. How about taking to wearing moccasins as part of your wardrobe? Soft leathery, flexible, whacky moccasins – hold on, they might be dirty from walking – well, bottoms can be washed, can't they? So down with the knickers and give her a dozen or so good sound whacks with your moccasin.

Holidays now. Don't forget an essential part of packing your suitcase must be the curling round inside the case of your specially oiled tawse. It will take up very little room, will fit into a rounded corner, and be available for the unwilling rear end presented to you over the end of the hotel bed. I know hotel walls are notoriously thin, but unless you have fine upstanding English rooming next door, who understand that these things are a part of the English way of life (by George), a foreigner will dismiss the sound as that of you banging the creases out of your clothes, unless of course the lady makes too much noise, in which case the cravat you remembered to pack will make a good gag!

Whatever happens, be prepared. Never leave home without something on or around you that will prove even more useful in your good right or left hand. It wouldn't do to let an opportunity go by, would it?

7

Party Games

This was written after we attempted to spice up our own love-making. There have been other articles on the same subject, with variations, but they all come down to the same thing in the end, two people making it fun to be together.

Here comes a very personal question. It's up to you whether you answer it or not. Did you get a spanking last night? If you did, was it the same boring old routine? You know how it goes, don't you, come on then: you're over the knees, your skirt's being turned back, your tights and knickers are pulled down, you're lying there, staring at the carpet and wondering how hard it'll be, or maybe you don't even need to wonder that! You're feeling cold and very very vulnerable and then the first hard slap makes you squeal, was it a bit like that?

Not a spanking, I hear you say, a caning. Oh well, that too can be rather boring, bent over the bed, the chair, the table, the desk or whatever, cold bare trembling a little. All jelly and butterflies inside, feeling the cold touch of the cane as he measures his distance, the sudden swish as the cane flies through the air to land with a thwack on your bottom, making you jump. Was it a bit like that?

From beyond the border I heard someone cry I got the tawse! Did you? Substitute the smack of solid leather for the swish of cane and the sensation is about the same. Likewise the belt. Or a birch. The only difference with the birch is the sensation, like being stung by a hundred nettles at the same time all over! You know only too well whether you bend over the chair, the settee, the table, the bed or bend and touch your toes for whatever it is decreed you're going to get this time - wouldn't you like a bit of variation?

I've got a new game for you to play. It involves a little thought and a little preparation. I think you'll enjoy the anticipation and excitement of planning almost as much as the game - almost . . .

Are you interested? If you're sitting comfortably, I'll begin, and you can be sure you won't be sitting quite so comfortably if you play the game properly!

You will need two dice (we made one of our dice red - you'll discover the reason why shortly), a piece of paper and a pen.

Now, in your place of residence, if you are an avid and loyal reader and supporter of CP magazines, you will have around you certain implements for inflicting pain and soreness on someone's rear end. I'd like you to pick six of these implements and write them down across the sheet of paper, then underneath you write the numbers 1-6. For example:

slipper	hairbrush	tawse	paddle	birch	cane
1	2	3	4	5	6

Are you getting the idea yet? (If not, why not?)

You throw the dice together. The first die will decree which implement is to be used, the second decrees how many you get. NOW do you see why we have a red die - all clever stuff, this!

I can hear the dominants protesting right now that you might throw a 6 and a 1. One stroke of the cane? Is that all? Disappointment reigns, that'll never do for an evening's entertainment! I agree, which is why we play the game like this.

Half naked, I roll the dice onto the hearthrug, it shows me 1 and 4. I go over his knees protesting (!) for four smacks with my slipper, which stings. I get up and roll the dice again. 3 and 5. Must I? I must. I bend over an arm of the settee for five stinging whacks with the tawse, get up roll the dice and decree myself three with the cane. And so it goes and *you* decide when your rear end cries enough! Then it's time for bed!

We decided, after some discussion that our punishment routine also needed sparking up a bit, so one evening he carefully cut out squares of white cardboard, about one inch square. He decreed the lowest figure I'd get, five in our case (you pick your own), and he numbered the squares in bold numbers 5 to 18. Then they were all turned over, mixed around thoroughly and on the back of each card he wrote things like brush, slipper, cane L, cane M, birch, tawse and so on until the squares were complete.

Then we turned the cards over and I began to get shocks and nasty feelings in the pit of my stomach. Fate decreed, by the mixing of the cards and random selection that I could, if I were unlucky, get eighteen with our large cane, seventeen with the tawse, twelve with the birch and so on. I only breathed easier when I got nearer the lower numbers!

These squares are kept in an envelope marked Lucky Dip, and it's all down to me now. If I'm insolent, sarcastic, difficult or contrary, or if I behave in the way any normal person would during the course of a day, I am told I will have to take one card. If I persist in my bad behaviour then of course I would have to take more cards out. It is now a common saying in our house 'three lucky dips tonight,' and if I am foolish enough to trespass on his goodwill and go past three lucky dips, then *he* takes the

49

fourth square out! I can assure you it is with considerable apprehension that I select those squares and, as I'm naturally short sighted without my glasses and don't wear glasses in the bedroom at bedtime, when I take out the card and give it to him to pass sentence, I wait fearfully for the sigh of satisfaction which means that I've picked out a high number.

It has improved the 'punishment' sessions no end, I can assure you!

Crazy? Perhaps. Unfair? Of course not, it all depends on the fickle finger of Fate. Fun? Definitely.

Enjoy yourselves . . .

8

With Friends Like That . . .

Friends, we all have them, but what would you *do if your friends acted like this . . .*

MONDAY

(Sue)
Bill came round. It's no good, I fancy him like mad, and yet I love John so much. I don't understand it. I suppose it's the 'grass is greener' syndrome, or something. Anyway, I flirted with him. Well, who wouldn't? He must be over six foot, dark, so very broody. Good-looking, enough to melt anyone. And John? He seemed to ignore it, somehow, at least, he didn't say or do anything. That's one of the annoying things about John, he never does say or do anything. I wonder what Bill would have done?

(John)
I like Bill, he's my best friend, I suppose, the one I'd confide in if I had anything bothering me, and I do like him coming around for a beer. But the way Sue was hanging over him; showing everything in that suntop of hers, it made me boil. It's a wonder neither of them felt the heat coming from me! I wish I could say something to Sue about it, but she may have been doing it unconsciously for all I know. I don't think so, though.

51

(Bill)

How John could sit there and let his wife flirt with me like that I'll never know! Man of iron, he must be, not so much as a flicker or look from him to disapprove of what she was doing. And if ever anyone was aking to be laid, she was, mine for the taking. If I didn't think so much of old John, I'd be in there like a flash. What that girl needs is a good tanning. If I get the opportunity, I'll mention it to him.

TUESDAY

(Bill)

Well, the opportunity came quicker than I thought. There was John all broody over lunch time pints, so we went off into the far corner and I said:

'Let's have it, old chap, what's the matter?'

'It's Sue,' he said, 'I can't get it out of my mind, the way she was hanging around you last night.'

John's like that, no pretence, straight out if you ask him; honest as the day is long. And never thought to ask how *I* felt about Sue hanging all over me, either! Trusting devil. What it is to have friends.

'Well, John,' I said, launching into my prepared speech. 'I think Sue needs a pretty firm hand, she's running rings round you, old chap, and you'll be hobbled and wearing an apron before you know where you are if you don't watch out.'

'I know,' he said, and he looks gloomier than ever. 'I just can't bring myself to shout at her, or anything like that.'

'Who said anything about shouting? What she needs is a damned good hiding!'

'What do you mean?' Oh, the innocence of him!

'You know, a bum warming, a spanking, a tanning, six of the best, call it what you like.'

'I couldn't do that!'

Shock all over his face, you can't help taking pity on him, can you? 'Look, pop round if you can tear yourself away from your blonde beauty for a night, and I'll show you some of my books. We can talk about it, all right?'

(John)

Never knew old Bill had such thoughts in his head! You should see the magazines he's got! All sorts of books, all with bare bottoms on the covers, and people getting smacked. Well, I never knew such things went on! Interesting, though, very interesting, especially the stories and letters about erring wives getting their just desserts. And do you know, if I were honest, I really did feel like tanning her last night when she was flaunting her boobs at Bill. But then again, she might take offence and leave me. I think I'd rather be her doormat.

(Sue)

Can't think what's got into John. Usually when he goes round to Bill's it's a few beers, a lot of chat then he's out like a light and snoring, except when he's in the loo, eyes shut, letting the beer out. But this time – well, if he's going to come home that randy in future, rock hard and ready, wow, he can go round Bill's every night, and I'll sit up in my best black nightie and wait for him, too! Wonder what they talked about?

FRIDAY

(Sue)

Same old John back again; the other night must have been a one off, if you see what I mean. Back to the old floppy cock and no guts, whatever did I see in him, that's what I'd like to know! Here we are, Friday morning, and I've had nothing since Tuesday night's booze up with Bill!

Wonder if Bill was as randy as John was that night? Perhaps we should have had the drinking session round here, then I'd have found out, wouldn't I? I wonder if I can invite Bill round again; wonder why he's never married; wonder if he's interested in me, or am I just John's wife? What am I doing being John's wife anyway?

(John)
Can't get those books of Bill's out of my mind. I know it's the right thing to do, but somehow – well, all right the thought of putting her over my knee and smacking her appeals all right, soft bum giving under my hand, turning red, but doing it – that's something else. I'm not sure I'm ready for that yet. I wonder . . .

(Bill)
So John comes up with this incredible idea, well, really, to be honest with myself, I've been fantasising about it for ages! I mean, who wouldn't fancy a tasty bit of blonde stuff like Sue; all boobs, curls and eagerness. I keep getting off the point, well, what I'm doing is savouring it, like you know, depriving myself of thinking about it. All right, I'm thinking about it. He wants *me* to give her a tanning for him! Well now, what do you think of that, Bill me lad, Sue over your knee, or Sue over your chair getting that pert bum of hers spanked red or tram-lined with your best bendy cane? Decide, decide, what is it to be? I know what I'd like – to have her over my knees for a bit, give her a long drawn out spanking; let her know what it feels like to go over a man's knee, helpless, knickers down and my hand tanning her bare bum scarlet. But would she stay there, that's what I have to ask myself; or would she even stay bent over for six stingers with my cane? Now there's a thought, six red lines neatly dissecting her cute jouncy cheeks.

(Bill)

Well, looking back at it, it was easier than I thought. Round they came, John and Sue, and I don't think he'd said anything. She was twitching like a mad thing; itchy crumpet, I suppose, flaunting those up-thrust boobs at me, and John, all embarrassed and nervous, wondering what, when and how, I guess. How Sue was going to take it. It was so easy!

'Sue,' I said, 'come over here.' And she comes all cock-teasing sure of herself. 'John's had enough of your flirting,' I said stern as anything, like my old schoolmaster used to be and how I've always wanted to be with someone. The women I've had, well, they were all mature ladies who knew just what they wanted, and that was six of the best – well laid-on, no messing, no games – and into bed for a good ride afterwards. I must admit I enjoyed it but I enjoy the games too. But for Sue, it was real, because I *had* had enough of her flirting, as much as John had. Well, how would you feel if someone kept sticking their tit into your ear and you knew you couldn't do so much as look at it, let alone grab a handful?

'I know,' she says, all coy and girlish. 'He said so.'

'What else did he say?' I asked, wondering how far John had gone on this.

'Nothing.' A toss of the curls and the arrogant look creeps back, the 'I know men and I've got you where I want you' look comes over her face.

'There's only one way to treat girls like you,' I said, reaching for a wrist and then tripping her up with my foot. She's over my knees before she can say jock-strap, and I've got her skirt up and her knickers down round her knees. John's eyes were like saucers, and a little grin came over him. Her bum was just as I'd imagined it, small, rounded, cute and very soft and I spanked it until she howled for mercy.

(John)

I never believed Bill would really do it, despite the magazines and his stories. Well, I suppose it's because I've never known anyone to do it before, yet there was Sue, bare-bottomed over Bill's knee, screaming and kicking and squealing every time his hand came down. How red she went; so quickly too and then she stopped kicking and lay there crying. I felt sorry for her then, she must have been sore. She was unbelievable tonight, we've never had sex like that before. I wonder if I have the nerve to do it? Maybe I should get Bill to tame her properly for me first, but then if he keeps doing it she might end up fancying him even more. Problems. Got to get some courage. Perhaps if she made me mad enough . . .

(Sue)

What a shock and I'm still glowing too! Never for a single moment did I dream Bill would do such a thing to me! I mean, when he called me over, I thought I'd got him at last. I'd about made up my mind that he was mine for the taking, but then suddenly, there was a moment when the floor left me and I was over his knees. Before I knew what had happened, my knickers were down; that was awful, the thought of John and Bill looking at my bottom, all naked like that, but there was hardly a second to think about it before I was getting smacked, and hard too. Wow it stung! And it went on stinging. It didn't matter how much I fought and kicked, he went on smacking. It seemed as if he did it harder and harder, and when I stopped fighting he stopped smacking. The heat was terrific; I could hardly get my knickers up again when it was over. But the glow, well, who can say when it settled down who I fancied most. And I thought Bill was a friend, too!

(Sue)

Well, I guess I asked for it. And I got it. I'm still not sure whether I'm sorry or not, I'll decide that later. Right now it's enough to lay here and feel the ridges with my fingers, but oh so gently as they still hurt! Who would have thought a cane could hurt as much as that? I certainly didn't or I'd never have teased Bill into it.

Well, there we were, drinking and I'd had a glass of wine too many, of course, as I often do, and I started teasing Bill about how he had enjoyed having me over his knee for that spanking. In response he went and got a pile of magazines which he dropped on the table.

'John's seen all these,' he said. 'Now it's your turn.'

I looked at all the ladies getting smacked, over chairs, benches, tables, beds, knees, desks. My – what a lot of different places, all with the same end result! The ones with the canes fascinated me most. All I could really remember of the spanking was the afterglow; nice that was. I wondered whether the sting of a cane would produce a better afterglow than a spanking, so I kept on about it. So much so that Bill went and got a cane out! I suppose I'd talked myself into it. John just watched and said nothing. I bent over the armchair and Bill pulled my knickers down. He said that no caning is a proper caning if it's not bare! I'm not sure I agree, but also have to admit there were not many covered bums in the magazines.

'Six,' he said, all stern like before.

It sent shudders through me, ever so strict and teacher-like.

'Six, and don't move.'

Boy did they hurt! I yelled and kicked and wriggled until he threatened me with double the number, tied down, if I didn't stay still! I took them. I had to. Now I'm lying here. John's done a real good job on me tonight, I feel tender and sensitive and ever so sexy still; feeling these ridges with my fingers. I wonder if John's still awake? I wonder if Bill would teach John to use a cane?

(John)
Tonight was another surprise, but seems Sue went willingly to the slaughter. Well, she asked for it, kept on at him, 'bet you've never really done it to a lady', and so on, till he got the cane out. Then she didn't seem to protest much when she bent over the armchair and do you know I felt myself go hard at the sight! I got harder as I saw the cane crack across her bare bum too; odd that, I thought I'd be upset, seeing Sue hurt, she certainly screamed and kicked enough but did she ever look good with the six clear lines across her cheeks! How she bounced at each whack! I think I'll ask Bill where he got the cane from. I think I could manage that easier than a spanking. I wonder if she's still awake? I'm still hard! I wonder if Bill enjoyed it as much as I did? Maybe I could go round again. Isn't it nice to have friends?

(Bill)
All right for them, isn't it. Here's me in bed alone, rock-hard and nowhere to put it! That Sue, she's impossible; tormented me into that caning, she did. How she asked for it: tease tease, 'bet you're just a dreamer, bet you never laid a cane on anyone, just sitting here night after night with your dirty books' – what else could I do but get the cane out and lay it across her cheeky bum six stinging times? And damn me if she didn't love every one of them as well!

Damn John, and Sue too. I'm aching and no one's home tonight.

With friends like that, who needs enemies?

9

Fire and Ice

This story is part truth, part fantasy. I did live in a flat with someone like this, but the rest is my fantasy. But it could have happened, it could . . .

I was into CP before I met Adele. I'd had a few boyfriends who liked to slap a little, and I'd encouraged that into full-scale spankings that left me red, tingling and begging for bedding. It made life interesting, added a touch of fire, you might say.

Adele was stunning. If I'd been a lesbian or even half-way inclined in that direction, I'd have fallen for her like a ton of bricks. Just as the men did. Her blonde hair was always swept up out of the way, elegantly. She was immaculately made up; jewellery always matching the model outfit she had on, and she floated in a cloud of perfume. All heads turned for her, male and female alike. Add to that a sweet laughing voice, and what more could you ask?

I was flat-hunting at the time, not being overly happy with my current living quarters. I had a room to myself in a house, but a flat would be more like it, somewhere to spread my wings a little, so I wouldn't always have to use the back seats of cars or park benches. Winter was fast approaching and I wanted some shelter for my love life. But the flats were expensive! I'd have had nothing left over for the necessities of life – like food.

Adele coming to work for the same firm was a godsend. She too was flat-hunting, being on the point of breaking up with her husband, and needing somewhere to go. She had the contacts and the cash; divorce settlement, you see. I left the flat-hunting to her, agreeing to go halves on rent, electricity, telephone and food. It seemed a fair enough deal.

The flat was more than fair – it was fantastic, to me, anyway. Large lounge, two bedrooms, one large, one small, kitchen, bathroom, garage and a bit of front garden. It was more than enough. Adele saw to the decorating and the furnishing and I let her play house. I happily moved in to the small bedroom with my bits and pieces, and made myself at home.

For a while things went very well. We shared chores, and ate well; sat up talking half the night and still got up for work in the morning. Our cars ran with the minimum of problems. The only trouble was that they needed constant supplies of that awful expensive commodity known as petrol. Other than that life – on the surface – was wonderful.

Talking into the small hours brings people very close together. We learned of each other's desires and hates, and I found out, to my surprise, that the blonde bombshell with whom I shared was cold as far as the old bedding game was concerned. She could have men simply by crooking her little finger, but all she wanted was their companionship. For her, it all ended at the bedroom door. It resulted in a spectacular fight one night with hairpins all over the lounge carpet where Adele had fought off a Casanova with designs on her slender body.

Me, I slept through it all.

In some ways it was frustrating for me, the fiery one, to be living with someone who was so capable of pulling men but who didn't want them. I wasn't that attractive, and always thought the men I met were interested in me so they could reach Adele. It didn't help my inferiority complex much.

During our talks, I told her of my interest in CP. It seemed to shock her, so I let the subject drop. No sense in upsetting a flat mate, is there?

The man I saw regularly at that time was a CP enthusiast. Unfortunately he sometimes had a tendency to overdo things just a little. I clearly remember the night I came home with some spectacular bruises which Adele saw through my filmy nightie. She asked me to show her. It was, momentarily, embarrassing, for we rarely saw each other nude. It was just something we avoided, without actually discussing it. But I did show her, and for a long time afterwards she was very quiet. I didn't ask. It wasn't any of my business.

Slowly, small envelopes began arriving, with shop names on the back. Why, I asked myself after a while, should Richard Shops or Dorothy Perkins write to Adele? But they were addressed to her, and it wasn't any of my business.

Then a man called one day, wanting a bill settled, a repair for Adele's car. I left him to her, but adding up the too-regular bank statements, the bank letters, shop letters and now a caller, it all fell into place. Adele was overspending at an alarming rate.

I confronted her with the revelation and she broke down, confessing all. She was bouncing cheques like tennis balls, it seemed, had a hefty unauthorised overdraft and was upsetting a lot of people. Some of it would rub off on me, if I wasn't careful. None of the cheques was mine but what if she defaulted on the rent?

'You,' I declared, pointing sternly at her 'need a damned good spanking!'

Why I said it I don't know, but I did, and it worked. She stared wide-eyed at me and then crumpled like a dropped rag doll.

'I know I do!' she whispered and that was that. I reached out for her, she came flopping forward like a Raggedy Ann doll, somehow ending up clumsily over my knees. I felt very strange for a moment, very powerful. The occasion could have been relished but there was something to do and I had to do it. I pulled up her dress, took off a slipper and held it firmly by the heel. It looked sturdy enough for the job. A bottom awaited me, small and rounded, I hadn't appreciated just how rounded it was until now, when the skin was drawn tight and it was presented to me. I was beginning to understand what my boyfriends saw in the whole business!

Without dwelling on what I was doing, I brought the slipper down first on one cheek then the other. Adele didn't yelp, so I hadn't done it hard enough. I don't have a particularly strong arm so instead I worked at keeping up a rhythm, bringing the slipper down on a different area, then back again, over and over again until she was blushing pink enough even through her panties. She struggled a bit but mostly lay there, rag-doll still, and took it. There were tears, of course, by the time the slipper hit the floor there were tears.

It always surprises me how quickly a spanking knocks all the stuffing out of someone. I know that after I've had an over-the-knee session with someone who possesses a hard hand or strong arm, I feel absolutely useless; floppy, tearful and ready to do anything. Adele was the same, except it hadn't fired her sexy feeling at all. Me, I would have needed an instant stoking to cool the flames, if you don't mind my mixing a metaphor or two.

Adele then, all floppy, helpless, tearful and promising humbly to stop spending so wildly and to watch the figures in future, and if they slid toward the zero mark, not to spend anything until the next pay cheque went into her long-suffering bank account. She promised to see the bank manager and come to some arrangement about the overdraft. It couldn't last forever. The overdraft I mean.

She confessed to feeling better, and to having a sneaking suspicion that she might get a spanking, after she'd seen my bruises. Although the two don't, in all honesty, quite connect, do they? I didn't mention the fact that my bruises were the result of a genuine Lochgelly tawse, extra thick, laid on brutally hard after a particularly stupid argument that I lost. In every way. It didn't matter, because the deed had been done, both to me and to her. I was glad something different had come into our lives. A positive move from mere flatsharing to a caring relationship. I cared enough about her not to want her to go bankrupt and, admittedly, I cared about a roof over my head, but then who wouldn't? I promised her another spanking should one more letter arrive concerning a cheque that hadn't been met, and I even threatened to lock up her cheque book!

For a while things were fine. No letters arrived that weren't openly talked of; the overdraft was slowly coming down, a few pounds at a time, nothing spectacular, but we were content.

I was able to bring my boyfriend home the nights Adele was out, so we could indulge in bottom warming (my bottom), in peace, quiet and warmth. I dislike exposing my nether regions to the cold, don't you? Much nicer to expose in front of an electric fire, both bars on and burning hot; as hot as you hope you're going to be after the birch, the tawse, the slipper or whatever else you had in mind, has finished landing rhythmically on the upturned cheeks. I don't think the neighbours care too much for it, I collect strange looks the next day, especially if I've been unable to completely control my oohs and aahs, not to mention the odd scream. Delight? Ecstasy? Pain? Judge for yourself after *your* next session. Do you expect me to reveal *all* my secrets?

I knew Adele wouldn't have liked it. The whole thing is far too noisy for spectators, unless they care to join in, or they are turned on by sights and sounds.

I finally got around to telling my boyfriend about my spanking Adele. It took me a while, because I felt I was breaking a confidence somehow, although I'd not said I wouldn't tell anyone about it. I thought he would understand.

He was very very interested. He asked how I felt, during and after. I tried to remember, but it all happened in the heat of the moment. I couldn't really say how I felt. I could only tell him what had happened. This boyfriend was one I could trust, as far as Adele was concerned. He wasn't interested. He said he could practically see the icicles dripping off the ends of her fingers and out of her hair, whereas I on the other hand sparked fire every time he looked at me. He wasn't tempted to get his hands on the beautiful Adele, except on her rear end!

I saw by the look on his face that he rather liked the image he had of Adele over someone's knees, knickers down, sobbing, as her bottom took its fair share of chastisement (although I did it). He smiled, knowingly. 'Next time, dear girl, see if I can do the chastising, would you?'

I promised to see what I could do.

Now I don't want you to think for one moment that what happened afterwards was a deliberate effort on my part to get Adele into what you might call a compromising situation. I'm not that devious!

What happened was, and you have to believe me when I say it, truly a coincidence. Those little white envelopes started turning up again. My boyfriend was round for a drink one evening and we were talking by the fire when Adele came in. She greeted us, and picked up the envelope from the sideboard, where we always left our incoming mail. Her guilty look in our direction was enough to tell us all.

'Trouble, Adele?' he asked, sweet as sugar, not a hint of what lay behind the question.

'No, no trouble.'

But the letter was crammed unopened into her bag, as she hurried out of the room, closing the door after her. We exchanged looks but said nothing. Later she came to join us, and we chatted for ages; she as light and as innocent as could be.

Two days later my boyfriend arrived unexpectedly asking me, as soon as I opened the door, 'Is Adele in?'

'In there.' I closed the door and went after him, wondering what was going on.

'No trouble you said!' he told Adele, staring angrily at her. 'No trouble. So what was that cock-and-bull story you told the bank manager about being seriously ill and having to have an operation?'

First she blushed and then she went as white as chalk. I couldn't believe what I was hearing.

'Well, I'd run up an overdraft again,' she confessed miserably. 'I saw some clothes and – well, you know how it is . . . How did you know?'

'Your mistake, Adele. I play golf with the bank manager. He knows I date Fiona, and that Fiona shares with you, so he asked me how you are.'

She looked down at the carpet, there was nothing she could say. I wondered if she knew what was going through his mind.

'I don't think you were spanked hard enough last time, Adele,' he told her grasping her wrist and pulling her to her feet. She offered no resistance, as if it was all inevitable, and she became all floppy and lifeless like a rag doll again. She stood by his side, all but collapsed over his knees, then lay over his lap, her immaculate hair falling everywhere, her hands just touching the floor. He didn't mess around, skirt up, panties down, even though they were thin enough to see through. Well, I could see the long dark crack of her elegant bum, saw the cheeks exposed properly for the first time, saw the hard hand come down first on one then on the other and heard her yelp. He was making a better job of it than I had! He spanked her hard and long, covering the entire bottom, from top to undercurve, then hard down on the thighs when she fought too much. Harder and harder it seemed, and her cheeks turned from pink to red in a very short time indeed. Adele howled and struggled, but she had to take it, every last slap.

The only trouble was, I was getting wet and wriggly, watching her being spanked. Foolish, I thought; I knew how much it could hurt and there was me, wishing that it was me across his knee instead of her! How daft can you get?

I got mine, though. After the sobbing, thoroughly-humiliated and chastened Adele was through, running off to the bedroom for cold cream and tissues, he advanced on me, grinning. He had seen my face and watched me wriggling.

'Very bad,' he commented, unbuckling his belt slowly, deliberately, tantalisingly, letting it slide out of the loops. I knew that belt, had felt its caress many times before, and it always devastated me. I got wet just looking at it, well, wetter than I already was. 'Very bad, to get excited watching a flat-mate getting her just desserts. Come over here, young lady,' he said pointing to one of the big armchairs. I went over, laid myself down, hands tightly wound together not to be tempted to put one in the way – I did that once and got the belt over my fingers, I didn't do it again.

The belt landed once, a band of pain wrapped around me, instant and sharp. Again, this time lower. I yelled, but the sound was muffled into the cushion. On the third one, the higher stroke, near the spine which sometimes hurts more than the others, I came. The explosion came in a mass of feelings; mixed and violent. He could see me wriggling, saw my legs go straight out, knew what was happening. His fingers were inside my panties in a second, deep in me, bringing the orgasm to its shuddering, shattering conclusion.

It was an unspoken condition between us that if I orgasmed, the punishment would stop. So, because I didn't get the thrashing I know I deserved, we made up for it another night, when Adele was out with another of her admirers who thought he could melt the Ice Maiden. I received a thorough thrashing with the belt, and exploded all over again.

'Fire and ice,' he murmured, when it was over. 'Fire and Ice. Adele and you. And I know which I'd rather have, any day of the week.'

It wasn't long after that I moved out of the flat, and left the Ice Maiden to her own frozen devices.

My boyfriend and I had decided to make it permanent, and that suited me very well.

10

World's Greatest Lover

No, I wasn't angry, in a mood, or involved in an accident to write this, but I did go to Wembley Arena market, and I did buy a World's Greatest Lover medal. I did also once buy a CP magazine in a newsagent, not these days, though!

Stephanie was bored. Completely and totally bored. Wembley Arena was crammed with people and kids, pushchairs and shopping bags waiting to bite at her ankles and shins. It was impossible to see the ground for the crush of people. She could, for all she knew, be walking in just about anything – her mind shied away from the thought and she sighed as once again she sought to keep her husband in view in front of her. Why he had wanted to come and see this collection of crafts she would never know. Yes I do, she told herself angrily, because his precious mother said it would be interesting, so he trots along so we can go round there tonight and he can say:

'Oh yes, Mother, the candlemaking stall was *so* fascinating and what about the miniature pottery urns? I could have spent a fortune on the things!'

You could have done, she thought savagely, kicking at a pushchair threatening to run over her toes, earning a glare from the harassed mother pushing it. You would

69

have done if I'd not kept a close eye on you and the cheque book!

Further along the area cleared a little, and she could actually see what was going on. A toy stall attracted her attention and she wandered over to it, keeping an eye on Gary as she went to make sure he didn't disappear. She might be bored, but she didn't relish searching the entire Wembley Arena for him if they lost one another.

The collection of 'medals' caught her eye, large gold circles on bright red buttons. 'Greatest Mum', 'Greatest Dad', an intriguing one which said 'World's Greatest . . .' The mind boggles, she thought, smiling to herself. Another one attracted her attention and she picked it up. 'World's Greatest Lover' it read in bright red lettering. She fumbled for her purse to buy it, thinking it would be a good joke for Gary. *When* she was in a better mood! She handed the medal to the stallholder to put in a little bag. He glanced at it.

'Congratulations,' he said winking at Stephanie. She blushed, handed him the money and backed away before he could make any more comments. She tucked it into her handbag and thought no more about it, looking around for Gary.

Finally he escorted her to the car park. The autumn breeze ruffled her black curls and she pulled her coat collar closer around her neck.

'It's cold after being in there,' she complained.

'We'll be warm in the car,' Gary said, tall and rugged, striding along by her side, seemingly impervious to the weather, 'and we'll have tea at mother's.'

Of course, Stephanie added silently, we have to have tea at mother's. She immediately castigated herself for her unkind thoughts. Gary was no mummy's boy, but it was just that she was bored, she decided, that's all.

Despite her earlier thoughts, Stephanie's mood grew steadily worse during the evening, as she sought to make small talk with her in-laws, while Gary discussed the things they had seen that afternoon. Finally Stephanie could no longer stifle her irritation and she snapped at Gary a few times. He raised his eyebrows at her, and his mouth set into a firm line but he said nothing to her until it was time to leave. Farewells were said, and Stephanie tugged Gary away to the car.

'I'll drive,' she announced.

'What's the matter with you?' he asked angrily as she slammed the door and jammed in the ignition key. 'You were almost downright rude tonight!'

'I'm tired,' said Stephanie in a sulky voice. 'I'm tired, I didn't like walking around the market, and I liked talking about it afterwards even less!'

'You're acting like a spoiled brat,' Gary told her.

Stephanie swung the car round the corner, making the tyres screech and throwing Gary off balance.

'Slow down!' he shouted at her. 'You'll have an accident if we go on like this!'

'I'm all right!' she said, but as Stephanie spoke, the car coming the opposite way overtook a parked car too wide and Stephanie did not have enough time to get out of its way. The wings collided with a frighteningly horrid sound of crunching metal.

'That's all I need to end my day!' she exclaimed, and slammed her fist against the dashboard.

'Don't worry, I'll see to it.' Gary got out of the car, leaving her sitting behind the wheel fuming. When he came back to the car he handed a piece of paper through the window to her.

'Put that away safely and you get on to the broker in the morning. And move over, from now on I'll drive, all right?'

Stephanie felt totally deflated and upset; she climbed awkwardly over the gearstick and into the passenger seat, holding tightly to her handbag and saying nothing.

Gary didn't look at her as he started the engine and set the car in motion. Stephanie stole a look at his set face and quickly looked away. He didn't look very happy.

But much to her surprise he said nothing more to her about the incident when they got home. He garaged the car and Stephanie busied herself with some supper, all the time waiting for the outburst that was sure to come. She had never escaped without a telling off before, but Gary seemed almost offhand with her. He had adopted an easy going attitude which was rare after one of her bad moods, and especially after the accident. Stephanie was puzzled and a little apprehensive. This could be the calm before the storm; she had no way of knowing. When she came out of the bathroom later, she found Gary sitting on the edge of the mattress, as if waiting for her.

'Why aren't you in bed?' she asked, and wondered at the stab of apprehension that hit the pit of her stomach. She had nothing to fear, as far as she knew. She wondered again at her train of thought.

'I've been waiting for you,' Gary took her hand and drew her closer to his side. 'I decided today that spoiled brats need to be treated like spoiled brats, don't they?'

Stephanie tried to pull away, her apprehension growing stronger; she didn't like the tone of Gary's voice or the meaningful way he was looking her up and down. His grip tightened fractionally on her wrists and he pulled her even closer to him.

'Do you remember what happens to little girls who show off and break things? They get their bottoms smacked, don't they, Stephanie?'

'No, Gary, that's ridiculous,' she protested violently. 'I'm a grown woman, you can't treat me like a little girl!'

'But I can and I will,' he replied stolidly, ignoring her frantic struggling to escape. 'You, I think, deserve a spanking for being in such a filthy mood, being rude and then crashing the car.'

'That isn't fair, the accident wasn't my fault!'

'I didn't say it was, did I?' he asked reasonably. 'All I know is if you hadn't been in such a bad mood you would have been driving just a little slower, and might have had time to avoid the other car. Therefore –', with a sudden movement he pulled her face down over his knees, 'you need to be taught a lesson and this seems to me to be the most effective way of doing it!'

He pulled back her filmy baby doll nightie which covered very little of her body anyway, and brought his hand down hard on one of her rounded cheeks. It produced an instant red mark and a shriek from Stephanie, who immediately renewed her frantic fight for freedom. She was raging with anger; it was almost a nursery punishment and she resented it bitterly. He took both her wrists and pinned them in the small of her back and proceeded to spank her soundly, turning her cheeks from palest pink to bright red while she cried and struggled to be free and pleaded with him to let her go, promising that she would be good in future.

When he finally did let her go, she rolled on the floor, sobbing. Gary ignored her and got into bed. Stephanie got up from the floor and inspected herself in the mirror, crying aloud at the sight of the flaming red cheeks that presented themselves to her in the brightly lit mirror.

'Beast!' she cried, flinging her slipper at Gary as he lay watching her with an amused grin. He caught it and threw it back.

'Any more of that and you'll find out what a slipper feels like across your backside,' he warned her.

Stephanie fumed and stamped and tears continued to course down her pretty face, but she heeded the warning and made no further attempt to retaliate. She got into bed and snuggled herself down on her own side, sniffing and grumbling into her pillow. Gary left her for a little while before sliding over and taking her into his arms.

'Go away, I hate you!' she snapped. Gary rolled away, still amused.

'Have it your own way.'

'I will.'

He switched out the bedside lamp and lay smiling into the darkness. Whatever Stephanie might be feeling at the moment, apart from her hot sore bottom that is, he was feeling very good indeed. There had been something very erotic about Stephanie's soft white cheeks turning bright red under his punishing hand; about the way she squirmed and wriggled to be free yet he was able to hold her with just one arm. He almost laughed at the memory but checked himself in time, it might upset Stephanie even further and he didn't want to do that. As if she had sensed his mood or read his thoughts, she suddenly turned over and reached for him.

'Gary, I'm sorry,' she whispered, her voice tear-husky in the darkness.

'That's all right,' Gary said, as he cradled her gently in his arms and she moved closer, pushing against him.

'Ready and waiting?' she teased, biting his neck gently, nibbling with small white teeth. 'You are a beast, though, aren't you?'

'No.' Gary gently pushed her onto her back and began to rub her nipple, very gently. It came erect under his fingers. He traced the fullness of her breast as she lay there, slid a finger down and encircled her navel, found her tightly curled hair and parted it, sliding a finger into the slit; searching for her erogenous zones and finding them.

'How's the bottom?' he asked as she writhed against his hand.

'Hot and sore.' But Stephanie was reacting to his touch. She pushed him back and eased on top, sitting up straight and allowing her wetness to envelop him, her thighs gripping his body, his hands cupping her cheeks. She rocked backward and forwards, her muscles working hard to bring them both to a powerful climax. Stephanie was surprised at the intensity of her own feeling. She soon fell asleep, tumbling down into sensuous dreams.

In the local newsagents the next day Stephanie saw a magazine on the top shelf that made her stop and stare. The girl on the cover was quite obviously about to get a spanking, and she felt her stomach muscles contract with the sudden memory. She realised that the magazine had been there in the past but she'd taken no real notice of it, that was, until she'd had a spanking, just like the girl in the picture. She looked at the price on the cover, thought about it for a moment, weighing up the expense against what was possibly only her curiosity, and decided to buy it. She waited until there was no one at the counter, and then walked quickly over, paid and crammed it deep into her shopping bag.

In the supermarket she began to berate herself mentally for spending so much money on a trivial thing like a semi-pornographic magazine when there were other things she had to buy. And then she berated herself for being so very nosy and wanting the magazine anyway. But her curiosity was strong, and last night's memory was sharp in her mind; the feeling of helplessness and indignity when she was sprawled across Gary's knees; the slightly shameful feeling of his eyes on her bare bottom; the pain of his hand slapping and slapping and the memory of the intensely passionate lovemaking afterwards which was the overriding memory. It was only the checkout girl calling impatiently to her that made her realise she was day-dreaming.

At the front door, searching her bag for the elusive door key, she heard the crackle of paper and remembered the medal she'd bought at Wembley. That, she decided, is going away safely until the day he earns it! Last night had been good, very good, she amended, as she packed away her shopping, but he can do better than that, hopefully, and then I'll give him the medal! She went upstairs and hid it under the tray of jewellery in her drawer; he'd never look there, it was safe.

Later, over a cup of coffee, she opened the magazine on the table and stared fascinated at the array of photographs; at the many different bottoms on display for men's eyes to savour; slim ladies, heavy ladies, small rounded cheeks, heavy cheeks that looked as though they could take a lot of punishment. Not like mine, she thought, instinctively touching her small rump.

The variety of implements used in the photographs astonished her more. Judging by the photographs the readers had sent in, a cane could do a lot of damage to a girl's bottom, but then she wasn't sure she liked the look of the tawse either! And come to think of it, Gary had managed pretty well with just his hand!

She settled down to read the stories, realising after she'd read half of them that the stories told of spankings and canings, tawsings and slipperings that were always connected with sex and passion; with excitement and interest. Stephanie found herself wondering whether there had been a connection between the spanking she'd had and the intense passion of the lovemaking later. The only way to find out, she told herself, was to ask for another spanking. She stood up and shut the magazine. I don't think I want another somehow, she decided, and then wondered at the tinge of regret that touched her mind for a fleeting second and then was gone.

It was some weeks later before the whole question of spanking and the magazine Stephanie had carefully secreted away came up again. Life had remained usual and routine: work and sleep, visiting and staying home. Nothing seemed to be happening to change what was, really, a very boring life. If only I had a job, thought Stephanie irritably from time to time, when the day stretched endlessly before her. Nothing to do but clean the house and go window shopping. Even if she had the money to buy half the things she saw and desired, there would be no room for them – their home was more than adequately furnished already. Part-time jobs were scarce, and she wasn't sure if Gary would like her working anyway.

Boredom inevitably leads to bad moods and, more and more frequently, Stephanie found herself losing her temper with Gary, shouting at him and generally being rude. Once the thought flickered through her mind that she was doing it deliberately to provoke him, but then she squashed the thought as firmly as she could, and continued in her sulky moods.

One day Stephanie found that everything was going wrong. In the morning she managed to burn the toast, and then a plate slipped on the soapy suds on the draining board and crashed to the floor, breaking into a hundred sharp shards, one of which stuck in her finger as she cleared up the pieces. She went to the supermarket in a thoroughly bad mood, compounded by getting to the checkout to find a bag of flour had leaked all down the front of her winter coat. By the time Gary came home for tea, she had spilled coffee down herself, banged her knee badly on the table and developed a blinding headache. When Gary walked in, announcing he had had a bad day, she exploded:

'*You've* had a bad day! I'm sure you've had nothing compared to the day I've had! Look, my dress has been ruined by coffee stains, I've cut my finger, I've had flour all down my coat, I've broken a plate –'

'All right, all right,' Gary said, as he held up a placatory hand. 'My wife has had a bad day, I'll say no more.' And he went and sat in the dining room without another word.

Stephanie put his meal in front of him and he ate it silently. She sat at the table glaring at him, willing him to speak so she could start a row and get all her pent up feelings out of her system; but he refused to look at her or give her any openings at all. She cleared away the tea things in an absolute fury; slamming around the kitchen, banging doors and drawers, making as much noise as she could.

Finally she came to sit down in the lounge and stared at the television. In the middle of the news she became infuriated with a trivial item and picked up the remote control to change channels. Gary snatched it back, his eyes glowing with temper.

'One more thing from you, my girl, and you'll be sorry,' he warned her quietly. But Stephanie had reached the point where she didn't worry about danger signs. She snatched back the remote control and flicked the switch. Without a word Gary walked over to her, pulled her to her feet and guided her back to the settee, ignoring her cries, as she realised what was going to happen.

'No, Gary, no. Gary, I'm sorry, I've been in a bad mood all day – Gary I –' She found herself helpless, face down over the arm of the settee, Gary's firm hand in the middle of her back, holding her in position while his other hand tugged at her jeans. He pulled them down around her thighs, then he removed her tight black knickers.

'You, my girl, are going to be taught a lesson. Remember last time? It worked a treat, you were good for ages!'

'Please, Gary, don't spank me!' Stephanie wriggled and kicked to be free but he held her down easily and reached for one of her mules. He gripped the heel and grinned to himself. Then he brought the slipper down hard on her right cheek.

'No Gary, it hurts!' She wailed as he brought the slipper down across the other cheek.

'I know it hurts,' he told her as he settled into a rhythm.

'I have every intention of making sure you don't sit easily tonight!'

The slipper made a resounding crack each time it met her bottom, turning white to pink and pink to red as Stephanie wailed and sobbed and fought and kicked against the spanking. No matter how hard she struggled, she was forced to lay there and take it, until her bottom was bright red all over and she had given up the fight to be free. Gary dropped the slipper and picked her up from the arm of the settee, then he sat down and put her on his lap, holding her close.

'You're making my shirt wet,' he told her, but without expecting a reply. He cuddled her as she cried and then said, 'You also look very silly with your knickers round your knees like that.'

Stephanie's sobs stopped and she smiled tearfully at him. 'I asked for that, didn't I?' she asked, pushing her damp curls back from her face.

'You did. You've actually been asking for that for a while, today was the final straw.'

'It hurt more than last time.'

'It was meant to, you deserved to be spanked harder this time.'

'I hurt.' Stephanie gingerly moved herself on his knees and rubbed her bottom tenderly. 'You've made me very hot.'

'So you should be after a spanking like that. Want to pull your knickers up?'

'Yes please.' Stephanie stood up and carefully eased her knickers over her sore cheeks, wincing as she did so. She pulled her jeans up but left the zip undone so they wouldn't pull tight. Then she sat on the soft cushion of the settee next to Gary, leaning against his shoulder. He pulled out a large handkerchief and she dried her face.

'I decided today that you can expect something like that every time you get in a bad mood,' he told her, winding her curls round his fingers.

'Really? I'd better behave myself then, hadn't I?' she murmured, feeling the stinging smart subsiding to a warm glow.

'Yes, you had. Now, darling, there is something I want to watch tonight, will you leave the TV alone?'

'Of course.'

Later that night as they lay side by side after their intensely powerful lovemaking, Stephanie resolved to dig out the spanking magazine and read it again. There had to be a connection between the glow she had felt after her spanking, the butterfly feelings in her stomach when she knew it would happen, and the lovemaking which followed. Somehow Gary seemed more potent after spanking her. She fell asleep dreaming of being over Gary's knees while he smacked her, not hard, but gently, erotically. She awoke in the morning, content but curious.

She read the magazine through twice, and the more she read the more aroused she became. The writers of the stories are exactly right, she told herself, that's how it happens. I'll have to get Gary interested – but how? The thought occupied her mind for a while as she turned over all sorts of conversation openers in her mind:

'Gary, about last night, er, could you do it again, do you think?'

'Gary, I broke a cup today, do I deserve to be put over your knee for a good smacking?'

'Gary, er, would you mind giving me a good hiding? It seems to turn me on.' All were dismissed as being useless, and embarrassing! The easiest thing to do was to leave the magazine lying with the evening paper and see if he took the hint.

It was with a sigh of relief that she peeped round the door later that night, while washing up after tea, to see the evening paper lying unopened on the coffee table and Gary absorbed in the magazine. She skipped away delightedly, and hummed softly as she finished clearing up.

Then she quietly went back into the lounge and sat down beside him. His eyebrows arched as he looked at her, but he said nothing just went on reading. Finally he put the magazine down and stared at her.

'Wasting housekeeping money on pornography now, are you?' he asked abruptly, and Stephanie quailed under his stern look.

'No – I mean – I was –'

'Nosy.'

'Well, yes, perhaps, if you like. I bought it after the first time you spanked me.' She waited for his reaction. To her surprise he started laughing. 'What's the matter?' she asked, puzzled. This was not what she expected after such a stern expression.

'You've done exactly what I intended to do!' he laughed. 'I was going to buy the same magazine and leave it for you to find! I never dreamed you'd get it before me!'

'Are you interested then?' asked Stephanie cautiously.

'Yes, I am, if we make it part of our love play,' he said thoughtfully. 'How do you feel about it?'

'I'd like to keep the painful spankings for when I'm naughty,' she confessed in a little girl voice. 'But there's nothing to stop you giving me – well, gentle ones, is there?'

'Nothing at all,' he replied, leaning over to give her a kiss. Stephanie snuggled against him, purring contentedly. Life might be improving after all.

'Love spankings' became part of their love play from then on; usually with Stephanie lying across Gary's knees, completely naked, her slender bottom on view, his hands sliding over her, caressing her. His fingers would gently penetrate her making her wriggle and gasp with pleasure before he withdrew them to slap her lightly, almost caressingly, slapping progressively harder until her bottom was a deep pink and she was gasping with excitement.

It became a ritual, and then, in time, stale, and Stephanie found she no longer looked forward to the love play any more. She had also noticed that Gary's erection was not as pronounced as it had been when they started the 'love spanks'.

She stared at herself in the mirror one morning, looked deep into her own blue eyes and told herself firmly:

'There's got to be more to it than this, Stephanie, my girl.' And she resolved right there and then to buy the next issue of the magazine to see if it had anything in it to excite and inspire their lovemaking.

When Gary came in that night, he had a large envelope under his arm. He saw the copy Stephanie had bought lying on the kitchen worktop and started laughing. It seemed he too had had the same idea as Stephanie, namely that their lovemaking needed something to perk it up a little, but while Stephanie had been buying and reading a magazine, he had been to buy a whippy cane . . .

Stephanie was eager to try the new toy, but restrained herself, deciding to wait for bedtime; it was better then, when they could make love and go to sleep.

When she went into the bedroom that night, she found Gary had laid the cane across the middle of the bed.

'In case you'd forgotten,' he teased when she laughed.

'I hadn't forgotten,' she assured him.

'You'll have to bear with me for a while,' he said, swishing the cane through the air. 'I've never used one of these, and it could be a bit naughty until I learn to handle it properly.'

'I trust you implicitly,' said Stephanie, but all the same she was a little apprehensive. The cane did make the most awful sound whistling through the air, and she suddenly remembered the colour photos the readers had sent in, bottoms marked with livid weals. She put on a brave face. 'How do you want me?'

'Bend over the end of the bed,' he ordered, and whacked the bed with the cane. Stephanie jumped.

'I don't think I'm going to like this,' she said doubtfully.

Gary laughed. 'You didn't like spankings once either, did you?'

'True.' She lay down over the end of the bed and waited, slightly worried, very excited. The cane was a line of coolness touching her skin. Gary stood to one side of her and then brought it down across her bottom. She jumped, bit her lip but said nothing. It stung, but not much more than the slipper had.

'That couldn't have hurt much,' he observed. 'Only the palest of pink lines.'

'I don't think you intended to hurt,' she retorted.

Gary paused for a moment. 'I don't know,' he said finally. 'I think that's been a lot of our trouble lately, you know. I've not hurt you very much.'

Stephanie turned her head to look at him and then got up to sit on the end of the bed. She couldn't feel any sensation from the stroke with the cane. 'Whatever do you mean?' she asked him.

'Well,' Gary began, and then stopped. 'When we – I mean, I – oh hell, what do I mean?' He started walking around the bedroom, trying to put his thoughts in order, tapping the cane on his leg as he walked. Stephanie watched it, mesmerised. 'When I first spanked you, I did it to hurt, and it did; and you were fantastic in bed afterwards. Now you've got used to the light spankings, it's stopped doing very much for you.'

'And you,' observed Stephanie tartly, and he coloured slightly.

'All right, for me as well.'

Stephanie was silent for a moment. 'You're right, but I'm not sure about this cane though, it could hurt!'

'I'm pretty sure six strokes with this, firmly laid on, will hurt,' agreed Gary, 'but whether it'll hurt any more than the spankings I gave you when you were naughty, I wouldn't like to say. And –' he added, 'you've not given me the opportunity to punish you lately, have you?'

Stephanie wrinkled her nose and looked at the floor.

'I was beginning to feel . . .' she began slowly and blushed. 'I was beginning to think it was about time I was naughty again, you know, so you'd spank me really hard.'

'And all you had to do was ask, didn't you, my sweet darling?'

'Yes, well . . .' Stephanie rolled over, face down on the bed. 'Let's see what it *really* feels like, shall we?'

Gary grinned. 'All right, you've asked for it!'

Stephanie buried her face in the eiderdown and waited, feeling the first prickle of excitement and apprehension hit her stomach. She yelled as the cane cracked across her bottom, bringing an instant red weal and intense smarting pain.

'Ow!' she cried, rubbing frantically at the line. Gary surveyed the weal.

'Not quite straight,' he commented. 'This is going to take some getting used to.'

Stephanie finally stopped rubbing and moved her hands away. 'Ouch!' She looked up at him piteously, pleading.

'All right, just a little easier this time,' he smiled down at her and swished the cane through the air, bringing it down again.

'Ow! It still hurts!' she complained, both hands flying to her injured rear.

'Hands out of the way!' he told her. 'No one gets less than six, you should know that, you've read your magazines, haven't you?'

'Yes, but nowhere in anything I've read does it say you *have* to have six!' she protested.

Gary aimed for and cracked the cane across the tender crease at the top of her thighs.

'Ow, Ow, Ow!' she complained, rubbing frantically. 'That wasn't fair!'

'Nor was your comment – six of the best has been a long-standing English tradition, and you know it!' He stood back to admire his handiwork. 'Come on, two more and you'll be about ready for me, I think.'

'Conceited swine! Ow!' The cane landed squarely across her bottom neatly between the other four lines. Gary waited until Stephanie stopped rolling around and brought the cane down again. She jumped up immediately and danced around the bedroom, holding her bottom and complaining like mad. Gary hung the cane in the wardrobe and then got into bed, waiting for her to join him there.

'Let me look,' he instructed her. 'I want to see what mistakes I've made, if any.'

She turned round, showing him her cheeks marked with six distinct lines.

'Not bad,' he remarked, 'but it looks like I've got to even things up just a little. Too much on the right hand side.'

Stephanie slid into bed and clung to him, feeling more sexy than she had done for some weeks. Gary was erect and throbbing, already feeling more excitement than he had done for some time, and judging by Stephanie's reaction to his wandering fingers, she too was more than ready. He eased himself on top of her, rested on his elbows and smiled.

'Ready for me, aren't you?'

'Yes, now now!'

He slid into her hot wetness, feeling her muscles contract around him, then relax, allowing him to penetrate deep inside her. She climaxed almost immediately, and then, as he continued thrusting deep and strong, she came again; clawing her nails down his back, shouting her pleasure.

As they lay holding hands in the afterglow of their lovemaking, Stephanie wondered at the improvement in Gary after a real painful session like that; it seemed to turn him into a better lover.

Suddenly she remembered the medal and leapt out of

bed, rummaging in the drawer, giving Gary an absolutely delightful view of her neat bottom with its decorative pattern of weals. Slightly bent over, she presented an exciting view.

'Here,' she said, as she held out the medal. 'I bought this for you ages ago, I've been waiting for you to earn it!'

'Minx! That deserves another caning.'

She laughed happily. 'Save it for another night,' she said ruefully, rubbing at her six lines. Gary looked at the medal, smiling at the thought of being the World's Greatest Lover.

'We need this on display,' he told her.

'It would have to be somewhere we can chart your performance,' she replied instantly. 'Make sure you *stay* the world's greatest lover! At least in my bed!'

'All right,' he declared, 'I'll accept that challenge. I'll put this medal on a ribbon and pin it to the wall, and you can move it up or down, depending on my performance!'

And that's where the medal is now, adorning the bedroom wall on a strip of white ribbon pinned to the ceiling and the skirting board. It has moved up and down a few times but in all truth, Stephanie will tell you if you ask, that it has never got to the skirting board; although once or twice it has slid half way down, but when that happens, Gary blames it on Stephanie's lack of response to his lovemaking. That is followed by a long session over his knee to have her bottom tanned bright red or bent over the end of the bed for six stinging whacks with the cane; practice has made him rather adept at using it.

And Stephanie isn't bored any more.

11

A Note for Benny

Quite a few years ago I read an advertisement in a contact magazine just like the one featured in this story. I'll never know if the advertiser had any takers for his service – what I do know, and can assure him should he chance to read this book, is that I have had many a happy hour and orgasm fantasising over being sent to him! And I got a story out of it as well. It would be nice to think he had some response too. On re-reading this story, I've realised it is virtually every man's dream – compliant women who will go along with the instruction to visit someone for punishment! Or, being the person who puts out the advertisement. Dream on, guys!

'Anne.'

'Oh!' I've just realised what I've said, and it's too late to do anything about it. I can't snatch words back out of the air.

'Right, that really is it, I've had enough – I'll write a note for Benny, and put a stop to your games!'

'Tom, no!'

'And you can walk there and walk back too!'

'TOM!'

He's walking off, he means it, I've done it this time. Oh no, not a note for Benny! Last time was bad enough! Tom's coming back, has he relented?

87

'...t did Benny give you last time?'

'Twelve with the hairbrush.'

'How?'

'Oh Tom it's –'

'I wasn't there, remember? I want to know, how else do I know what to tell him to give you this time?'

'I leaned over the arm of his big armchair and I got twelve with a wooden hairbrush over my knickers.'

'Obviously didn't do you any good, or you'd not be insulting me now. So we'll make it on the bare bottom this time.'

'Make what?'

'You'll find out when you get there.'

I've gone all cold and my insides have turned to jelly, Benny *hurts*!

'Tom, won't you do it, just this time? I really am sorry, I didn't mean to call you that, please, I'm sorry!'

'Despite what you just called me, and the fact you've been looking for an argument for three days now, I love you very much. If you started crying I'd have to stop, and you wouldn't get punished then, would you? Why else do you think we send our wives to Benny?'

'I know, I was just hoping –'

'That this time I'd give in. You're lucky, you've only been once to Benny, I know Jack has sent Susie four times now!'

'Four times? Wow!'

'I've put up with a lot from you, it's time you had your knickers taken down and were given a hiding you won't forget in a hurry.'

There's nothing to say, is there? What do you say to a husband who looks as angry as Tom does, and who is writing busily, explaining my 'crime' to Benny and working out a punishment? How I wish Benny had never come along. We used to be happy around here! I remember when the advertisement came through the door, duplicated on a sheet of yellow paper. It simply said:

'Naughty erring wives chastised, hairbrush or cane. Moderate charges. Contact Benny Silman, after 7pm', and the address. That was enough to start off a chain reaction all right! Most of us treated it as a joke, but we were slowly finding out that our husbands didn't, and that was when it started. I think Susie was the first to go, at least, she was the first to talk about it. Jack had sent her along to Benny one night and she told us all about it at the supermarket next morning.

'He's big,' she told us with huge eyes. 'He's bigger than any of our husbands and must weigh half a ton! So good-looking it isn't true, and he treats you so nicely – "come in, sit down" – and then he reads the note. He said, "Oh dear, you have been naughty, haven't you?", and didn't listen when I protested. All he's interested in is the note you take.'

'What happened then?' asked Gina, wriggling excitedly. The baked bean mountain was in danger of going over as her elbow almost jogged the middle tins. I swear she had damp knickers or something. Susie had a quick look round to make sure no ears were straining in our direction; you know what shelf fillers are. Gossip magnets. Well, they are in *my* supermarket.

'He led me over to his big settee and asked me to lay down over the arm, which I did. I was scared silly. I was shaking so much my knees almost gave way! He pulled my dress up out of the way and then picked something up.

' "Just a hairbrush spanking," he said. "Ten should do you." And it did! Oh it hurt! I forgot all about being tough and dignified, I just bawled like a baby. When you've got that hairbrush smacking your bottom, you don't think about anything else!'

It was the general opinion of us all that we'd better tread carefully. All of us, that is, except Mary who shyly confessed that she got spanked or caned at least once a week anyway, so Benny's arrival didn't make any difference to her. We all looked at Mary with surprise but said nothing. She looked so quiet and shy, now we knew why.

I resolved to be very good, I wasn't having any strong-armed man spanking me!

But of course I didn't, and it wasn't that long before I ended up on Benny's doorstep, shaking from head to foot as I rang the bell. This blond giant came to the door and smiled so nicely at me that I felt a lot of my shaking stop. I handed him Tom's note and he invited me into this beautiful lounge, filled with heavily-stuffed, comfortable furniture and elegant tables and chairs. There were lovely paintings on the wall, really nice. I fleetingly wondered if Mrs Silman was there, waiting upstairs for a frantic lovemaking session when Benny was through spanking errant wives for the evening. After all, that was surely what he was getting out of it, wasn't he? Surely he wasn't only doing it for the money! I longed to ask, but didn't dare.

'You've been getting out of hand, Anne,' he observed quietly, looking at me as he read Tom's note. 'I think twelve with my hairbrush will stop your games, for a little while, anyway!' He led me with quaking knees to the big old-fashioned armchair. 'I'll collect the hairbrush while you make yourself comfortable over the arm of that chair, all right?'

I think I muttered something. I can't remember. I laid myself down over the arm of the chair and buried my head in the thick cushion. I was going to tough it out and not give him the pleasure of having me cry and fuss! I felt silly and childish, which is of course, what he intended. And he gave me time to think about it. I felt my bottom muscles tightening and relaxing, the fear quivering through me like a fever of some kind. Where was he, where had he gone?

Then I felt Benny lift up my dress and my slip and smooth down my frilly nylon knickers. I remember sighing silently with relief when I realised he didn't intend to take them down, that would have been too much. At least I had a little protection!

Just as I was beginning to feel even sillier lying there, my bottom was on fire – the first of my twelve. It felt like a solid thump against my cheeks and a flame shot through me; it stung and burned at the same time, and all I wanted to do was yell. Everything Susie said was right, you did forget about being big and tough, you just cried because it hurt. It hurt a lot. Each one hurt more than the one before, because they all landed on top of one another.

My struggling to get up resulted in him crossing my wrists in the small of my back, which hurt even more; I couldn't fight like that! He carried on as though I'd done nothing. No one, but no one escaped Benny's punishments, and he let you know it as well!

By the time Benny had counted twelve with that unrelenting hairbrush I was sobbing helplessly, hot and sore, and ready for absolutely nothing. He let me get up, handed me a tissue and escorted me to the door. 'Tom can settle with me later.'

The door opened, and I was outside, crying like a baby, my bottom on fire; so hot I thought everyone could see the red glow through my clothes.

The car was there, I could just see it through my tears and Tom was waiting for me. It hurt just sitting down in the car.

Now I've got to go back to Benny again. I don't know what I'm going to get. And, having annoyed Tom in the morning, I have to wait for nine hours before I get my punishment! That means there's time to be nice to Tom, he might relent if I'm lucky.

It's nearly seven and he hasn't relented; in fact he has hardly spoken to me all day. It's been one of the longest most miserable days I can remember. Tom mad at me – and me scared. I really will be glad when it's over. Tom glances at the clock.

'Time to be on your way, Anne.' He is so cold, so hard. 'Here's the note for Benny.'

I pick up my bag slowly, hoping all the time he'll say it doesn't matter. But I'm at the door and he hasn't called me back – I suppose I'd better go.

It's a long walk to Benny's house, it takes me ten long, agonising fearful minutes to walk it; every minute I want to turn and run. But I daren't.

Benny's door is open but I ring the bell anyway.

'Come in!' he calls. Trembling, I step inside. 'Go in to the lounge, I'll be with you in a minute.' The lounge is empty and immaculate. Mrs Stilman must be kept busy!

I can hear muffled voices from another room. Someone else is here before me, perhaps more are waiting. I wonder why they're not in here? I came in this room last time. The yell startles me, whatever is he doing to her? The screaming is too much, he must be caning her! Oh God, what if Tom's asked for a caning for me! Oh, no, I'm not staying here, listen to her! Oh no, I'm going home, Tom will understand, he must!

'Anne, what are you doing back? Is it all over?'

'There was someone there, she was screaming. Oh Tom, I can't go back to that!'

He looks cold again, cold and hard, just like he's been all day.

'Please Tom, don't you understand?'

'I understand you've run away from a punishment. Come on.'

'Where are we going?'

'Benny's, where else?'

Tom has a tight grip on my wrists and is walking me back along the street I just ran along. I hope no one is looking out of their window. It's all I can do not to cry. I steal a look at Tom's face and realise there's no point in arguing with him.

'What's the matter, Tom, Anne?' Benny actually looks concerned.

'I sent Anne along with a note, someone was already here, making a fuss. Anne ran back home, thinking I'd take pity on her.'

'I wondered why there wasn't anyone here when I came out,' said Benny, looking sternly at me.

'What were you doing to her?' I have to ask. I have to know.

'Oh, she'd been specially naughty, Anne. She had to have the cane and she made *such* a fuss! I was asked to make sure she went home well and truly punished – so I gave her twelve. Took me a while, she wouldn't stay still!' He smiles, a slow, knowing, calculating smile, watching my face drop; watching my spirits hit the ground and the fear sweep over me like a long cold breeze off an ocean. 'I know you're going to be much better than that.'

Tom pushes me towards Benny. 'I'll wait here. Oh, you will add something on for running away, won't you, Benny?'

'Of course.'

I hand Benny the note Tom sent me with, and he reads it quickly.

'We won't be long, Tom. Come on, Anne.'

We walk into the lounge where I'd waited before, no chance now of escape. He has an amused look, this really is a pleasure for him.

'Do you know what Tom wants me to give you?'

I shook my head, not daring to answer, too afraid of what he might do. *Why* did I run away?

'Come on, can't you speak? I bet you can cry though!'

I'm saying nothing, I've said too much already.

'Well, Tom wants me to break my usual practice and

93

put you over my knee. OK? With me so far? He then wants me to take your knickers down and spank your bare bottom until you cry for mercy. All right?'

I have nothing to say, I feel sick!

'Then when I've done that, I'll give you three with my little cane for running away. I don't think you'll do much running after that!' He's being deliberately spiteful, knowing the words hurt almost as much as the punishment will; fear is the greater enemy of all.

What can I say? There is nothing to say – my heart is thumping like a sledgehammer and I've gone all cold. I really feel ill. Should I tell him? He's sitting down now, getting comfortable.

'Come on, over here.'

I take slow careful steps, I'm only prolonging the awful moment, I know that. As soon as I'm within reach he grabs my wrists and pulls me face down over his knees. This is worse than going over the arm of the chair; my hands are on the carpet; all my long brown hair falls over my face so that I can't see; my toes are just touching the floor; my bottom is stuck up in the air, and I'm scared. He pulls back my dress and slip and tucks them firmly into my belt. Then he pulls my knickers down around my knees. With them goes my last shred of dignity!

Then the spanking starts. This isn't the hairbrush, solid and hard, every whack sending shudders through me, this is different. This is a hard, male hand slapping my totally unprotected soft, pampered bottom; the slaps hard enough to sting every time. To hurt. They move all over my cheeks, they miss nothing, and then start over again. Slap follows slap and my bottom's getting sore, getting tender; I can feel tears coming. I won't beg for mercy. I must be burning red by now, I'm crying because it really hurts. He'll stop in a minute, he'll take pity on me, he must stop in a minute, he's got to stop in a minute or I won't be able to sit down for days!

'Please – Benny!' I let out an involuntary cry for mercy and he stops immediately. I slide onto the floor and lay there crying.

'What a well-spanked girl you are!' he says almost admiringly. 'I thought you'd never ask me to stop! Tom was right, he said to keep on until you begged for mercy. Proud, aren't you, Anne?' He walks away, has he forgotten about the cane? 'Come on, over here.' No, he hasn't.

I painfully get to my feet and pull my knickers off before walking over to the armchair. One plea, I'll just try one more plea.

'Bend over, please.'

'Please Benny, I'm really sorry, I won't say anything like that to Tom ever again and I promise I won't ever run away again.'

'You won't speak to Tom like that again, I'm sure, or my punishments aren't effective! But you still have to be punished for running away. You ladies must learn to do precisely what you are told. Come on!'

I bend over the arm of the chair, carefully. Oh, my bottom is on fire! I hate to think what it looks like!

'Three I said, didn't I? Three ought to make sure you behave.' The cane touches me, I'm so hot it actually feels cold!

'Please don't get up; I'll have to add one more if you do.'

'Please, Benny.'

'One.'

That was me screaming, I can't help it! The agony of the lines of fire leaping across my bottom! I must touch.

'No hands, now, Anne. Come on, only two to go. Two.'

I can't take any more of this!

'You'll be good in future, won't you – three!'

And it's all over. But I cannot move.'

'Come on, Tom's waiting.' Tissues are pushed into my hands and he leads me out of the door.

'I'm sorry, Tom, I really am!' Loving arms hold me close.

'Hush, it's all over now.'

'I gave her the spanking you asked for, Tom. You were right, she took quite a lot before crying out, and then I gave her three with the cane for running away.'

I can hear the rustle of notes but I'm not looking. I don't want to know what I've just cost him, all I want right now is to be held tight.

'Come on, love, let's go home. Thanks a lot, Benny.'

'Any time, Tom, any time.'

We walk slowly back down the road. I must look a mess. I certainly feel it, eyes all swollen and hair all over the place. My knickers are pushed into my bag. Now Tom is loving and kind after the coldness of the day.

'I'm sorry I've been so hard on you,' he says softly as if he has read my thoughts, 'but if I'd been nice to you, I'd have relented and torn up the note, and you know and I know you had to be punished.'

'Mary's husband spanks her,' I offer tentatively. He frowns thoughtfully.

'Does he? I might have a word with him about it.'

Back indoors I rush upstairs to inspect my bottom in the mirror. Scarlet cheeks and within the scarlet the deeper red lines of the cane. It looks awful!

'Very pretty.'

I didn't hear Tom enter the bedroom.

'Very sore.'

'And so it should be, you won't forget that in a hurry!'

Isn't it odd, I remember last time after I'd been to Benny the lovemaking was as marvellous as this. I think I'll wait a while before I have to go to Benny's again, but in the meantime, there's Tom, I wonder if he will . . .

12

Reminiscences

This, unlike most of the others, is a true story. This is about a man I met at the offices of the CP magazine for whom I was writing, who was so persistent that I finally agreed to go and visit him – and no it wouldn't happen today, so don't think YOU can try it on with me!

Do you remember what it was like, the first time?

Of course, could anyone forget?

Want to tell me?

Why not?

There was the long journey to London first, checking and re-checking the letter, thinking over all the assurances I'd had; all very well but the doubts were creeping in, did he mean them? Won't hurt, he said, well, won't hurt much anyway. I squirm a little on the rough moquette seat of the coach.

It's a long journey to London, with time to envisage everything that might happen, from the over-the-knee spanking which would surely sting and redden my some-what generous bottom, to the tawse. I know he has tawses, oiled and ready, and a martinet. Anticipation thrills. It sits like a coiled desire deep in the pubic area, almost a physical pain but a most enjoyable one; my knickers become wet with the prospects of delights and pains to come!

Victoria Coach Station, people spill from coaches like milk from a broken bottle, running in every direction. A good many of them, like me, heading for the loos. It has been a long ride, and there is moisture to mop up, so that I become at least partly respectable before I carry on my journey.

Away across the complex set of lights and bus lanes which are a novelty to a country dweller, then on to the rail station. It is a blaze of lights and indicator boards, booming tannoys, taxis and commuters; they all know where they are going and are anxious to get there. Claustrophobia as I stand at the end of a very long line of people buying tickets they cannot get from a machine; low roof-lights and crowds. Will my turn never come? Following the lights and clutching my yellow ticket tightly I find my way down the escalator descending into the deep dark depths of . . .

Come on, it's only an underground system after all. Over-active imagination, that's your trouble! The trains are surprisingly empty, the people I queued with have dispersed among the many different trains on many different levels. It approaches lunch time, the restaurants and sandwich bars overhead must be packed solid by now.

I have an appointment and I still feel apprehensive about it. I tell myself there is always time to turn back, all I need to do is get out at the next station, cross the platform and take the train back to Victoria, a quick telephone call and I'd be free.

But I don't. I sit there, staring at the edge of the blue sheet of paper peeking from the compartment at the back of my travel bag. It contains a map and precise instructions to get from the station and assures me I can't get lost. Want to bet? It's been years since I commuted, and then not to this part of London but to the City. Of course I can get lost.

The question has to be asked, why don't I get out, go

back the other way? Why do I sit there, heading toward a man who will surely hurt me? Because the tingling sensation which the mere thought brings; because the anticipation of being told what to do and obeying him without question comes before all else. A double thrill – double pleasures. The anticipation of what is to come and the obedience of taking orders without question. Submission. His will over mine.

My station at last, and a long climb to the surface. Surprisingly, for I'd forgotten on the long train ride, the sun's shining. I turn right at the side of the pub and begin the walk. My heels are high and the pavements aren't brilliant. I must be careful, I don't want to spoil the outfit with grazed knees and torn tights.

(Yes, tights! Tights in which I am comfortable, rather than stockings in which I am not. Do you realise it's fourteen years since I wore stockings? Must have been mad to wear them then, would certainly be mad to wear them now! And before Puritan spankers start writing to me to complain, let me tell you that no one's complained yet about the view when I'm uncovered and ready, suspenders or no suspenders, it doesn't seem to make any difference.)

Apart from the indignity of falling, I don't want to spoil the mood, the anticipation is exhilarating, I'm quivering even as I walk. A wet quim adds a good deal to a stroll in the sun, even if the stroll is towards an appointment with pain. Now *there's* a good title for a story.

Quick look at my watch, I'm late. It has taken me longer than I expected, but here's the road at last, and I suppose he lives right at the end? Naturally. A head or two turns as I pass, do they know? Of course not, just curiosity. No one could know, *I* know and *he* knows why I'm here, the person who lives over there behind that door – yes, that door over there. I'll climb the steps and ring the bell in a moment. First, deep breaths and severe clamping down on butterflies. Shall I be a butterfly and turn and fly away from here?

I'm ringing the bell, now it really is too late.

'Come in, lovely to see you.'

'Thank you, sorry I'm late.'

'That's all right, don't worry about it. You found it all right, then?'

'Yes, I found it all right, your map was a great help, it just took me longer to walk than I realised.'

'I'm sorry, I should have told you there were buses.'

Too late to tell me of buses, as I sit here looking at you, shorter than I remembered, thinner than I remembered, but with eyes that tell me that you are the boss here, and I shall not and will not question what you say. And I am wondering whether you like what you're looking at as much as you did when we first met.

'Worried?'

'No.' But I'm lying.

'Tea?'

'Tea would be nice, thank you.'

'Or would you prefer cider?'

'That would be even better, thank you.'

And that gives me time to make small talk and relax my tight muscles and nerves. My sense of euphoria is suddenly violently shattered when he says:

'Well, I think you deserve a spanking for being late, don't you?'

Flustered, I find myself agreeing, fool that I am. I should have protested but now it's too late.

'Come on then.'

He has put a straight-backed chair in the centre of the room. I kick off my high heels, instantly shorter, and lay aside my precious glasses. No need to see when your nose is going to be three inches from the carpet, is there?

Now, the fluttering really begins, the feelings press so hard against every nerve I possess I think I'm going to burst. I lay across his knees, submissively. Slowly, so very slowly, he turns back my skirt and slip and, stupid person that I am, I help by moving my body so that he can lower my tights and knickers.

'Beautiful.'

I know I have a lovely bottom (conceited, aren't I?) and it's nice to be admired.

'Almost a shame to smack it but that's what you're here for.' The hard hand descends on the left cheek and then the right in quick succession. Intake of breath, it is always, always harder than I anticipate, and they sting!

'You were almost half an hour late.'

I gasp and wriggle as a flurry of smacks start the reddening process.

'Keep still,' he commands curtly.

I, being in no position to argue, keep still and take the spanking he's delivering in crisp, hard smacks to my unprotected bottom. I wriggle and cry out occasionally, but pride makes me determined to take as much as I can. I finally say, 'That's enough!' When I feel I simply cannot tolerate any more without a show of tears which would be treacherous right now. We are, after all, only at the beginning of the session.

'Just six more,' he says with quiet emphasis, and six more I get, three on each cheek in turn and I know I've been spanked. I am able to stand up, we cuddle, and I can restore clothes and dignity for a moment, sinking gingerly into a soft armchair.

There is something unreal about the situation. We talk about anything and everything; from writing, to trains and coaches and, all the time, I'm aware I'm sitting on a hot, red bottom and he hasn't mentioned it once and neither have I! In the middle of this strange situation and polite conversation, he produces a tawse and asks, so politely, if I'd like to lay across the bed, that is, if my bottom has cooled off. It has, and I do. I don't really have any choice, do I, now that I'm here and alone with him, and I've already accepted a spanking. To refuse would spoil everything. He knows as well as I that there is really no chance of my saying no.

Anticipation comes in a surge that is almost an orgasm in itself. The quietly spoken request is almost an order; there is no sense in saying no. This is a bedsit, and the bed is close, there is no need to walk further than the table to remove my glasses, walk over to the bed lay down and wait.

The spanking has forewarned me that he means to make me sting if not actually hurt and I'm a little apprehensive and rightly so; for with tights and knickers down again he immediately tells me that my bottom is no longer red, there is no sign of the spanking I've had, therefore it wasn't that hard! I'm capable of taking ten with his tawse and almost immediately the leather cracks across my bare bottom making me jump, and cry out.

'That wasn't too hard,' he says reproving my protest and he whacks me again and again. I count the strokes aloud, feeling the width of the tawse create its own wide bands of pain, overlaying each other, knowing with relief that I can take it even though I'm protesting like mad. Who wouldn't? The tawse has been well oiled and is very stingy indeed.

It's a different sensation from the intimate touch of the hand; a tawse says, 'this is punishment, this is meant to hurt!' and oiled leather certainly does. It wraps itself around the cheeks as if made for it. Well, it was, wasn't it?

And then it's over for a while. When I've cooled off from that session, and my equilibrium is fully restored, he tells me I'll experience the martinet. He waves it in the air for me to see, the long leather thongs look as though they can't wait to wrap themselves around my bottom. There's a lot of me, and they look as though they could cover it all.

We talk again of this and that (almost of cabbages and kings!) while I feel the glow subside and settle, wrapping itself around the sexy nerves that live somewhere down there, below my stomach, right behind the bush of hair that protects me from the sharp edges of chairs over which I have to bend at times.

And when he considers I've cooled down, I have to kneel in the chair, holding on to the back of it, and thrust out my bare bottom for the martinet. It's different again; the sharp sting of each of the thongs is electrifying. He uses it gently, luckily, but the cumulative effect is devastating. Again and again the thongs wrap themselves around my ample cheeks, bringing their own wire-thin strands of pain which build and build to a painful whole. The tips of the thongs wrap around my hip bones, yet don't cut, not once, they just add to the bite of the instrument.

I take it without a word of protest passing my lips. It has all come together to push me towards a screaming climax when he stops. Did he know, I ask myself, and for a long second I'm on the point of demanding a few really hard lashes with the martinet to complete and satisfy the excitement I'm feeling. But the moment passes, there is no point in anticipating the ending, for we are not through yet, and he knows it as well as I do. I climb down from the chair, and we cling together for a long moment.

He's as excited as I am, but we both know I have yet to sample the delights of one of his collection of canes. No disciplinary session would be complete without the cane, and he is an expert. I have to warn him not to mark me so I cannot have the caning I would like; we must be careful. I've only been allowed to come here on condition I don't go home marked by cane weals.

He has planned my visit well in advance, giving thought to every aspect of it. For the last session a small work-bench is pushed into the room, covered with cushions, and I am invited to bend over it; again a request but almost an order although I have no thought of refusing. He produces wide webbing with which he secures my wrists and ankles, and I cannot move. I surrender all responsibility for what happens to his capable hands.

An ice-cold bottle of water is passed over my cheeks, cooling, almost freezing them. Then he begins tapping me all over with the end of the cane until every bit of me feels as if it is on fire. I cling to the rail, fighting the bonds, wriggling and squirming and trying to escape the bite of the tip which is war-dancing all over me. It seems to last forever.

When I'm good and sore come the mandatory six of the best, not hard, but after such careful, painful attention with the cane they bite enough to make me jump – then I release the excitement I've been building all the time – the climax has come and gone while I'm being caned, it's all over. The feeling is unbelievable and indescribable.

Bonds are released, I stand up, rub frantically, and join him on the bed, where we lay together, and he finds his (safe) release.

Then I get dressed while he makes more tea, and the unreal feeling is back. We talk as if nothing has happened; as if we were friends meeting to have tea and nothing else; as if I'd not been across his knees, across his bed and everywhere, having my bare bottom tanned with the variety of disciplinary instruments he keeps on hand; as if my involuntary wriggling was normal.

Then there is the walk back to the station, the thanks, the goodbye kiss, and clutching my ticket I make my way back down into the depths of the earth. It is as if the film rewinds and reverses, quickly rushing backwards through time: the same train going the other way; the same escalator going up instead of down; back through the anthill of Victoria Station; along the road; across the lights and into the coach station to find my coach home.

'Had a nice day?' asks the driver as he takes my ticket.

'Not bad,' I reply. My smile is inner, secret and very real. The moquette feels just as rough as it did earlier but for a different reason. Then there is the long contemplative ride home.

Will I go again?

Of course, if I'm let off the leash again. There was talk of a note next time, to ensure adequate punishment for 'crimes' committed at home. My objection was that it's a long way to be sent for punishment – but boy is it worth it!

13

Teacher's Pet

This is another story to take care of the 'school' brigade and is pure fantasy. All the tutors I've had at evening classes have been – well – dull . . .

I'm not all that quick to catch on, so it took me until the middle of the Autumn term to realise why every single woman attending the evening class in English was well-dressed and made up. Now I'm not saying that the women going to the other classes, Spanish, French, basket making and so on, weren't dressed up too, but there are always a few, aren't there, who don't bother; who arrive in sweat shirt and jeans. But in our class, not a one. Every single female was immaculate. And it was all his fault, John Catherington, the English tutor.

What a name! Smooth as cream, rolls off the tongue, doesn't it? And cream suits him too as a description. He always wore those creamy coloured shirts, and brown tailored suits, or casuals, but always looked as if he'd just walked out of an advertisement for a men's tailor shop. His dark hair was greying just a tiny bit at the temples, making him look so distinguished. And as for his looks; was it any wonder a whole class of women were gazing at him with bedroom eyes? Was it any wonder I didn't realise I wasn't the only one for so long? I spent all my time gazing at him and hadn't noticed the others doing the same thing!

Oh, the dreams I fashioned around him; how he was swept off his feet by the pure poetry of my prose, the precise logic of my reasoned arguments, the purity of my grammar.

Dreams. The reality was that the 'A' level I needed was approaching faster than I cared to think about and my assignments regularly came back covered in red ink! *His* red ink, which made it easier to take, but red ink on an 'A' level paper probably meant no pass – and that wouldn't do.

The first problem was how to stop daydreaming in class and get some work done. The second problem was how to get this incredibly good-looking person, who seemed impervious to all attempts to beguile him with cosmetics and perfume, to notice little me. I felt swamped by all the elegant beautiful women around me.

I have to confess to the other dreams too. There were the moonlight and roses ones, and the others, when I'd be invited to his bedroom and gently he'd take my hand, lead me to the side of the bed, ask me so nicely to lay across his knees and I would. Of course I would.

Then with a touch of tenderness he'd gently peel back my clothes. I'd be so proper, with silk petticoat and suspenders to entrance his eyes. He'd lower the knickers, black, edged with lace, of course, until my creamy white bottom met his eyes. Then he'd tell me again, so nicely, that I'd been a bad girl and proceed to spank; left, right, back again. Hard ringing slaps against a background of the litany of my offences; the wrong spelling, bad grammar, misplaced punctuation, all firmly spanked home with a hand that looked firm and strong and probably was. And I'd squirm and writhe against an ever growing bulge – for surely he would enjoy doing it! I wasn't that bad looking! – until we'd both be panting with the effort, me with sore cheeks, him with a stinging palm and then we'd collapse on the floor in a veritable orgy of passionate lovemaking.

Perhaps I'd be allowed to climb atop him, to ride the erection that would go deep, deep inside me, filling every last centimetre of me, length and width. To feel the pressure of his balls on my clit, to feel his hands on my breasts, and to feel my tongue meet his when I finally collapsed onto the big manly chest that was surely hidden beneath the creamy shirts.

Dreams. To be satisfied right now with only a slippery vibrator and some KY jelly; not the same thing at all.

Dreams. And like I said, dreams wouldn't get me a pass. Something had to be done.

But copies of CP magazines kept intruding between me and the boring English study books. I was going mad for a spanking and no one, but no one, was around to do it. Here's where I also confess that I'd never been spanked, but the idea was tantalisingly sexy and interesting. I was turned on by the stories and pictures and wanted to find out for myself what it really felt like. All my dreams were pinned on John Catherington, and he didn't know I existed, except as a name on top of a sheet of paper. When I realised all the other women were yearning after him too, I was frantic with worry. What if one of them got where I wanted to be – in his bedroom? What if she intrigued him so much he didn't think of anyone else? Worse still, what if he didn't want to spank me, even if I got that far?

But first I had to get that far. And that was a problem all on its own.

There was one particular night when he didn't smile as he handed out the corrected papers. It was then that another terrible thought hit me. There might be a Mrs Catherington at home, with curlered head bobbing as she moaned about the lack of money which is why he was teaching evening classes anyway. After all, teachers had enough to do without taking evening classes as well.

I stared at him over the top of my book, longing to comfort him, to take the serious look from his face. Then I looked down at the paper.

Not lay heavy but lie heavily.

You naughty girl!

Now, to be honest, I don't really remember which was the right way round after all! You'll have to take my word for it that it was one of them. The words leapt at me, glowing out of the page. I had the next assignment by my side, waiting to be handed in. I tore off half a sheet, wrote my name at the top and added *naughty girls get punished, don't they?* and slipped it in among the papers. Daring! I never thought I'd have the nerve to do such a thing but the Devil drives where needs must, or some such expression. All through the class I denied the temptation to take the note back. I was determined to do *something* to get noticed, even if it was as extreme as writing the teacher a note. 'Don't ask, don't get' is one of my favourite mottos, and even though I might get more than I originally asked for, if I somehow became teacher's pet, it would be more than worth it. And after all, he could just laugh and tear up the note, couldn't he?

Can you imagine the week I suffered? I studied precisely nothing. No, that's an outright lie, and I'm being honest with you – I studied the colour photos in the magazines, trying to decide which were rouged bottoms and which had actually been smacked before the shutter clicked. But I didn't do the next assignment, because all I could see were his eyes and all I could imagine were his hands.

Monday night dragged itself into my life somehow. I dressed with special care and danced happily down the stairs, out of the door and into the cold night air, where another terrible thought hit me. What if he mentioned it in front of the whole class? What if he really did treat me like a schoolgirl and called me out front? No, he wouldn't

110

do such a thing, surely! But I worried all the way to the Centre.

He stopped briefly by my side and dropped the assignment on my desk, and said nothing. But he smiled, a sort of secret smile. I scanned the pages to see how much red ink I'd earned this time. Half a bottle, by the look of it. And in the middle of the sheets, a tiny note.

I agree. Naughty girls should be punished.

5 pm tomorrow at the above address. I'll be expecting you.

My heart leapt about like a mad thing; butterflies went berserk in my stomach and I felt a curious wetness down there, you know what I mean. I'm not spelling it all out for you.

What chance of concentrating after that? None at all. I somehow went through the motions; listened, asked a question or two, answered nothing, copied off next week's assignment and walked by his desk without handing in the last assignment. His eyebrows went up but he said nothing. I'd have given a lot to know what he was thinking, though!

So, what to wear? A night of fantasy and churning excitement. I settled on a plain skirt and blouse, as near a uniform outfit as I could find, and finally went to sleep, only to dream of his dark eyes.

It got to be five o'clock somehow.

I tapped on the door so quietly he didn't hear me the first time and I had to knock again. Stern-faced, he opened the door.

'Ah Rosemary, yes. Do come in.' Sort of cold, hard, not like the soft smile he'd given me the night before. I wasn't sure I liked this person very much, but on the other hand, we were role playing, weren't we? I sincerely hoped we were.

He led the way into a study, lined with books and furnished with huge leather armchairs and a big desk.

'Now, Rosemary,' he said, as he sat behind the desk, tapping a pencil in his hands, leaving me standing like a sheepish schoolgirl in front of him. 'I understand you think naughty girls should be punished. Is that right?'

I swallowed twice before replying, 'Yes.'

'Why?'

It seemed a foolish question, but I tried anyway:

'Well, it seems wrong, somehow, getting away with silly mistakes. If I'd been at school –'

'You'd have been reported to the headmaster a long time ago for daydreaming and sloppy work!' he interrupted, shocking me with his accusations. I definitely didn't like this John Catherington at all, and turned to go.

'Where are you going?'

'No, nowhere.' And to be honest, I wasn't. The impulse to leave flashed through my mind, I'd half given way to it, and then stopped. I'd come for something, and I was going to get it, no matter what.

'Come round here.'

I walked round the desk, dropping my bag as I went. I stood, eyes downcast, waiting for instructions.

'Rosemary, you've been my worst pupil this term. You've stared at me all through lessons, you've turned in consistently bad work, and last night there was no work at all! What have you to say?'

'Nothing.' And there wasn't anything to say, not really.

'I'm going to punish you, at your suggestion, remember. I can but hope you'll take more notice in future.'

'What are you . . .' And I stopped, because it seemed silly to ask what he intended to do.

'I'm going to give you a good spanking. Bend over!'

As I bent over his waiting knees, my stomach flipped right over. Here it was at last, what I'd fantasised about. Was I brave enough?

Skirt tugged up, silk petticoat kept for just this occasion, and yes, the suspenders and black lace-edged knickers, too. He said nothing but I felt the sharp intake of breath. I think I knew then I'd picked my man accurately. I hoped I'd picked the right man, I'd be in a pretty predicament if I hadn't!

What I hadn't envisaged was how much a man's hand hurts, when it meets soft, pampered flesh with a considerable amount of force. I think I yelped as the first smack stung like mad, and it seemed only seconds before my whole bottom was on fire and every subsequent smack hurt more than the one before. The pain grew more intense; my bottom got hotter and I kicked and struggled and pleaded for mercy, long long before he stopped. And when he did stop, my bottom was completely blazing hot; from the very top, right down to the tender join. I fervently hoped that there wasn't a surly, curlered Mrs Catherington somewhere listening to me getting well and truly spanked, and crying over it too!

I got up when he told me to, tears running down my face. I rubbed frantically at my sore bottom, not that it helped any.

'Right, now, bend over my desk.'

Had I heard right? There was more to come? I backed away, pleading for mercy but there was none to be had.

'Rosemary, I've just spanked you for daydreaming and sloppy work. Now I intend to give you six with this ruler for not handing in the latest assignment. Now bend over.'

The ruler looked pliable and painful, and I was sore, but I had no choice. After all, as he'd pointed out, it was my own suggestion.

The ruler hurt every bit as much as I thought it would, and then some. After the second whack I stood up, asking to be let off but there was still the strangely cold look on his face, and I was ordered down again, with the threat

113

of him starting all over again if I didn't. I bent over, hanging on to the other side of the desk, determined to take the other four. I did, but only just. When he stopped I collapsed at his feet, the six bands of pain hotter than the original all-over pain had been.

Suddenly, here was the whispering, tender, gentle, creamy-smooth John Catherington holding me and caressing me, with exploring enquiring fingers that found the wetness. The carpet was prickly and stabbed my bottom with sharp nylon tufts. I didn't get to go on top after all, but was crushed to the floor, a cock hard and long, harder than any I'd experienced before, plunging deep into me, me, waiting and willing. The sore bottom added impetus to my writhing as I wanted to get off it, so I thrust against him over and over. And he, in turn, rode me all the way to the climax. It wasn't quite moonlight and roses, but every bit as good.

Afterwards, sitting in one of the soft, leather armchairs, feeling the glow spreading from my spanked bottom to parts it shouldn't (not after the climax I'd just had) he told me how thrilled he had been to find my note.

There was no Mrs Catherington, he lived alone in the huge rambling old house with only the odd girlfriend and a supply of spanking magazines for consolation. Rarely had one of his girlfriends consented to go over his knees, and when they did, they hadn't liked it and he was beginning to think all the stories were fantasies, until last night.

He apologised for the cold hard act he'd put on, and I had to admit in all honesty it was convincing, and added tremendously to the whole thing, making me feel just like an errant schoolgirl. He said he'd worked it out all night, while he was trying to decide whether I meant what I'd written or whether it was all just a game. I made him promise to do it again, next time.

There's not much else to tell you.

My latest assignment has just dropped on my desk, with another note.

This work isn't up to standard. Please report to me at 5 pm tomorrow.

What price being teacher's pet? This time I've been promised the cane.

14

Dommie

Having read SF for years, it seemed natural to me to have a go at an SF story. This was the result. Will household robots ever get that good, we ask ourselves? And you're no doubt asking yourself why my heroines are invariably bored. Well, because housework generally and being a housewife in particular is the most boring job in the world, if you think about it. Role reversal films have proved that! Sometimes we have to do something to liven up our lives – other than drinking or turning to crime, that is.

Terry had been gone for a week now, and Stella was bored. There was nothing to do, and Dommie was not exactly a conversationalist. She sighed heavily. Perhaps if they'd had a baby she would have had something to occupy her days, but there was no baby, no Terry, there was nothing but the long empty days – and Dommie. He was the cause of most of her problems.

Dommie was six foot tall, dark, very good-looking – and a robot. And you just could not flirt with, tease or interest a robot. She could walk around the house naked, *had* walked around the house naked, and provided she didn't try to open the front door to anyone in that state, Dommie would merely respond to her with a 'Yes, Madam', as he always did when spoken to. Dommie never started a conversation. He made statements.

'Dinner is ready, Madam.'

'Your friend has arrived, Madam.'

'Your transporter awaits you, Madam.'

And that was about it.

Dommie was short for Domestic, his robot status. Stella, young, pretty and frustrated, was fast developing a violent crush on Dommie and he remained totally, robotically unaware of it. In fact, the only time he really made any effort to get near was when she did try – just once – to open the door naked. She was pulled rather sharply away and Dommie stood in front of the door, ignoring her commands to move, Stella sighed again. So tough, so strong, so inhuman. Such a waste.

She picked up the holographic image of Terry and it smiled at her. Why in all the Universe did she go and marry a Space Captain? It had seemed romantic at the time, marrying someone who flew to Mars as casually as she went shopping, but she had overlooked the boredom his long absent periods would result in. Dommie was the latest addition to a house full of gadgets, and had given Stella much amusement and interest at first, testing his capabilities around the house, but now the novelty had worn off, and she was bored.

'Someone here, someone here,' sang the door softly.

'I'll open it, Dommie,' called Stella, eager for something to do. Dommie stood in the doorway.

'Madam, you are inadequately dressed!' he said in his stilted not-quite-human voice. Stella looked down at the almost transparent Glassex negligée she had thrown on in the morning.

'I'm not naked, Dommie,' she answered swiftly, 'and it won't be anyone important.' And before Dommie could respond to that, she ran to open the door. Outside stood a young blond man, wearing the bright orange Helpers Inc coveralls.

'Mrs Black?' he enquired, trying and failing to look at her face. 'Helpers Incorporated, you called us.'

'Yes, I did.' Stella felt a prickle of excitement. 'Come on in.' She swung her head a little, sending shivers of light over her sleek black hair. She led the man to the kitchen and pointed to the waste-disposal unit.

'It's the waste-disposal, it refuses to dispose of waste!'

The man smiled at her small joke, and again tried not to look at her body as he opened a tiny box of tools. Stella began to move away some of the accumulated rubbish.

'You have been having problems, haven't you?'

More than you know, thought Stella, but replied brightly. 'Yes, just a few days and look at the rubbish! I was hoping our Domestic would have been able to fix it, but this is something outside his programming.'

The man looked up as Dommie glided silently into the kitchen.

'That your Domestic?' he asked.

'Yes.'

'He was one of the expensive ones, I bet.'

'Yes, he was.'

'You're lucky, my wife would give a lot for one like that.'

Stella suddenly felt as though Dommie was staring at her and she said abruptly, 'It's all right, Dommie, you can attend to your other duties.'

'But Madam –' Dommie began, but Stella cut him off.

'That's a command.'

'Command accepted.' Dommie turned and silently glided away.

Stella turned back to the repair man and caught just the glimpse of his look as he eyed her near-naked body. He resolutely turned back to the disposal unit. Stella crept nearer to him, on the pretence of being interested in the workings of the unit. The man tried to pretend she wasn't there, as he checked and probed, but when he reached out for a tool from his bag, his hand touched her leg. He looked at her.

'Mrs Black, I'm trying to fix this for you. You're getting in the way, just a little.'

'Sorry.' Stella backed off a bit, slightly subdued. She caught sight of Dommie watching her from the hallway. So what, she thought defiantly. What can Dommie do about it? For the first time she was glad he was only a robot. At last the man stood up and shut the tool box.

'Only a small problem, Mrs Black, it'll be all right now.'

'Thank you.' She leaned back against the cooker, her full breasts pushing at the filmy material, nipples erect. Being around a man always did that to her, especially when she was lonely and bored.

The man swallowed a few times and made for the door.

'The – the office'll send the bill.'

'I'll see you out.'

'Thank you.' He was going red now and Stella smiled seductively at him.

'Come back any time you're passing.'

'Goodbye!' he said, and beat a hasty retreat.

Stella turned away and walked into Dommie. 'Get out of my way!' she snapped, but he caught hold of her wrist in an iron grip. Stella tried to pull away from him.

'What're you doing, Dommie?' she demanded. 'I command you to let me go!'

'Your command is not accepted, Madam.' The impassive face of the robot hardly moved as he spoke. 'I have been specially programmed by Mr Black for just this occasion. Your commands cannot override my programming.' He glided away, towing a frantic Stella behind him.

'Where are we going!' she cried, furious that he would not accept her orders. 'Dommie, where are you taking me?'

Dommie ignored her and dragged Stella along the highly polished hall and into the kitchen where he sat stiffly on a high kitchen stool. Stella stood by his side, held firmly in an iron grip that she could not break, no matter how hard she tried, without bruising herself extensively. It was easier to wait and see what he would do next.

What happened next surprised her considerably. Dommie pulled Stella over his knees and put one arm around her waist to hold her still as she struggled and fought to get free.

'Dommie!' she shrieked. 'Stop it!' She struggled even harder when she felt her negligée being pulled back, exposing her bare bottom to the air. A dreadful feeling came over her as she began to realise what was happening, that Dommie had been programmed in a way she would never have believed possible.

And every fear became reality. Dommie brought one hard hand down SMACK on one of her plump cheeks. Stella squealed with outrage and pain and Dommie brought his hand down equally soundly on the other cheek. His hands were hard and unyielding, and each smack covered a large area. He waited while she shouted and yelled, while the pain coursed through her. Then he smacked her again, once on each cheek. After three smacks Stella was crying but had stopped struggling, it was no good trying to reason or fight with a programmed robot, she had to stay where she was, hoping it wouldn't last too long. Dommie deliberately paused between each set of two smacks, once each side, making her draw in a breath with dreadful anticipation of the next sound SLAP that a plasti-iron hand could deliver. Someone had programmed him very carefully; the smacks covered all her plump cheeks, and were delivered with the same strength each time, no variations. She stared through tear-filled eyes at the patterned floor, hoping he hadn't been programmed to deliver *too* many smacks!

Dommie stopped after the twelfth and helped Stella to stand up. She stood in front of him, holding her bottom, tears freely pouring down her face.

'Why?' she shouted, still not understanding.

'Madam,' said Dommie precisely. 'I have been programmed to punish you for any flirtation with any person other than your husband.'

'I might have guessed Terry was up to something, buying you,' she said furiously. 'When did he program you?'

But Dommie had clicked off, and Stella knew from experience there was no point in trying to talk to him.

She ran upstairs to the bedroom and slammed the door after her as hard as she could. Terry! Damn him for a distrusting man! No wonder he'd been so keen to have Dommie delivered before he left. How dare he not trust her! It's only a game, this flirting, and only because she was so bored when he wasn't around. She had no doubt that he was unfaithful to her on his flights, how could he not be with all those space attendants hanging around wearing skin-tight coveralls? She dried her tears and sniffed, then went to the mirror to inspect her hot bottom. It was bright red and glowing. She sniffed again. He'd pay for this when he got back!

A few days later, when Stella's boredom had reached screaming point, there came a welcome diversion. Her friend Isabel called to take her on a shopping trip. Isabel was a slim petite and pretty blonde, with a reputation for gossip and slander, just the sort of person Stella needed to take her out of herself for a while. The two women set off in high spirits. They spent a considerable amount of time window shopping and buying items they didn't really need.

As the hour grew late, Isabel suggested they stay in town to eat and Stella agreed. She called Dommie from a visibooth to cancel her lunch. As they entered the restaurant Stella confessed:

'I don't know how I managed before Dommie came along.'

'I bet it gives Terry some peace of mind while he's away. There isn't much Dommie can't do, is there?' asked Isabel, openly envious of the expensive robot.

Stella wriggled her bottom on the chair, suddenly remembering one of the things Dommie *could* do. 'He's marvellous to have around,' she confided, 'and you wouldn't believe the things Terry's programmed him to do!'

'I'd believe anything of someone as gorgeous as Dommie!' said Isabel.

'Yes, but this you won't believe, Terry's programmed him to spank –'

Stella stopped suddenly, realising she had said far too much to the town gossip but it was too late. The word was out, and Isabel pounced on it.

'Spank you? Has he, really? Darling, do tell.'

Stella sighed inwardly. She'd done it now, and there was no point in not saying anything else, she'd given it all away.

'Terry's programmed Dommie so that if I flirt with anyone I get spanked.'

'And did you?'

'How do you think I found out? I found myself over his knees, skirt up, getting my bottom smacked just like a little girl!'

'Did it hurt?' Isabel was all eagerness.

'I'll say it did! There's no fighting Dommie, he's too strong, and he's got a very hard hand too!'

'I don't think I'd mind being held tight by someone like that,' sighed Isabel.

'Yes,' said Stella, 'but he's a robot and completely unaware of women, except as someone in the house to obey.'

'There's a thought,' giggled Isabel wickedly and the

women laughed. The manager came over to the table and smiled at them.

'Enjoying your lunch, ladies?' he asked.

'Yes, we are,' smiled Stella.

'I saw you laughing over here and thought I'd share the joke.'

'Not this one you can't,' laughed Isabel.

Stella was looking up at the tall blond, eyes sparkling, lips slightly parted, and Isabel narrowed her eyes a little. It was no wonder Terry had programmed the robot like that. Look at the minx, she thought suddenly, right now that man doesn't know I exist, look how he's looking at her!

'I don't remember seeing you in here before,' said the manager, to both of them, but looking at Stella.

'We don't usually stay in town long enough to eat,' Stella smiled. 'But my husband's a captain on the Mars run, you know, and I had nothing to do.'

'If he's a captain you must spend a good deal of time alone.' The man was sitting down now so he could look into Stella's eyes more easily. Isabel got up.

'I'll just visit the rest room, Stella, back in a minute.'

'Right.' Stella didn't even look round when Isabel left the table.

In the rest room Isabel stared at her image in the mirror, raging with jealousy. I'm every bit as pretty as she is, she thought angrily, so why should he sit and talk to *her* and not to me! If that robot was around, she'd be sorry. Isabel followed the thought through and smiled suddenly. She left the rest room cautiously but Stella had her back to her and didn't see Isabel walk to the visibooths. Isabel coded the Black number and Dommie appeared on the screen.

'Mrs Black is not at home,' he said instantly.

'I know, Dommie, she's with me. I wanted to tell you she's been flirting with the manager at the restaurant here.'

'Are you sure, Madam?'

Isabel stood aside. She had chosen a visibooth that was in direct line with the table, and Dommie could clearly see Stella sitting with the manager.

'Thank you, Mrs Wyatt,' he said, and the screen went blank. Damn, thought Isabel, I wanted to ask him not to tell Stella I called. She looked through her bag but had no more tokens. She shrugged, deciding she'd have to take a chance on Stella's reactions if she found out.

Back at the table Stella was deep in conversation with the manager, and Isabel deliberately interrupted her.

'Time to get back, I think.'

Stella blushed a little.

'We were just talking.' She got up and fumbled for her bag for her share of the bill.

'Please come in again next time you're in town.'

'I will.' Stella gave him her most dazzling smile.

You wait, thought Isabel viciously. You've got a surprise coming to you!

She chatted idly of nothing in particular until the transporter drew up outside the house and Stella waved to her from the doorway. She drove away, grinning gleefully to herself as the pictures went through her mind.

Inside the house Stella found Dommie barring her way.

'Let me pass, Dommie,' she said, surprised at him.

'I had a telephone call.'

She stared. 'So what?'

'I saw you sitting at a table talking with a man other than your husband.'

'Isabel! The bitch! I'll – I'll scratch her eyes out, I'll tear –'

'Come, Madam.' And once again Dommie grasped her wrist in his iron grip. Stella hung back, causing Dommie to drag her along.

'I wasn't doing anything, it's all a mistake!'

But Dommie was deaf to her protests and once again

125

Stella found herself in the kitchen, waiting while the robot carefully and stiffly sat down and pulled her face down across his knees; experiencing a strange mixture of fear and excitement as she felt Dommie's plastic hands turn back her clothes and then tug at her knickers. They were tight, but not tight enough to stop the robotic, iron hand sliding them down, exposing her to the cool air. The fear was in knowing what was to come, the excitement was remembering the afterglow she had had last time, even if Terry wasn't around to do anything about it! There was always the solar vibrator . . .

She waited apprehensively, hanging limp over his legs, which felt like chair legs, they were so hard, so unyielding. Passions raged through her, causing her to go hot and cold in turn. It seemed to take forever, but then came the first smack. It was far worse *knowing* how hard he did it. It was as hard as last time, and as deliberately long and drawn out, ensuring she remembered each and every separate smack on her exposed cheeks. Despite her best intentions, Stella fought and struggled, while knowing she had to take the programmed twelve resounding whacks before she was allowed up. Individually they stung, together they made a painful whole that glowed down her thighs and up into her stomach. She ran for the bathroom, and stared at her tear-stained reflection. All she could see was a vision of Isabel telephoning Dommie and shopping her to the pre-programmed robot, knowing what would happen.

'I'll get her for this!' she shouted, stamping her foot. 'I'll show her what it's like!' She suddenly realised what she'd said and stopped crying instantly. She cleaned her face and ran back downstairs, calling to Dommie. 'I'm going out.'

She set the coordinates in her transporter for Isabel's house and sat, getting angrier by the metre, as the transporter rolled along, the glow from her bottom painfully reminding her of what she had suffered because of her so-called friend.

Isabel opened the door and stepped back in surprise and shock when Stella stormed in.

'I want a word with you! Dommie just spanked me, all because of you!'

'I didn't mean any harm,' protested Isabel, 'it's just that you weren't taking any notice of me, flirting with that manager, and I –'

'Got jealous and called Dommie. Thanks very much! Now I want you to know just what I've suffered!'

She ran into the kitchen looking around for a suitable implement. In the corner lay Isabel's sandals which she'd kicked off when she came in, and Stella grabbed one, eyeing the solid sole with glee. 'This'll do,' she announced. Isabel had followed her, wondering what she was going to do. Stella's temper was raging through her now, and anything could happen. Isabel made the mistake of getting too close to Stella, who instantly grabbed hold of one of Isabel's wrists, just as Dommie had with her. She sat on a chair and pulled the protesting Isabel over her knees, wrapping one arm around her friend's waist. Dommie taught me a lot, she thought, as she snatched at Isabel's flowing skirt, not wanting anything to get in the way. Isabel was fighting too much for Stella to worry about her knickers which, in any event, were thin and wouldn't give much protection.

'Now see how it hurts!' Stella brought the sandal down with a resounding whack on Isabel's rounded bottom. Isabel fought, shouting her protests, and Stella had the utmost difficulty in holding her. She smacked her again, her temper giving her the strength to hold on, her outrage giving her a strong arm to deliver some stinging slaps. She only managed six whacks with the sandal before Isabel broke away and collapsed on the floor.

'You – you,' she spluttered, lost for words.

'Now you know how much it hurts,' said Stella, 'and double that, because I got twelve from Dommie, thanks to you!'

Isabel slowly got to her feet, rubbing her bottom.

'Sorry, Stella,' she said, genuinely abject. 'I never realised it hurt so much.'

'I'm glad I did it then,' remarked Stella, putting the sandal back on the floor. 'Now the score's settled – this time.'

The feeling of revenge was good, and Stella also recognised the first stirrings of a serious erotic feeling too, which surprised her. It was time to go home and find that vibrator.

Terry came home a week later, bringing Stella a sculptured piece of Martian rock. They immediately fell into bed, making love with the wild abandon that only separation can bring. When the first passion of their reunion had abated a little, Terry casually asked Stella about Dommie.

'Oh Terry, he's marvellous,' enthused Stella. 'He really looked after me.'

'Took very good care of you?'

'Yes, he did!'

'Any problems?'

'No, no problems.'

'That's good. As long as I know I have nothing to worry about when I'm gone.'

'Nothing to worry about at all.'

Next morning, before Stella roused herself from bed, Terry went to the kitchen to speak to Dommie.

'Did you have occasion to punish my wife in my absence?'

'Yes, sir.'

'Why?'

'On one occasion she flirted openly with a man here, and on that day she was also wearing what I understood

128

to be insufficient clothing. On the second occasion Mrs Wyatt telephoned me. I could clearly see Madam with another man in a restaurant.'

'Mrs Wyatt called, did she?' Terry grinned broadly. 'Thank you, Dommie, I don't think I'll be changing your program.'

He went back to the bedroom.

'Dommie tells me he had to spank you,' he said, sitting on the edge of the bed and letting one of Stella's long black ringlets slide through his fingers. Stella blushed, rolled over and hid her face in the pillow. 'Did it hurt?'

'Yes, it did!'

Terry laughed. 'I'm not changing Dommie's program, you know I want you to behave when I'm gone.'

Stella wriggled in the bed. 'You're hard, Terry, I'd never be unfaithful to you, it's only fun.'

'I know, darling, but often fun gets out of hand, and I'd rather know you were being kept in check. What made Isabel call?'

Stella sat up, pretty in her disarray.

'We went to town and had lunch. You know that place in the Plaza? The manager came over to talk just after I'd made a bad slip and told Isabel how you programmed Dommie. Because the manager talked to me more than her, she got jealous and called Dommie. He was waiting when I got home.'

'What did you do about Isabel? You surely didn't let her get away with it.'

Stella began to giggle with the memory. 'I was so mad I went over and gave *her* a spanking!'

Terry roared with laughter. 'Good for you, it's what that meddling girl needs.'

'The trouble is, she struggled so much I couldn't give her the twelve I wanted to, but at least she apologised afterwards.'

'And I bet Ken doesn't know about it.'

'I bet he won't, either!'

'I'll have to have a word with him about getting a domestic, and programming it so that Isabel gets a tanning every time she gossips or meddles.'

'That would never do, she'd be over the robot's knee half the day!'

Terry looked at Stella, at his watch and back at Stella again.

'Just about enough time,' he murmured, sliding back into the bed.

The night before Terry was due to leave for another trip, they invited friends round for supper, and Stella went out of her way to be nice to them. When they left, Terry turned to her.

'I think I'll have to increase the number of smacks Dommie gives you.'

'Why?' asked Stella, surprised.

'Because if you can turn a man on by just being nice, like you were tonight, you're going to need a lot of taking care of!'

'I didn't turn anyone on and I didn't flirt.'

'You did, and you didn't have to, my love, your being nice is enough. Didn't you see the dangerous looks Diane gave you?'

Stella laughed. 'She's so cold and hard, a little jealousy might do her good!'

Terry grabbed her and held her tight.

'You, young lady, need a good deal of taking care of, as I said, and I'm not going to leave it all to Dommie. Why should he have all the fun?'

He pulled her to a relaxa-chair and sat down, pulling her firmly across his knees. Stella squirmed round, trying to get free, glad at least that Terry's legs felt warm and human, unlike Dommie's. Terry held her tight and took his time pulling down her lacy panties, revealing the soft cheeks. He gently caressed them.

130

'I programmed Dommie to do this, but it's wasted on him,' he murmured, and he brought his hand down hard on her left cheek, raising an instant pink hand-sized flush.

'Ow! That was even harder than Dommie does it,' she wailed, renewing her struggle to escape.

'No, you're not getting away from me. You were right, you didn't flirt, but you came close enough to it for my liking.' And Terry smacked her again, raising another pink hand-sized flush, and another squeal. Despite all her objections, he spanked her long and hard, much longer than Dommie would, and considerably harder, aiming for the top of her thighs and other tender spots until she was an abject and quivering limp rag doll. Then he sat her by his side and held her close while she shivered and cried a few tears, while rubbing frantically at her sore cheeks.

'You really are a beast!'

'I know,' he said and kissed the top of her head. 'That was from me, something to remember when I'm gone. Dommie's are only a reminder to behave while I'm away, the *real* spankings will come from me!'

Stella wriggled as the painful spanking settled to a warm glow. 'Terry . . .'

'Mmmmm?'

'I feel all sexy, I don't feel like that when Dommie spanks me.'

'I should hope not – he's only a robot!'

'Yes, I know but he's more real than some robots.'

'Getting designs on Dommie, are you?' he jested. 'Getting a sexy thrill when he spanks you? In that case, I'll program him to spank you if you flirt with him, shall I?'

'No, you'd only take my fun away, and besides, what's the good of feeling sexy when you're half way to Mars?'

'Not much, I must admit,' said Terry thoughtfully, running a finger down the side of her face. 'It won't be for much longer, anyway, then you'll have me around to spank you, instead of a cold robot. Let's go, I've got a flight tomorrow.'

'And leave me alone again,' pouted Stella as they climbed the stairs.

'You've got a nice red bottom to remind you of me.' He patted it gently, playfully, and she moved out of reach of his hand.

'That's still hot,' she protested.

'And so am I.' He held her close. 'You'll be all right while I'm gone, you'll have Dommie to obey your every command, well, almost every command.'

And that, decided Stella as the bedroom door closed behind them, is something I'll be looking into, when he's gone!

15

Girl Talk

*Once upon a long time ago, I wrote a three-part novella.
It was going to be published, then the magazine changed
hands, changed editor and the copy went walkabout. I
offered the copy to another editor who lost the carbon
too. I know you should never let a carbon go out, but this
was pre word-processor and I didn't fancy typing it out
all over again. And it wasn't the sort of thing you took
to the local shop for photocopying . . . So, I tried to
recreate the story, and this is as far as it went. The ideas
were there but . . .*

What do girls talk about when they meet for coffee? If
you come with me, we will do a little eavesdropping on
a group of girls sitting with their cups of coffee, their
eager ears ready for titbits, eager thighs ready to part.

No, not yet.

First we must make our way there along this smart
suburban road. See how nicely the gardens are laid out,
how neat the fences, how free of weeds each drive. This
is suburbia, where the women all wear designer jeans to
go to the supermarket, in their Audis and Volvos, of
course.

Here is the house occupied by the Stephensons, Joanne
and Nigel. It's a typical four-bedroomed detached, highly
desirable property. Joanne is considered by Nigel to be a

highly desirable property too. She is blonde, petite, with a neat attractive figure. They have been married for five years and hardly a month has gone by, during that time, without her getting her bottom well and truly warmed by his hand or one of the many implements they keep in the bottom drawer (highly appropriate) of a chest of drawers. Joanne also considers Nigel to be a highly desirable property, not least because he is six foot tall, extremely good-looking and fun to be around.

No good pausing here today, though, Nigel is at work in the systems design office where he is top man, and Joanne is along the road, drinking coffee and swapping tales with her friends.

On the opposite side of the road is the home of Sonya and Joe Marrin. Sonya is dark haired, with burning eyes that appear to eat up every man she looks at. It's all an act. Joe loves it, it gives him a thrill to see men turned on by his wife's look, knowing all the time it is only meant for him. Sonya looks like a tough lady, looks as if she would eat men for breakfast, but over someone's knee (preferably Joe's), being well and truly spanked, she shows herself to be a true submissive; loving every moment of it, even as she cries and pleads for mercy. Joe isn't a tall man like Nigel, but he knows how to give a spanking. No doubt about that.

Joe is at work today in the insurance office: work which he is good at but which is sometimes a bit on the boring side. There he entertains himself with fantasy sessions with Sonya, fantasies which (lucky man) he can turn to reality as soon as he gets home.

Next door to Sonya and Joe live Heather and Alan Henderson. They're CP fans too. Heather is a little on the plump side, it must be said, but pretty with it; a cluster of brown curls around an ever smiling face. Alan is a more serious person, befitting his position as a technical adviser for a local firm. Do I have to say they aren't at home either? Alan is at work and Heather is along the road.

Come with me just a little further along the road. See that house there, set back from the street – the one with the long drive? That's the home of Anne and David Portram. Yes, it is the most expensive house in the street, and that's where the girls are now, drinking coffee and swapping tales.

All right, I won't keep you in suspense any longer; I'll take you close so that you can press your ear against the window and hear what the girls are saying.

The girl talk may surprise you.

'Did you enjoy the ball the other night?'

Heather sips black coffee and looks at Anne. David Portram, Anne's husband, is the local close-to-being-a-millionaire, running his own engineering business and a leading light in the Chamber of Commerce, the Round Table, the – well, you get the picture. It means Anne gets invited to the elegant dinner dances the others don't.

'Yes, we had a wonderful time.' Anne's eyes light up with the memory. I danced with half the town, I think, boy, did my feet ache by midnight!'

'What did you wear in the end?' asks Heather. Anne's ballgown had been the subject of much discussion prior to the great event.

Anne jumps up. 'I'll show you. I went and bought something new in the morning after all.'

She hurries out of the room, leaving the others speculating on how much might have been spent on a single evening. Not that they are overly jealous, you understand, well, just a little, well, perhaps more than a little. But not too much. Some girls can be bitchy, but these girls share a passion for –

'Here,' says Anne, as she comes back into the room, slightly breathless, carrying a scarlet dress. Unselfconsciously she slips off her summer dress and struggles into the layers of silk and taffeta. The dress is a beautiful thing. The other girls sit speechless as she swirls and parades in front of them, silk whispering around her legs, taffeta floating above it in a tempting wicked-woman cloud of red. Anne's shining blonde hair looks even brighter against the scarlet dress.

'Well, it was a special occasion.' Anne unfastens the dress and steps out of it. She turns to lay it on the table. The other girls look closely and yes – there they are – distinct lines from a caning showing under filmy black panties.

'Your turn,' laughs Sonya. 'Come on, let's hear it!'

Anne puts her summer dress back on, blushing.

'I wasn't going to show,' she protests, laughing at the same time. 'I truly wasn't going to show you.'

It is one of the rules of this group of friends that one of the girls gets to show the others the evidence of a session they have recently had. It is one of the rules because there is nothing more erotic for a submissive than seeing the real, genuine evidence of a session on another woman. It stirs the loins, it gets the juices flowing, it sparks anticipation (and if I keep on like this I will have to take my ear from the window and lead you away so you can . . .)

Hell, let's listen.

'So we saw.' Joanne leans back in the huge armchair, totally relaxed and pleased with life. She has marks too, and was hoping someone else would be the one to tell all this morning. Hers were gained through an embarrassing incident in the local car park she doesn't want to relate to the others. 'Come on, Anne, let's hear it.'

'Well,' Anne sits down, carefully, they note, and leans forward. 'We went to the ball. Silbury House looked lovely! All decorated with gold and white and touches of green everywhere, huge ribbons, lovely flower arrangements, and the table! I can't begin to tell you how lovely the table looked. David looked pretty good too in his evening wear. You haven't seen him in dinner jacket and bow tie, he looks fantastic! Well, I think so, anyway.' Nods of approval from everyone else. They expect everyone to think their own husbands are the best in the world. (I happen to think mine is.)

'So we had our dinner and then the dancing started. I danced with ever so many different people and ended up with the mayor. And I had had a touch too much to drink by then and I danced – well, a bit close, shall we say – and he was seen in the men's loos coping with an erection soon after. Seen by David!'

There is much laughter all round. Given the scarlet dress, Anne's looks and the opportunity, they would all have done the same thing. While they consider their husbands the best in the world, it doesn't stop them flirting and tormenting and amusing other men, just so they know they can still do it.

'So, when we got home, I was told to get upstairs. I went, in a hurry! You know that tone of voice, there's no arguing. He said I was to strip off the dress and get over the end of the bed. I did, got over the bed in nothing but black lace undies, and waited. I heard him rummaging in the wardrobe where we kept the things, not knowing if he was getting the cane or the tawse or even our riding crop. He was mad enough to have used that! He said 'twelve' in that cold, cold voice, and I still didn't know twelve of what. I lay there, shaking a bit, trying not to say sorry, hanging on to the cover, and then he started. He's not been that mad for ages, he really laid into me with that cane!'

Anne stands up, turns around and lowers her knickers so they can all see the clear lines, all twelve of them.

'Bet that hurt,' breathes Sonya almost enviously.

'Certainly did!' Anne pulls her knickers up again and

137

sits down in the chair, carefully. 'That's me told. We went to bed, laid on our own side for ages until he got soft and came over to my side. And the rest you can guess!' She leans back in the chair. 'Anyone else got a story to contribute today?'

Joanne looks round at the others.

'Not a story, but I must tell you about this man I saw getting out of a taxi at the hotel last week. He was small, not much taller than me, very slim, elegant beard, sort of – oh I don't know, like one of those Spanish noblemen you read about in books – you know what I mean? Anyway, as he shut the car door and went to pay the driver, I saw his wrists. Very very slim but they looked as if they were like steel. I instantly imagined him holding a cane, and damn near creamed right there and then on the pavement! I've been fantasising about him ever since.'

'I know what you mean,' Anne smiles knowingly. 'Good job our men don't know about our secret fantasies, isn't it? But they're nice to have, as long as we keep them as fantasies.'

'I know,' sighs Heather. 'You see a man in the street or on a building site or something, build a complete fantasy around him and then can't do anything about it.'

'One day,' Joanne smiles at them all in turn. 'One day we'll have to talk to our men about realising our favourite fantasies.'

'Yes!' chorused the others. Seems like a popular idea.

'Right, if there are no stories, we'll have some action instead. Whose turn is it today?' Anne is looking round at her guests, waiting.

Heather looks at the others. She is wondering whether she should volunteer to be today's victim for bottom warming at the hands of the others – another of the rules – or whether to let someone else volunteer, or be picked on, if no one speaks up. Heather has had a session the night before and she isn't madly keen on getting spanked all over again, still feeling a bit tender from her session over Alan's knees for being cheeky.

Joanne looks out of the window, hoping they will ignore her. She has tawse marks from her latest escapade, reversing into a post in the car park. Nigel was very very annoyed. It showed in the tawsing she had to take, wriggling and struggling and protesting, bent over the side of the bath, still wet and pink and every stroke stinging like crazy. She lost count of how many she got, how many times the flexible leather wrapped itself around her, delivered with force, but she was still grinning with secret satisfaction today even if it was something she wouldn't forget in a hurry.

'Sonya,' announces Anne suddenly, making them look round with large smiles.

Sonya hasn't been spanked by the girls for – oh must be all of a month. Sonya blushes madly, as she does every time. 'Must I?'

'When was the last time Joe warmed your bottom?' demands Anne.

'Oh –'

'Come on, the truth!'

There can be no lies between friends as close as these girls. They have seen each other naked, spanked each other and seen their husbands administer punishment to the other wives, too. There can be no secrets.

Sonya groans. 'All right, it's been a fortnight.'

'Great!' Anne rushes out of the room, returning almost immediately with a rubber sandal. Sonya backs towards the window.

'Oh no, that's not fair, that's not nice, you know that hurts!'

Heather and Joanne are on their feet now, pulling Sonya into the centre of the lounge where a large leather pouffe waits for someone to lie over it. Somehow it is demanding someone lie over it, someone whose bottom needs attending to.

Which is precisely why Anne and David bought it in the first place.

Sonya fights, but not very convincingly. She knows she is overdue for some CP and she knows that she will take it willingly from her friends. With a sigh she pulls down her panties and lays across the pouffe, grinning stupidly. Her bottom is large, white and very inviting.

'Who's going first?' asks Anne, holding out the sandal.

'You can.' Joanne has one of Sonya's wrists to make sure she doesn't try and wriggle away and Heather has the other – it is easier at that moment for Anne to start.

'OK then.'

WHACK! the sandal comes down in the middle of one cheek then the other. Sonya squeals and wriggles but Anne does it again and then again, quickly settling into a rhythm, a tattoo of rubber meeting flesh. Joanne and Heather are watching, a sparkle in their eyes, their teeth showing white between red, almost bitten lips, as the excitement builds. Sonya, the recipient, absorbs the smacks, sensing every one fluttering through every nerve, into her stomach, down her thighs, along her spine and touching her nipples, making them come erect. The pain spreads, glowing relentlessly. When she is showing distinct signs of pink, edging into red, Anne hands over the sandal to Joanne and takes Joanne's place holding onto Sonya's wrists.

Joanne is adept at giving a good spanking as the others have found to their cost. The sandal appears to come down twice as hard, quickly turning pink flesh red, and making Sonya wriggle and gasp aloud a few times. Although she knows she would take the spanking, Sonya is glad the others are holding on to her wrists so she cannot even begin to think of escaping. Sonya loves bondage, but there isn't always the time or the need to be carefully bound for a session. Being firmly held by two other women, determined you are not getting away with a single stroke, is almost as good as being tied down to a bench by a loving and determined husband.

Finally it is Heather's turn to use the sandal which she does, hard, remembering the times when she has been over the pouffe, and Sonya has had her turn. It is a chance to pay her back for every whack she has had in the past. It's the same every time; they all remember past punishment sessions and get revenge on their friends in the only way they know – by giving as much when it is their turn.

Finally Sonya is allowed to get up, gasping and protesting and clutching her sore bottom. But it isn't over and she knows it; she has to stand in the middle of the room, skirt raised, panties lowered, until the others say she can sit down. The bottom they are looking at, in turn, is very, very red and will be sore for quite a long time. This usually guarantees firstly another punishment session with their partner and secondly a marvellous session in bed. It is always worth the pain and humiliation of standing with a well-spanked bottom on show. It is an oddity of CP that getting it is one thing, standing with the evidence on display is quite another, even when the people who are looking are the people who did it.

And at this moment I think we should tiptoe away down the drive, quickly, before they see us. The session is over and soon the girls will be walking – with wet pussies – back to their homes to await their husbands who, knowing there has been a meeting, will come home with erections demanding to be satisfied, one way or another.

And that is something we don't need to spy on, do we?

16

Trial by Jury

You've no doubt seen many times a so-called pilot film which was supposed to be followed by a series, and often isn't. Well, this was a pilot story. I had every intention of writing a series about the Club. The series never came off, as the editor never asked for any more. There's no incentive if you find you are writing in a void, sending work out and never getting a response, so as with 'Girl Talk', the ideas were there . . . When this story first appeared a (male) friend complained he could not find enough description, couldn't see the eroticism of it. So, before I get the same complaint from all you (male) readers out there, the eroticism, the whole point of this story, is the exhibitionism. I wrote it after a (female) friend said she rather fancied being punished before a group of people, almost a public execution, as it were.

The sleek dark sports car fitted itself neatly into the drive of the luxurious detached house and stopped. Its engine sighed into silence and the lights faded out.

Inside the car, Marjorie and Darren Johnson exchanged smiles in the half-light cast by the porch lantern. They touched hands.

'Ready?'

'Always ready for one of these nights.' Marjorie's response was husky, whispered with excitement, and Darren gripped her hand tightly.

'Who do you think will draw what tonight?' he wondered aloud, but the point was academic. No one knew what role they would play until they got inside the glassed porch of the Grayson's residence and drew a ticket from the appropriate box, a ticket which would set their role for the evening.

Inside the elegant house, standing so cool and tranquil in the dark night, a trial was to be staged. And every person attending the trial had an essential part to play. But what that part was no one yet knew. In time all would be revealed. Literally.

'Come on, let's go.'

Marjorie opened the car door and stepped on to the gravel path just as a gold Rover drew up. She waved to Dianne, who was grinning excitedly at her through the window. Darren locked the doors of the car and walked round the still warm engine to wait beside Marjorie for Dianne and James Kenning to lock their car before hurrying up the drive.

'Cold, isn't it?' commented James, rubbing his hands and then tucking them deep in the pockets of his sheepskin coat.

'It is,' agreed Marjorie, huddling deeper into her fur. 'The sooner we get inside, the better.'

'And collect our ticket,' added Dianne, anticipation sparkling in her eyes. 'Let's go!'

Giles Grayson opened the door, greeting the arrivals as casually as if they were there for an informal gathering. Coats were removed and handed over in the flutter of greetings and embraces until almost shyly, each arrival took a ticket from the boxes, clearly labelled Men and Women. Well might you ask why. That way they ensured that the defendant for the evening was always female –

144

no women's lib allowed in the Scottsdale Spanking Club, you understand.

Annette Grayson was waiting for them, nervous and bubbly. 'Come in by the fire, and get warm. Have you got your tickets?'

'Yes.' Darren stopped to give her a brief kiss before approaching the huge log fire. 'Have you taken yours?'

'No!' Annette rushed to the hall. 'Giles, we haven't taken our tickets yet!'

'Come on, then, before I get involved with more people arriving.'

They looked at their tickets, and then at each other, trying to read from their expression what ticket they had drawn. But not a word was said. Part of the fun of the evening was the not knowing; by long standing tradition, you see, no one revealed what part they were to play until the Court was declared in session and everyone took their place.

Annette rejoined her guests, mixing drinks and putting on a tape of background music to help relax everyone. Giles responded to the summons of the doorbell to admit Sandra and Alexander Danes. They too stopped for tickets, which they glanced at before going into the lounge.

Shortly afterwards Rosemary and Stephen Trace arrived, with Estella and Christopher Deacon hot on their heels. The members had arrived. The fun would soon begin.

Gentle readers, devotees to a man (or should I say person?) of the exciting, exhilarating genre of corporal punishment, I have a story for you. Well, not so much a story as facts carefully disguised as fiction, for that is the only way to describe the games and goings-on of the Scottsdale Spanking Society, not its real name, of course, under which banner a good deal goes on and not all of it concerns CP. Not by a very long cane weal! Rather than risk libel proceedings, it is easier and safer (if not cheaper) to change the names of the guilty, thereby protecting the innocent.

Now, you will recall before I diverted your attention to me, unforgivable thing for a writer to do, that all the guests were gathered in the lounge of the Grayson house, each clutching or perhaps pocketing a ticket. We have frozen them with a stab at the freeze-frame button; they are suspended in a moment of time, drinks in hand, or half way to mouth, the flames are frozen in the very act of leaping up the chimney and the stirrings of anticipatory lust are, for the moment ceased, held in limbo.

Or somewhere.

Now that they are frozen in that way, we can examine them in detail, and peek over their shoulders to see what ticket they are clutching or pocketing. What secrets are stirring in their minds? What do they think of the role they have been called upon to play?

Marjorie and Darren Johnson arrived first, did they not? Parking the sleek sports car in the drive. Not only is that a safe place, it is also a good way of ensuring they are the last to leave, their car being blocked by the others. This suits Darren, who we have to admit is rather fond of drink. You will also appreciate that drinking is banned in courtrooms, so he has to do all his drinking both before and after the trial. So he comes early and stays late.

Darren is a large man, blond touched with grey so it is almost indistinguishable. His face tends towards redness, and his body towards being large. He has a healthy appetite for all that life offers him. Not really a devotee of spanking he will be the first to tell you, but he has yet to refuse the offer of having a writhing woman across his knees, bared bum, for him to spank to his heart's content with all the subsequent joys that brings! Of all the people frozen in this timeless moment he is possibly the least interested in the spanking of a bottom; he prefers it for its natural use, something to hold on to at the moment of orgasm. He contentedly clutches his ticket, which marks him as a juror. It means he can relax and indulge in sexy daydreams of the afterwards.

Marjorie was with him, a petite person looking even smaller than she really is against his largeness. She dresses expensively on the proceeds of his insurance broking firm. She is as dark as he is blond, black of curls and deep hued of skin, as if perpetually under the hot sun or a sun bed. This being the height of an English winter (I mentioned frozen flames a while back) I leave you to judge which it is. Marjorie likes being spanked, she likes the feel of a man's hand slapping her cheeks, likes the feeling of total domination. She isn't quite sure about having the event carried out publicly, which is why she is more than glad she has drawn a juror's ticket again tonight. She surreptitiously looks round, trying to decide who has 'the ticket'.

If you can remember that far back, Dianne and James Kenning drew up behind the Johnsons, blocking the sports car with the Rover. Dianne is one of those seemingly limpid ladies who lie elegantly in armchairs or drape themselves along the arms of settees, floating gracefully. She has long shining brown hair which flows in ripples down her back. Her face is delicate, her eyes change colour as you stare into their depths. A beautiful lady, a sharp business woman too, who is more than capable of summing up an opponent, male or female, with one single all-embracing glance. She is fascinated by CP and all the implements that go with it. Their bedroom, in their own expensive luxury house, paid for out of the proceeds of the small engineering business, looks somewhat like a black museum, with whips and canes adorning the walls. She would be only too pleased to be on display even if it was face down over the padded stool for the executioner to mete out his sentence on her creamy white bottom, which blends so smoothly with her long, muscled thighs.

But tonight Dianne clutches a juror ticket, for in any trial there must always be seven jurors, and one accused. Still, there is always later, and she looks, in this frozen moment, towards her husband with a sparkle of anticipation for what is to come, not only here but back in their black museum, where no restraining straps are needed.

James Kenning has read her look, and knows what is in store. He looks down at his juror ticket, and slips it into his pocket, trying to decide whether he is disappointed or not. Tall and lean, muscled, with not an ounce of fat, James Kenning is the epitome of the business man who has come up from nothing and made it into this rich society on the basis of his own determination. His hair is streaked with grey and he kids everyone that it is the result of all his worries and cares. In fact it is the result of the natural aging process that he doesn't care to think about. CP is his love and his major hobby. In a locked bookcase in their bedroom is a collection of every *good* spanking magazine that has ever been printed. If they ever need any inspiration, and even the most devoted followers sometimes do, they play a game of selecting a book at random, allowing it to fall open and giving Dianne double whatever is on the page, no matter how severe.

There *is* always later, as Dianne's look has already promised him. It has also told him that she isn't the victim, or her look wouldn't hold as much promise as it does. You can see nothing? But then you aren't married to the lady, you don't know her every whim and mood. But I bet you'd like to.

While Annette was mixing drinks and adjusting the volume on the wallpaper music which, incidentally, isn't frozen and has been drifting violins into the air whilst we speak, Sandra and Alexander Danes arrived. Born rich, these two were bored with life until the Spanking Society got started, and they were quick to join as soon as they read about it. CP was a new game for them, and still is, in some respects, but they have joined in with great enthusiasm and a good deal of sexual satisfaction, which goes to show that spanking is for the rich as well as the poor. The only difference as far as I can see is the quality of the silk knickers and the price paid for the cane.

The result, I'm happy to say, is exactly the same. Cane weals look like cane weals on a rich or poor bottom, and the squeals, whilst perhaps not quite so refined in the lower classes, are just as loud and indicate just as clearly that pain is being administered to a female who is dearly and clearly in need of chastisement. Aren't they all?

Alexander, then, portly with good food and wine, slightly balding from too much good living, blue of eye and firm of jaw. And, to his great delight and expectation, holding the executioner ticket for the first time since joining the club. He is anxious to know who the victim is, and is hoping desperately that it isn't Sandra, because the executioner, by right, gets to bed the victim. It isn't half so much fun bedding your wife – he can do that later.

Sandra on the other hand is clutching her juror ticket in carmine-tipped fingers, and is quivering with suppressed excitement. As thin as her husband is portly she carries her clothes a bit like a skeleton, with ribs and shoulder blades protruding but, surprisingly, she has a round bottom which invites the open hand as she wiggles her way through the gathered company. Or she will do, when I release the freeze-frame button. Even being a juror is all right with her. She delights in seeing someone's rear end well and truly thrashed. Make no mistake about it, a sentence from this court is a severe one, when it is carried out in public. Perhaps it is better to be an observer after all. It all depends on your inclination. What's yours?

Rosemary and Stephen Trace arrived next, and as coincidence would have it, drew the victim and prosecutor tickets respectively. He saw her ticket, which gave Stephen plenty of time to consider how best to ensure that his wife receives the maximum sentence he can persuade the court to award, as she has been getting out of hand lately and he isn't strong enough to dish out the just desserts the lady really needs. Stephen, you see, is a bit on the weedy side, as opposed to being thin. No muscles to speak of, his eyes are a washed out brown, his weak chin is hidden behind a neat goatee, which gives him a stern look he doesn't actually deserve.

And Rosemary, excitedly clutching the victim ticket, knows it. Her eyes dart around the gathered guests, wondering who is the executioner. Who will be laying it on hard later? Stephen's hand isn't hard, nor his arm strong, and Rosemary, a tiny waspish lady with tight bouncy brown curls and a ready entrancing smile, does love a hard hand. And a hard anything else that also happens to be going in the right direction. I should, for her sake alone, release that freeze-frame button, as she is going to be rather wet with excitement before the trial starts.

But we're not through yet, for Estelle Deacon, with defence counsel ticket, and Christopher with judge ticket, came last, but not unwilling, by any stretch of Estelle's imagination. Rarely does this intelligent-looking lady, peering through tortoiseshell rimmed glasses at the world, actually experience the stinging slap of a well laid-on tawse or the burning line of a well-applied cane, because Christopher is gifted with a golden tongue, and has talked to her of so many delights that she comes, swiftly and dramatically, and rarely experiences the real thing! Which is a very good reason to join a spanking club, gentle readers. Practical experience. There's no substitute. And if I keep writing lines like that, I'll go drifting upstairs to my bedroom for some practical experience, and I'll not finish the story. For the sake of all the people gathered here, that will never do.

Christopher, appointed by chance the judge for the evening, is in fact a good choice. He is a studious man, a perfect partner for Estelle, and he too suffers the disability of poor sight. Not that that stops him spending hours reading and researching various obscure items for hefty tomes, the like of which are not seen on the shelves of W. H. Smith. Tall enough to look distinguished, he will arbitrate well in this trial, and mete out fair sentence to the unfortunate victim, whoever she may be.

Before I release the freeze-frame, I must mention our hosts for the evening, in whose home we have intruded with our video and whose idea the club was.

Annette and Giles Grayson, rarely apart, always referred to as a couple, these two are almost identical twins. Round happy faces with dark, cropped hair, ever-ready smiles and laughs, and an overwhelming interest in all things corporal, they are the perfect hosts for such an evening. They have drawn juror tickets too, and Giles has appointed himself clerk of the court.

And now I'll release the button and let the guests go back to the buffet and the drinks.

They'll need them.

Annette's eyes flickered constantly round the group, watching levels of drinks descending and indicating to Giles who needed a refill. Keeping plates well laden with food, and the talk drifting happily in all directions, she is the perfect hostess. Giles will find no fault with her tonight. Not that that will mean her bottom won't be well and truly reddened later with the first thing that comes to hand; even the excitement generated by the sight of the victim getting her just desserts won't be enough for the Graysons. They'll need the added excitement of Annette over the end of the bed being laid into with something hefty – she felt her body twitch at the mere thought of it.

When Giles had gauged the moment at which everyone

was pleasantly full of drink and food, he rang his small bell, and immediately all talk stopped, and eyes turned to stare at him.

'Thanks for coming.' A spontaneous burst of laughter greeted him. Double meaning, you see. 'If you would like to depart to the courtroom . . .'

Immediately people put down their glasses and moved towards the door, fluttering feelings of anticipation increasing in all of them. Rosemary in particular found herself going positively weak. Would she stand up long enough to be tried? Would the judge be strict? Would the executioner be hard on her? Oh let him be, let him be!

The dining room had been set up as a court. Down one side a double row of chairs, at one end a throne like chair on a dais, and in the centre, the high, padded stool. A little behind the stool, and just to one side, so the judge can see him, will sit the executioner.

The jurors filed into place, nodding at each other as they saw who took the jurors' seats, and laughing as they pointed out the defence and prosecution counsel, approving with a grin Christopher mounting the dais to the judge's chair, and their hearts going out, partly in sympathy, partly in jealousy, as Rosemary stood behind the stool, and Alexander sat gleefully in the executioner's chair.

Rosemary gasps audibly as she realises that Stephen is the prosecutor, knowing guiltily that she has been out of hand these last few weeks, knowing she has been asking for a tanning and has not had it. But she would tonight. The feeling of fear and anticipation increase. Alexander is an unknown quantity. In all the times she has come to the club he has never been executioner, so she has no idea of his skill – or otherwise.

The bell rang, sharply. The court was in session.

'Your name?' The judge leans forward, the better to hear. Rosemary clears her throat, nervously.

'Rosemary Adriana Trace.'

'What crimes are brought against the accused?'

Stephen steps forward, his goatee beard quivering as the nervous tic in his neck affects the muscles of the jaw. He's nervous and trying not to show it. Grim determination to ensure Rosemary goes home well and truly thrashed helps in overcoming some of his nerves.

'The accused, Your Honour, has during the last few weeks been insolent, neglectful of household duties, lax in her marital duties and has dented the offside wing of the automobile.'

'I see.' The judge leans back, giving defence counsel the chance for a swift discussion with the accused.

Stephen has played a dangerous game, as far as Rosemary's behind is concerned. The offences outlined have no real defence, and Estelle knows it. She stands up and bows deferentially to the judge, setting her glasses on her nose.

'Your Honour, the accused has no real defence to the matrimonial crimes of insolence, or household duties unperformed, except perhaps – and here I speculate just a little on behalf of my client – she was angling for a touch of the very interest that brings us all together.'

She pauses for the swift round of applause from the jury, most of whom have at some time or other practised the same deceptions themselves.

'She wishes to state, however, that she has not been lax in her marital duties, in fact on several occasions she has been the instigator of a session. She also wishes to state in her defence that the accident to the automobile was not her fault, as witnessed by the fact that the insurance company is paying up.'

Rosemary watched anxiously as Stephen assimilated the information, knowing he was trying to find a way round the defence, trying to ensure a severe sentence for her. She also watched Christopher, calmly waiting for all the sides of the argument to be put to him.

'Your Honour, it is true that the accused has instigated several marital sessions, but we are talking about a time span of some six months, during which a few occasions have been lost due to overall neglect.'

Estelle sprang forward. 'Your Honour, I protest –'

But Christopher waved her to silence. 'The point is fair made. I will accept it as it stands.'

'But Your Honour, I would point out that in this trial, the prosecutor is also the spouse of the accused, and as such is biased.'

'That point has already been considered, and due regard will be made to that point when sentence is passed.'

Rosemary sneaked a look behind her. Alexander sat, arms and legs crossed, as if he had not a care in the world, and was watching a TV show, but he winked at Rosemary to let her know he was awake, aware and waiting. She shuddered again in pure bliss.

Stephen edged forward and glanced at Rosemary.

'Your Honour, it is the prosecution's case that the accused has been merely neglectful of her proper position as a wife,' (this too brought laughter and applause from the jury, who are a most disrespectful crowd) 'and I would merely state that it is the duty of the court to ensure that sentence is severe and fitting to the crimes of which she is accused.'

He walked away to stand near the jury, knowing there was nothing much else to say.

Estelle stood next to Rosemary, one hand resting lightly on her arm.

'Your Honour, members of the jury, you have heard both sides of this particular marital dispute. It is clear from the evidence presented that the fault lies on both sides. I maintain that the accused cannot be wholly to blame for the charges brought against her. I would ask for leniency.'

'Members of the jury, would you please consider your verdict.'

The jurors conferred together, delighted with the performance. Usually outrageous charges were brought, invented by the prosecution more or less on the spot, and bearing no relation to the accused whatsoever. This time the charges had been real and the defence well argued. Rosemary whispered her thanks. No one could have done more for her. Estelle had certainly ensured that she got a fair sentence.

Finally Giles stood up to deliver the jury's verdict, after what seemed to Rosemary a length of time resembling eternity.

'Guilty, Your Honour, but with mitigating circumstances.'

'Thank you.' Christopher considered the various combinations of sentencing he could give, knowing Rosemary's desire for a good session, and yet not wanting it to be too severe, as she was unused to it and might not be able to stand too much. Not like Dianne, for example, whom he knew could take almost anything that the court would wish to sentence her to.

He looked up. Alexander was grinning broadly and expectantly for Rosemary, for the first time, looked a little worried.

'The sentence of this court is twelve strokes with the tawse, followed by six with the cane.'

The jury applauded again. It was a fair sentence, severe, and yet not beyond what Rosemary could take.

'The executioner will kindly carry out the sentence immediately.'

Giles hurried to the end of the room and came back with the tawse and the cane. Alexander put one hand firmly in the middle of Rosemary's back and bent her over the stool, where he swiftly tied her wrists. The stool was not secured to the floor, but Rosemary knew, from watching others, that if she struggled so much that the stool toppled over, the sentence would start all over again, as if it had only just begun. Unless you had a tough skin, it wasn't worth risking that!

Alexander turned back her clothes and lowered the lace-trimmed, pale blue knickers, revealing Rosemary's plump white cheeks to the assembled court. He took the tawse from Giles and flexed it in his fingers. Then he looked round, caught Sandra's eye and grinned. He knew she was enjoying it as much as he was.

'Sentence is about to begin,' he announced, simultaneously bringing the tawse down with a crack across Rosemary's unprotected and very vulnerable bottom.

The shriek came at the very instant that a broad red stripe sprang across the white skin and almost drowned the gasp of pleasure from the onlookers. Again and again the tawse cracked down, never harder, never softer and each time a broad red line leapt up across the whiteness until the whole of Rosemary's soft cheeks were covered in red bands. She moaned and cried out but made no attempt to struggle.

'Six,' announced Alexander, and Rosemary yelled then, as if to say 'no more', but there were six more to take, and Alexander laid them on with deliberation and precision, exactly across the earlier six. He might have come late to the CP game but he is now quite experienced, and delighted the onlookers with the severity and accuracy of the tawsing.

Rosemary, face down and helpless, is awash with conflicting feelings. Reality always far surpasses fantasies, and while she has fantasised about having a 'real' tawsing, she is finding the actual experience far more painful than she could ever have imagined. And there are still six more to come and the thought of the cane landing across the already burning lines is fearsome – and extremely exciting.

There is no need for me to detail the caning. You've all had them, or given them. Or both. Suffice it to say that Rosemary had six scarlet lines etched across the red lines dealt by the tawse, and screamed at every one.

Stephen, watching with avid excitement, knew that this was what she needed and despaired that he couldn't bring himself to do it.

Estelle watched with glistening lips and glowing eyes, hoping someone would do exactly the same for her later.

Christopher watched sadly, knowing he too was incapable of giving such punishment and his wife had to go to others. He vows to try again. Soon.

Sandra watched her husband's performance with pride, and anticipation of something close to that with someone at the end of the session.

Marjorie and Darren exchanged knowing looks. Dianne and James watched approvingly, yet knowing their sessions have surpassed this many times. Annette and Giles watched happily, knowing another successful trial is over, and another good spectacle has been laid on – in every sense of the words – for their guests.

Finally Rosemary is released from the execution stool, and leans on her executioner, who dries her tears and offers to rub it better for her, but not too soon. Without looking at anyone, they leave the room for the master bedroom; the prerogative of the accused and the executioner.

This is the signal everyone has been waiting for. As if by pre-arranged agreements, people began to pair off. Christopher held out his hand to Dianne, knowing she needed no more than release right then, as he did. James offered an arm to Estelle, delighting her, as she knew she could expect something good from an expert. Darren reached out for Sandra, and Marjorie, with only a moment's hesitation, left with Stephen. After all, anyone different was worth trying.

Annette and Giles left together, as they always do. They are possessive and jealous of each other, these two, and everyone knows it.

It is time, gentle reader, for us to disappear into the night. If you pause for a moment, hand on door knob, in the very act of pulling the door shut behind you, you might hear the sharp slap of leather on skin or the whistle of a cane about to land on an upturned willing bottom; but not all the pairs are re-enacting the sentence or in fact need the stimulus. From those rooms you will hear little more than cries of ecstasy. Which is how it should be.

We can leave now, for I can tell you what will happen later. With dignity restored and alcohol intake stepped up to compensate for non-drinking time, the various legal couples will join up to go home.

It is at home that we may one day meet up with the couples we have seen tonight, but that is in the future, and another edition.

For tonight, at least, the trial by jury is over.

17

The Master

This story aroused all sorts of emotions when it first appeared, ranging from comments such as 'it's too intense', to admiration and people wanting to write to me. Unfortunately I have to decline such invitations due to pressure of work, but the compliments are nice. It was actually a fantasy which kept me going for some months, until I committed it to paper and lost it. Your gain my loss! There are times when I would wish I were free to make a fantasy come true . . .

I made a foolish mistake today. I reached out to take a file from my boss, and he saw the bruises on my hand. Instead of giving me the file he grabbed my wrist and held it tight.

'Do you have any more of those?' he asked. His voice was strange, and a little frightening.

'Yes,' I admitted carefully, and showed him my other hand, also marked with three clear lines. He let go my wrist and sat down in his leather chair.

'Are there any more marks – anywhere else?'

Tactfully worded, I thought, and was grateful for that. 'Yes, plenty of them.' A further confession. Would I regret confessing? Only time would tell.

'Want to talk about it?' His voice was strangely tense, still strangely frightening.

'Too long and complicated a story,' I said lightly, trying to dismiss it as a mere nothing.

'All right,' he seemed to make up his mind suddenly, and stood up again. 'Take some time off from my work, and write it out for me. How about that?'

'Is that an order?' I asked as flippantly as I could. His look hardened, went cold, as I did.

'Yes.'

I left the room with the usual anticipatory tingle which came from being ordered to do something, which always produced a violent reaction in me, and went to sit at my desk, carefully, on the large cushion I had thoughtfully left in the office for just this occasion. So, he wanted the story, did he? Then he would have it. In all its gory and glorious detail.

I'm late. Nine and a half minutes late. I rushed everywhere, but the bus was delayed, people got in my way and slowed me down. The Master hates odd numbers, so it will be rounded up to ten, no doubt about that. Ten sound whacks of the leather slipper before I confess my sins and am punished for them. Not an auspicious start, by any means. Try excuses again? No, last time he doubled the amount because I tried to excuse my lateness.

The door is shut tight. I ring the bell and wait fearfully on the immaculate doorstep. Not a leaf or a grain of dust in sight. The Master must be as tough on his housekeeper as he is on his penitents, if not tougher. After all, he pays her to do the work, while we pay him for our punishments. We? Oh yes, he once admitted there were quite a few of us. A rare moment of cordiality long ago, when we first met, before he became the Master.

A glance at my watch and I realise I am now eleven minutes late, because The Master is being deliberately slow in opening the door. Come on! Don't make it worse for me, please! At last, I hear the lock turning.

He is there, tall, dark, coldly good-looking, oh so stern and looking at *his* watch.

'Late,' he snaps. 'Get changed.'

I slip carefully past him, sensing the rigidity of his muscles, the cold radiating from his look, a faint hint of after shave that tingles as much as the anticipation churning madly in my stomach. I actually feel sick, but dare not allow myself to do such a thing, not here, not now.

I go into the small room where the clothes are laid out; the sports top and wrap around games skirt are all that I am allowed to wear. They lay on the narrow bed where I will lie later, taking all that he can give me. Before then I have to take all that he decides to give me. The clothes are small concessions to modesty, but modesty somehow goes out the window when punishment is being administered. Hurry to the loo, quick nervous evacuation of bladder and I think I am ready. If only the butterflies and sick erotic fear feeling would lie down for a moment.

The Master is waiting in the punishment room. It's a large place, probably sound-proofed, and cold, always cold. At the moment it is shadowed by huge wooden shutters he closes across the large windows. The lights will be switched on later, when decisions are taken as to what punishment I am to receive. For now, the Master needs no light. He is already sitting on the hard wooden chair that I have learned to hate and is holding the leather slipper I have also learned to hate. I cross the room as slowly as I can without incurring further anger and carefully place myself across his knees. My hands touch the floor, my toes touch the floor, all else is available for his attention. My skirt has ridden up already, showing a white bottom free of bruises or redness. I have avoided all contact with anything painful so I could come fresh and unmarked for his pleasure – as much as my own. I

161

would have done that anyway, but it happens to be one of his rules. He wants a clean canvas.

'Eleven minutes late,' he says, resting the slipper against my tense bottom. It's cold and it sends thrills through me. I cannot say he deliberately delayed opening the door, what would he do if I dared accuse him? Eleven minutes equals twelve whacks. The Master hates odd numbers. The slipper leaves me, then is brought down hard, leaves me, then is brought down hard on the other side. Every spank is soundly delivered, making me cry out and jump. But I lay there and I take them. I will remember; next time I will be on time. Even if I stand at the end of the road for half an hour.

With burning bottom and the prickle of tears (which come quickly as he has been far from lenient with me!), I kneel at his feet and confess three months of sin. Things I have done that I wish I hadn't, things I haven't done that I wish I had, not being careful enough with my money, not careful enough with the words that fly unchecked from my mouth. Enough sins to warrant a very severe thrashing. I know it, I expect it, I have not come for anything less. He listens without a word, absorbing all I offer.

The Master thinks over what I have told him. I remain kneeling. He stands up and walks over to press the switch on the wall. Spotlights spring into life, each picking out an element of his punishment room; the rack of canes, all twelve of them, a row of tawses and whips, a martinet, a paddle, a riding crop. A light shines directly onto the wooden chair, and another lights up the stool with its straps for wrists and ankles, only used for caning, because when the Master canes, no one but no one stays in place. So I believe, anyway.

'Come here.'

This means the decision has been made, the punishment is about to begin. I know from experience that the twelve whacks I have already taken have no place in the thrashing to come; it is as if they never happened. That's why it is so important for me to be on time!

I stand up, and go across the Master's knees for a second time for a thorough hand spanking, relentless, and very hard. I sometimes think his hand is as hard as the slipper, the slaps sting so much and I writhe and kick, muttering my protests at the punishment being delivered to an unprotected and already reddened bottom. But there is no escape, and when he is done there cannot be an inch of skin left untouched by his stinging hand.

'Get up.'

I stand up slowly, carefully keeping my hands away from my burning cheeks, and stand by the chair. He moves away and I sit down. I have fifteen minutes' grace now to compose myself, to allow the pain to subside just a little, to stop crying, before phase two begins. The chair is hard, uncomfortable and does nothing to comfort my poor bottom – it is designed not to, that much I do understand.

There is a large plain clock on the wall, just above the canes. You cannot look at the clock without subliminally seeing them, all part of his dread design for this terrible room. I sit and feel the pain settling just a little, wanting to rock from side to side, to ease myself off the hard wood, to move around, but I dare not. I clasp my hands, aware of the tears trickling down my nose, and stare at the clock, wondering what else he has for me.

The fifteen minutes go so fast, and yet so slow. At least the burning sensation has settled down now, has translated itself into the sick erotic feeling I know and love.

His voice comes from behind me. 'Over there.'

And I walk to the leather armchair, put myself face down over the arm; smell of polish, of body, of other people's pain and suffering, perhaps someone else's tears?

I go instantly. Obedience learned after painful digressions from the main punishment when I was not quick enough to do as I was told. Face down, waiting, scared, remembering.

It was agreed, when I signed the paper, that once in the punishment room the Master would give no explanations unless he chose to. Therefore, it was up to me to work out what the orders meant, and I would find obedience thrashed into me if I didn't either decide or do what he wanted fast enough. I signed, because I thought it would be easy.

I have since wondered how many others made the same mistake. On my first visit, 'Come here,' meant little until I was grabbed by the back of the neck, pushed face down over the wooden chair and given six hard strokes with a heavy tawse, and was *then* spanked soundly. 'Over there,' was beaten into me with the nasty leather covered paddle, twelve sound slaps before the tawsing that was decreed. I learned fast.

So far I have not broken the 'no touching' rule. I do not know what retribution that would bring. But oh the temptation to rub and rub to ease the pain!

The tawse. It always follows the spanking, coming with devastating pain over the red skin, bands of agony that build and build until I think I can take no more. The tawse hurts. This time it feels like a heavy one, it sounds like a heavy one. I count, silently. Something else I learned, after one occasion when the Master stopped and asked how many I had taken. I was foolish enough to say I didn't know. He immediately started all over again, and that time I made sure I counted. Twenty today and I am crying again because there is no way I cannot cry after that. I am on fire.

'Have you had enough?'

Oh tricky question! 'Yes,' and he will say it is not enough and perhaps do it all over again. 'No,' will no doubt have the same effect.

'It is not for me to say, Master,' I say in a muffled voice because I have not yet been told to get up. I talk into the cushions, feeling the pain, feeling the moistness gathering between my thighs, longing to stand up.

'Indeed it is not.'

Oh thank you, I managed the right answer.

'Get up.'

I spend another fifteen minutes sitting on the wooden chair which has now grown cold and is, for a few wonderful seconds, easing the pain. Sitting quiet and still, hands cupped in my lap, feeling the tears pouring down my face, feeling foolish and hurting and wanting it to be over, knowing it isn't over, I secretly rejoice in the fact that there is still more to come. To stop would disappoint me. He knows it as well as I do. We have been through this several times before, it never fails to have the same effect, a thrill, a fear, an adrenalin high to be ridden for up to two weeks later.

From somewhere behind me the door opens then closes. The Master has left the room! Glory, it has never happened before! I jump up and start rubbing madly at my swollen painful cheeks.

Stupid idiotic fool that I am not to have looked around, to think I would be left alone! Even as I rub, I hear the cold hard voice –

'Come here!'

With sinking heart and deathly coldness creeping down my spine, I turn, both hands clutching my bottom. The Master is standing by the door, pointing at me with a cane.

'*If* I decide to leave the room at any time, you will stay just where you are. Do you understand? It is not an excuse to break the rules. Come here. Hold out your hand!'

I walk across to him, jolting my cheeks with the effort of walking; I stand before him, looking at the floor, holding out my right hand. He has never done this before, I do not know what to expect.

The cane swishes down with incredible speed and creates a line of unbelievable pain across my palm. I cry out and snatch my hand away. The cane waits, I reluctantly hold out my hand again for a second and then a third stroke. I cry out each time.

'Now the other hand.' It is fair, he caught me with both hands on my bottom. Three more incredible lines of pain; it takes all the willpower I have to stand there, one hand burning and shrieking at me, and holding out the other one for an equal amount of punishment.

Sobbing, I return to the wooden chair, and glance up at the clock. Seven minutes left; seven minutes in which to cope with this new agony. I never knew hand caning hurt so much! He used the tawse on my hands once, when I was stupid enough to put my hands behind me in an effort to stop the beating, but not the cane. Oh I wish I'd been more sensible!

The Master is standing in front of me, swinging the martinet from side to side. There are still five minutes to go, but he torments me with the vision of what is to come. I shudder involuntarily. The martinet is agony on agony; the thin strands in themselves harmless, combined are devastating to a bottom already raw and swollen, as mine must be.

And I must be firm with myself. Last time – was it really as long ago as three months? – last time I was foolish enough to get up in the middle of the martinet session, to plead with the Master to stop, saying I couldn't take any more. I was dragged by my hair to the stool, strapped down and slowly, with the greatest deliberation and yes, say it, cruelty – he caned me six times with a heavy, thick cane. I screamed at every stroke. Then he unstrapped me, led me by my hair back to the leather armchair, pushed me down and started whipping me with the martinet all over again. I know, because I counted every one of the twenty-four strokes.

And I still got the mandatory six of the best before the punishment session ended. I vowed never to interrupt the Master again, particularly when I found it almost impossible to walk afterwards, and near impossible to sit comfortably for close on a week!

The time is up; I push memories aside and obey his gesture which means walk over to the leather armchair and bury my face in the cushion again.

My hands still hurt, my bottom still hurts, my thighs are (so far) unmarked but I don't think that will last. He wastes no time, almost immediately the martinet is lashing across my cheeks. Thin strands bite into my painfully-thrashed cheeks, upward of a dozen at once cutting into me. Again and again they fly through the air, wrap around me, and this time he goes for my thighs, agony on agony, they are so tender, so vulnerable to the thongs! I count silently, but aloud cry out my sobs and protests. It is a severe whipping: thirty strokes, before he stops and tells me to get up. I am close to passing out, almost too giddy to make it back to the wooden chair. Perhaps the Master knows he has gone too far, for out of character he thrusts a handful of tissues at me, and allows me to dry my face.

No, banish the thought, the Master can never go too far, his wish is always my command. If he wishes to beat me until I am unconscious, it will be done. All this was discussed, agreed, the contract signed, long before my first visit. His will is supreme, my obedience is guaranteed no matter what he does. After all, I made the appointment, I came with sins to confess, I needed absolution in the only way that satisfies me, severe corporal punishment.

The punishments take the same form every time, a good solid spanking, a tawsing, the martinet, the cane. It is the length of time I am spanked, the amount of strokes I get, the heaviness of the tawse, the thickness of the cane, which varies depending on my confession. Disobedience during the punishment session is entirely down to me and,

167

foolish person that I am, I manage to do something ridiculous every time, and earn extra strokes. Entirely my fault, but I will learn. I am learning fast!

My fifteen minutes are up; ahead is the most unbelievable agony of all. He nods, and I walk slowly and reluctantly to the stool and lay over it, waiting for the Master to buckle the straps firmly round my wrists and ankles. I cannot move, I have tried before, believe me I have tried. The straps are three inches wide, the buckles large and solid, they hold me rigidly in place, legs splayed, arms outstretched, all my weight resting on the padded top. No pressure can be brought to strain against the straps, so now I don't even try.

The Master is taking his time choosing the cane, I hear them moving on the rack. A heavy one, to cut me? A light one, to bite me? No matter, they all hurt.

He comes close, the cane is whipped through the air, every time. I wait, almost breathless, feeling so sick. The caning begins. Each time I tell myself no one can hurt that much, and each time it seems worse than the time before. Only six, only six but each is a nightmare in itself because he takes his time; they are delivered slowly, with great force, or is it that I am already so thrashed any pressure would hurt? I scream at him to let me go, but know even as I cry out that it will make no difference. I am afraid that one day I will shout something and he will increase the caning to twelve. Then what would I do?

Lay there and take it.

And then it is over, I am unstrapped, I can stand up, I can fall down at his feet and thank him for the thrashing.

He acknowledges my thanks with a small smile. He switches off the lights as I go to the small room where I remove all my clothes and lay face down on the narrow, hard bed – and wait. I am still crying, the pain is intense, I do not know what to do with my hands, or my poor thighs and bottom. The air is cool, at least that helps, but

168

a new feeling is taking over. The feeling that will only be satisfied by fucking. It builds hard. I long to reach down to massage my own sex to bring myself to orgasm but that would ruin what is to come.

The best bit of all.

In a short time the Master will come, and spread cold cream on my burning bottom; ease the pain, send his fingers walking into my wet places, for now I am very wet and waiting. At a signal, a tap on my neck, I will lift myself up onto my elbows and knees and wait, thighs splayed, for him to enter me with his long hard cock, longer and harder than anyone else I know! And he will thrust at me and I will push back against him putting pressure on the marked cheeks, even as he does, until I will explode with an orgasm that makes the whole thing worthwhile.

My boss has read this from end to end, several times. I have sat uncomfortably still and watched him read it, watched the glow in his eyes and the look on his face. I never knew, until now.

I told him how much I pay the Master. He says he will do that for me, and more, for nothing. It is an offer that is impossible to refuse.

But I will still visit the Master occasionally, because he was the first and because unless my boss turns out to be brilliant and fantastic, the Master will still be the best. Even the thought of his coldness sends me into anticipatory glow, the memory of his beatings set the juices flowing.

In truth, in my life, there is no one like the Master.

18

On Course at Cornfield

This story was written in an effort to appease and please all lovers of school scenarios, without going into an actual school scene; headmaster, teachers, schoolgirls in uniform, and so on. Or, come to that, adults playing school games, as it is beyond my understanding or approval. Readers of my regular columns in various magazines will know the way I feel about such things! So, here's a novella dealing with ladies who are unsure, but curious, and ladies who are bold enough to seek what they want, within a school framework. This story was read and vetted by a very dear friend, since departed this mortal world for the place where all ladies are willing and no one bats an eyelid at the sound of a session. It is dedicated to his memory with my love and thanks for my memories.

Tall, distinguished, good looking, hair greying just a touch at the temples, Richard Edwards looked every inch the successful businessman. His suit was well cut and an expensive shirt and tie completed the overall impression of elegance and wealth.

And why not? Business Dynamics Ltd, was going from strength to strength and the acquisition of Cornfield School had only added to the prestige of attending one of the residential courses offered to the business world. It

171

seemed, even in this financial climate, that firms were prepared to pay to educate their up and coming young executives, if only to give them an edge on their competitors, and in return Richard was only too pleased to take the money and supply a fortnight of unashamed luxury. The young executives lived in style, attending a rigorous course in business studies. An iron fist in a velvet glove. The studies were hard, the discussions often heated but held in such elegant surroundings it could only help create the right impression on impressionable minds. Add first-class meals, and the formula was complete. The courses were booked solidly until the end of the year.

All this, and Emmy too, thought Richard, smoothing the dust-free surface of his desk. Emmy was as much a find as the school, indeed, as the whole concept of Business Dynamics had been in the first place.

He sat down in a large leather chair and selected a fine cigar from the box. With any luck Emmy might drop by to discuss the imminent arrival of the next twenty trainees, and to share in a little extra-curricular activity or, as he preferred to call it, discipline. Blowing a cloud of smoke into the air, Richard opened the centre drawer of his desk and ran his finger along the pliable rattan cane. It rested on a bed of white blotting paper, which cushioned its rest between periods of duty: inflicting all that pain, giving all that pleasure.

Business Dynamics had moved from a small house in the village up to Cornfield School when the number of trainees proved too much for the place. Once an expensive boarding school, but slowly bankrupted by the loss of parents willing to pay exorbitant fees, Cornfield School had come onto the market at just the right time.

A number of people had applied for the various posts and Richard had interviewed them all himself. Mrs Williamson had stood out as an exceptional housekeeper-cum-trained nurse, able to supervise the overall running of the school. The chef had been enticed from the five-star hotel in the village by an offer he could not refuse – a good salary and a self contained rent-free flat. The gardener had come willingly from the ranks of the local unemployed, and finally he had chosen Emmy and Penny, general maids for want of a better description.

At first he had had difficulty in telling them apart. They were both buxom country girls, well endowed in all the right places, with round faces, deep blue eyes and a mop of dark hair. But there was a difference, a considerable difference, as he was to find out later to his amusement and happiness.

It had been so casual at first he hadn't quite realised what was happening. Emmy had been busy dusting the study which had once been the headmaster's office, when she asked casually: 'Did old Mr Harpener leave his cane behind, Mr Edwards?'

'Did he what?' Richard had been jolted out of his contemplation of the accounts to take in her question.

'Did the old headmaster leave his cane behind?' Emmy repeated patiently.

Richard thought furiously. Was she? Wasn't she? Was it a casual question? It couldn't be – no one asked that kind of casual question these days!

'As a matter of fact, er . . .'

'Emmy, sir!' A half smile and a deep blush.

'Thank you, Emmy. As a matter of fact, he did. Any reason why?'

'Well now,' she said, as she leaned over the bookcase to dust the framed diplomas on the wall. Richard took in the generous backside straining at the seams of her uniform while waiting patiently for what he hoped would be the answer he desired.

'There are them as might like it, if you get my meaning, sir.'

'Would you be one of them, Emmy?' he said, smiling,

as the blush grew deeper. 'Whatever you say won't go any further than this room, I can assure you of that.'

'And I believe you, sir that I do. Yes, I would be one of them.'

'Well, perhaps later.'

Richard had turned back to his papers to give Emmy a chance to recover from her blushes. Nothing more was said on the, oh so delicate, subject and finally she left the room.

When she had gone, Richard sat up, tapping his fingers on the blotter and whistling softly to himself. There had been a few, far too few, ladies who hadn't minded the odd slap or two, but only one who had actually dived across his knees for bare-bottomed spanking at the mere suggestion of the word; but that had all been a long time ago and he had despaired of ever finding anyone again willing to submit to a tanning of any kind. It had crossed his mind that by occupying Cornfield School he would be taking on the role of headmaster but he couldn't exactly order willowy young ladies with delectable rear-ends to wait outside his office for their just desserts. Nor could he ask the lecturers to send people to him for discipline either although, from comments he had heard from time to time, there were no doubt occasions when they wished they could do just that!

He had to wait a full three days before Emmy shyly knocked at his door and slid into the room, her eyes downcast, her cheeks red with embarrassment.

'What is it, Emmy?' He hoped this would be the first of many interesting visits, if he played his cards right.

'I called to see you, sir, about what we was talking about the other day.'

'Oh, you mean Mr Harpener's cane?'

She nodded, staring at the thick pile carpet.

'Well, Emmy, I've got the cane right here in the desk, but I've a confession to make – I've never caned anyone in my life.'

'Haven't you, sir?' She looked up, eyes flashing with curiosity. 'But you are interested, aren't you, sir? I didn't pick the wrong one, did I?'

'No, Emmy, you didn't pick the wrong one, as you put it, I'm very interested indeed, but until now I've not owned a cane and up to now I've not had the opportunity to do it. There have been a few ladies who didn't mind a slap or two, but that's all, and before you ask, no, there isn't a Mrs Edwards, so if you're agreeable you'll be the first. But I warn you, I might not be as accurate as you'd like.'

'But you'll learn, sir, you'll learn. I'm sure of that.'

To Richard's surprise she pulled down her white cotton knickers and leaned over his desk, waiting. He stared in astonishment at the expanse of white flesh, and then opened the desk drawer and took out the cane.

He flexed the cane a few times, feeling its strength and flexibility, and then went to stand at one side of Emmy, who was so very still. He had no idea of what she was feeling; embarrassment, anticipation, apprehension, genuine fear knowing he was a novice? Whatever it was, he should not out of all kindness keep her waiting.

Richard brought the cane down across her very wide and plump cheeks, marvelling at the instant red line which sprang up, noticing with pure pleasure how the skin dented and then rebounded again. The lines weren't straight, far from it, so he tried again, aiming carefully. This time creating a perfectly straight line, and a movement from Emmy, a sort of shiver. Pleasure? He hoped so, for it was giving him a lot of pleasure. With a sigh of pure happiness he carried on.

Over the next few weeks Richard learned a little of Emmy's past, how she had been regularly beaten by her father for all manner of misdemeanours, usually with a thick leather belt. For a while that had put her off any kind of bottom warming, but a boyfriend beat her, half in anger, half in fun, with a hazel switch which had implanted in her a desire to feel the cane. But until she had come to work at the school, there had been no opportunity.

Richard learned to use the cane properly. To his great surprise and gratitude, Emmy was more than willing to stay bent over his desk for what seemed like an age, being whipped again and again with the stinging flexible cane, which left large angry weals across her ample cheeks. He learned to place the strokes exactly where he wanted them, to leave a small space between each mark and not criss-cross the lines so that every single stroke was a sharp pain in itself. The day he produced a cry from Emmy's otherwise sealed lips was the day he felt he had finally learned his craft. That was also the day when she slid to the floor, wet and waiting, and held out her arms for him to enter her. Richard did it with the same willingness he had learned to cane in the first place.

There wasn't a jealous bone in Emmy's body. She knew Richard would appreciate a varied diet. She became his spy, seeking out people she thought might be interested, dropping sly hints, judging by the reaction whether they were interested or not. Occasionally a magazine or book would reveal a trainee's interest, and she would leave a small note when she cleaned the room. Inevitably the person would end up in Richard's office, bent over his desk, or with their head pressed deep into the thick cushions of the chair on the other side of the desk, bottom bared for the stinging strokes of the cane. It worked wonders for those lagging behind in their studies, and for those who had guilty consciences about their lack of enthusiasm for the course. It was a bonus for the devotee of the gentle art of CP. Sometimes they offered more than a willing bottom, and Richard was ready to oblige, every time.

And there was always good old, reliable trusted Emmy, of whom he was inordinately fond, for comfort and solace when he had caned and hadn't been rewarded with the sexual release he craved.

The huge wrought-iron gates stood sentinel at the start of the long winding drive which ended before the mellow stone of Cornfield School. The autumn sun showed the building in its finest light, the golden rays touching leaded windows, and the vivid scarlet of the creeper climbing around the porch.

Carole Davidson looked at the floor plan of the school framed in the huge cool hallway. Her suitcase was heavy, despite the fact that she was only staying for two weeks. Somehow there had seemed to be so much to pack, things she simply could not live without. The case had grown heavier and heavier as she carried it from the station to the taxi and now into the school. She experienced a sense of relief when one of the maids appeared and offered to take her case for her.

'Here's your room, Miss.' The smiling girl put the case on the bed and quietly left without giving Carole an opportunity to offer a tip.

'Well trained staff,' thought Carole, looking out of the tall windows across the sweeping lawns to the swimming pool which reflected the rays of the dying sun.

She looked around the room. The drapes were heavy red velvet and beneath her feet a rich red carpet gave a look of warmth and luxury to the room. There was a large desk under the window, the fireplace was filled with a gas fire and was flanked by two comfortable looking armchairs. In the recesses bookshelves waited. There were already books in place, paperbacks and heavier more studious looking tomes. Behind her was the bed, the wardrobe and the dressing-table. It was all the brochure had said it would be – and more.

Carole opened the suitcase. She unpacked swiftly, putting clothes and books away, and finally arranged the homely touches, the silver-framed photograph of her fiancé David, and the small stuffed donkey which went everywhere with her.

When it was done she sat down at the dressing-table to comb her long dark hair and study her skin for tired lines. Her deep brown eyes saw a face that pleased her, smooth brow, and pointed chin completing an oval. The hair fell forward, framing her face and she sighed, partly with relief, partly with tiredness. A bath would have been nice but there wasn't really time for a long relaxing session before dinner. It would have to wait until bedtime. She paused, comb suspended in the air. Bedtime. A fortnight without David didn't seem that long, not really, but a fortnight without the sting of the cane across her shapely bottom was something else. She would just have to work hard and try to forget about it until she was in David's arms again or over his desk, whichever came first . . .

Hazel Jennings paid off the taxi and turned to look at the building that had SCHOOL written all over it.

I'm grown up now, she told herself. But it didn't stop her feeling remarkably like a schoolgirl again as she walked through the large doors into the hallway. Notice-boards are noticeboards, she thought: tacked with rusting pins and showing out-of-date announcements; bet this one's no different. But it was. The plastic-capped pins weren't at all rusty and there wasn't a single out-of-date notice there, only lists of lectures and invitations to out-of-hours meetings and social gatherings.

Well, well, she thought with a smile. Things are looking up. But it still feels like school.

A maid appeared from nowhere, asking her name, and picking up her case. Hazel followed, wondering what she was doing there.

I'm being silly, she told herself for the millionth time.

This course was for adults, for grown people who didn't have teachers shouting at them or sending them outside or handing out detention or – she grinned wryly – trying to knock some sense and manners into you with a strap. This was far removed from those days yet the mere thought of going back into a school environment had been enough to stop her signing on earlier, when it had been proposed.

'No fear,' she had replied, startling her boss with her vehemence. 'I had enough of school when I was there, no chance of going back, thank you!' And all his reasoning hadn't made any difference, then. But Harry had been persuasive, anxious for her to improve herself as much as she could. Holding back from a chance of training and promotion over something as silly as unhappy school memories was nothing short of foolish. In the end she had given in, convinced by logic.

The maid touched the door and it swung open silently, revealing a luxurious room. So far so good, thought Hazel.

'Dinner is at seven, Miss,' said the maid, who was gone before Hazel could look round. Everything was very impressive, they certainly had gone to a lot of trouble. She closed the door after her. A full-length mirror gleamed, showing her plump but attractively rounded body, her now smiling face topped with a thick bunch of tight brown saucy curls. I think I'll cope, she told herself silently. It's going to be all right, I know it is.

Susan Mintell paused on the steps of the school for a quick look round. So far the school had been a delight, the mellow stone, soft velvet lawns, the majesty of the ancient trees. It was a place for lovers to walk and dream. She shook herself. Her father had told her over and over she was too much of a dreamer to appreciate real life, which is why she was being sent on a course.

'No room in my business for dreamers, young lady,' he told her. 'I've enrolled you in the Business Dynamics

179

course, see if they can get some sense into that head of yours. Time someone did!'

She had felt about ten years old all over again. She loved her father dearly and was content to make the family business her life, but surely there was time for the odd dream, wasn't there?

'Excuse me.'

Blushing, Susan realised she was blocking the doorway with her case and she quickly moved aside to let a well-dressed woman with expensive luggage pass her by.

Perhaps Dad was right after all, she thought, look at me, dreaming away, blocking the door, and I'm not even inside yet!

She followed a porter to her room, which she decided was made for dreamers. Such luxury, such beauty! She made herself unpack swiftly, giving herself time to dream later.

At the bottom of the case was a battered brown envelope. As she lifted it out, a spanking magazine fell onto the bed. There were footsteps outside, and Susan hastily thrust the magazine under the mattress, before realising foolishly that no one would just walk in, this wasn't home. But it was better left under the mattress for now. If she remembered the timetable correctly, she just had time for a wash and change before the dinner gong sounded.

As she brushed her blonde hair, she saw the colour flood into her face again as she thought of the magazine. Blushing like that could be a distinct disadvantage at times, and she wondered if she could learn to control it. Not here though. Two weeks wasn't long enough really.

She could hear voices outside, people gathering to go down for dinner, it was time to move. Susan wondered briefly if she could spot the dreamers among her co-students on the course. Doubt it, she told herself. On the surface we all look normal, don't we?

* * *

180

Richard looked down at the group sitting in rows in front of the small raised steps. A mixed bunch, he decided; a few dreamers among them possibly, a few hard-headed ones who would go away with something out of the course, and perhaps one or two who would really do something with what they learned, not very different from last time.

He paused for a moment to reflect on the group who had just left. With Emmy's contrivance, a total of five ladies had succumbed to his oh so gentle persuasion that they needed just a little more than the odd sharp word from the lecturers to get the message home. Five lovely ladies and indeed, face down over his desk, bottoms uncovered, waiting for the sting of his cane, they *were* lovely. Five was an all-time record. How many this time?

Putting all sexy thoughts aside, he launched into his standard introductory remarks, dealing with the purpose and methods of the school, the type of instruction, the degree of student participation, timetable and free time. He introduced the lecturers, and the resident housekeeper, mentioning her nursing abilities along with her capable running of the whole school.

He answered the standard questions and then left the platform to mix with the students, to make lightning assessments of their abilities. It was a constant source of amazement to him that some of the sophisticated and elegant ladies standing around holding glasses of sherry would, sooner or later, come creeping into his office, the very image of naughty schoolgirls, ending up lowering their knickers and leaning over his desk for some extra-curricular discipline. Looking at the women, listening to their refined and intelligent conversation, then picturing them as they would be in his study, it was all he could do not to laugh. That would never do. He was the boss, the all-powerful, the one who supervised the course, he was the epitome of authority.

A few enticing bottoms caught his eye and he felt the pressure in his trousers increase; the start of an ominous bulge. Hastily he excused himself from the gathering and hurried away to see if Emmy was in her room alone, waiting.

She was, with a new magazine to delight him, too. What joys life held!

What more could a man ask?

After only a few days at Cornfield School, Susan felt as if she had been there forever. The schedule ran like clockwork, everyone was friendly, the meals were good and the lectures varied and fascinating. In fact she had completely forgotten about the spanking magazine tucked under the mattress. When she returned to her room one lunchtime to collect some notes she found her magazine lying on the dressing-table. Her heart pounded wildly and the colour flooded into her face as she realised that the maid must have discovered it that morning. But the bed had been made every morning since she arrived, yet the magazine had only just come to light.

Susan walked over to it and picked it up. A tiny slip of paper fell out and she retrieved it from the floor. It was a hastily scrawled note, very much to the point:

If this is what you'd like, see Mr Edwards.

Susan blushed again to the roots of her blonde hair. She screwed the note up and threw the magazine into the dressing-table drawer, determined to forget the whole thing.

But she couldn't. During the afternoon session on business relationships her mind kept wandering, trying to put a face to the person who might have discovered the magazine, and with it her guilty secret. Had they looked at it each day since she had arrived? Or had it worked its way towards the edge of the bed with her nightly tossing and turning, until it met the fingers that tucked the sheets in that morning? No, it's a duvet, not sheets. Unless the lower sheet had been changed. That had to be it!

What did Mr Edwards have to do with it? Was he a secret spanker? Susan grew red again at the very thought, admitting in her secret heart that she had fancied him ever since he had stood, so tall and dignified, and so very strong, on the platform on the very first day.

With a supreme effort she brought her thoughts back to the discussion and contributed an intelligent remark or two, to the pleasure of the lecturer. He praised her and Susan coloured all over again as eyes turned to her.

That evening she escaped to her room immediately after dinner, not lingering over coffee as she had done previously. She went straght to the dressing-table to see that the magazine was still there. There were no more notes. Don't be silly, she thought, a maid wouldn't look in the drawer. It's just that I was foolish enough to push it under the mattress.

She sat down in the armchair holding the magazine. The words were familiar, the photographs provoked familiar thoughts. How much did it hurt? Did the lines last very long? Could you sit on the lines afterwards? Was she strong enough to take six of the best? And what had Mr Edwards to do with it? Could she just go down, knock on his door and say: 'Mr Edwards I'd like you to cane me please.' No of course not. Susan blushed again just thinking about it, and put her hands to her burning face. I'd never have the nerve to go and ask him, but what an opportunity to find out, once and for all, realise my fantasies, my secret desires, and no one need ever know. If I bruised, the marks would be gone by the time I went home.

All it needed was courage, a considerable amount of it, and a little encouragement from Mr Edwards – which came sooner than Susan anticipated.

* * *

'Susan Mintell, eh?' Richard thoughtfully tapped his pen on the blotter, trying to put a face to the name. Then he recalled the blonde with green eyes, and a pretty face. He'd labelled her as a bit of a dreamer, but she seemed to be doing all right according to the reports. At least there were no adverse comments, as there had been about some of the others.

'Thank you, Emmy,' he smiled across the desk at his loyal partner. 'It's been a long time since someone turned up here with an actual magazine! At least, one you've seen, anyway! Anyone else?'

'I'm not sure,' Emmy thought for a moment, looking down at her strong capable hands. 'That Carole Davidson, you know, the dark one, all pert and spark. I wouldn't mind betting she's interested but I don't know why. Just a feeling.' She smiled at Richard, whom she loved with total adoration. 'As for anyone else, well, I'm looking for opportunities.'

'Thank you very much, Emmy. I know I've said it before, and thought it before, but what would I do without you?' He pulled a sheet of paper toward him and wrote swiftly. 'There you are, a note for Miss Mintell, see if we can encourage her into the den of iniquity, shall we? Leave it in her room next time you're passing, and we'll see what reaction we get.' He looked thoughtfully at her. 'And while I'm waiting for the blonde Miss Mintell to make up her mind . . .'

'We mustn't let the cane get out of practice, sir.' Emmy responded, grinning as she stood up and began to unbutton her skirt.

'Emmy, what *would* I do without you?' Richard murmured as he took the cane out of the drawer.

Carole relaxed in the deep armchair in front of the fireplace, letting her eyelids droop in tiredness. The course was as demanding as the brochure had said it would be;

with discussions and written assignments, lessons in acting, with each person taking the part of someone involved in a business deal or office routine. Something going on all the time to keep the mind alert, the brain cells functioning. But underneath it all was her longing for David and his arms and body. And, she had to confess, for some discipline too. Funny how quickly you become addicted to regular sessions of being put across the knee for a slippering or spanking, or bent over something, waiting for the cane or tawse to land with surprising severity; for the leap of pain followed by the vivid glow that makes it all worthwhile. A week and a half to go before she could get back to David, and every part of her aching for some attention, somewhere, from someone.

Now, if this were a *real* school, she could play up and be ordered to the headmaster's study for six of the best, and right now that would be great. But it's futile, thinking like that. She'd just have to put up with it.

Next morning, as Carole was leaving her room, Emmy arrived to clean and tidy for her. Carole paused for a moment, last night's thoughts still fresh in her mind.

'This was a school, wasn't it?' she asked, watching Emmy make the bed.

'Yes, it was.' Emmy risked a calculating look at Carole and dropped the usual large hint. 'Mr Edwards uses the headmaster's study for his office; kept it just as it was, he has, even the cane is still in the desk!'

Carole laughed a little self-consciously, and dared to ask, 'Does it ever get used?'

'Depends on who's asking.' Emmy busied herself with a duster, leaving Carole to walk out of the door, thoughtfully considering the answer. So, there was a cane still in the school, and in use, if what Emmy said was right. What next? Go and ask? No, better to contrive an interview and bring the subject round to the original use of the building, and so on.

Carole went to her first lecture in a brighter frame of mind, unaware that her thought processes had been duplicated many times before by other interested students.

Hazel clutched a large batch of notes under her arm. She had to admit the course was fascinating, and everyone was so pleasant and amenable, but still the aura of school hung over her. She found herself jumping every time someone walked into the room, as if they were 'the authorities' checking up on her. She knew she was stupid, but she also knew she couldn't help it, no matter how hard she tried. The fact that no one shouted or got stern was a help, but somehow –

In the end she tried to discuss it with the girl in the next room, but she only laughed.

'Why don't you ask Mr Edwards if you can have a chat with him?' the girl suggested. 'He'll soon put all your fears to rest, he's so *nice*!'

Sensible advice, thought Hazel. She would write Mr Edwards a note, asking if she could see him. It would be a shame to waste the firm's money over some silliness she couldn't control.

Susan found the note in her room when she returned from the last session of the day. The memo was brief, and to the point, exactly the sort of thing she wished she could write.

I like to see all the students at least once during their stay. I wonder if you would care to visit my office at five o'clock tomorrow for a brief chat. Richard Edwards.

Susan felt her stomach turn over completely, and settle down into a mass of raving butterflies. It was the answer to her prayer, but only half the answer. She was going to be inside the office, but what next? Should she broach the subject of her interest or would he? Don't be foolish, she reproached herself, how could he? He doesn't have the remotest idea I'm interested! She pulled open the drawer to find a comb and saw her magazine. Her stomach did another impossible flop.

Someone might have mentioned it. What if they had?

Even worse, what if they hadn't? This was a once in a lifetime chance, to turn dreams into reality, to see whether she liked it or not.

If he doesn't mention it then I will, she decided, setting the comb down on top of the happy bare-bottomed lady. And tonight I won't need the stories, that's for sure!

The next day passed in a sort of haze. Several times Susan found her attention wandering to an alarming degree as a picture of Richard Edwards, cool, suave and so authoritative, floated before her eyes. Five o'clock seemed an age away and yet as she trailed from the lecture hall to the afternoon session the clock hands appeared to be speeding.

At last, with trembling fingers, she knocked on his office door just as the hands touched the hour. The door opened and she saw Richard sitting behind his desk. She felt awkward and clumsy as she responded to his invitation to sit down. They chatted about trivial items for a few moments, and Susan felt herself relaxing under the influence of his friendly smile and benevolent gaze. She assured him she was enjoying the course, and learning a good deal from it.

Then he dropped the first large hint. 'Is there an area of interest the course doesn't cover, Susan?'

She felt herself blush, very slightly. Were they thinking of the same thing or was she jumping to conclusions? 'I'm not sure I know what you mean.' She raised tentative eyes to his and saw the friendly smile change to an outright grin.

'I think you do.'

This was the moment, thought Susan, it's now or never. She took a deep breath to bolster fast-flagging courage.

'Yes, I do know what you mean. There isn't any discipline in the course, is there?'

It was said. The words lay on the desk between them, charged with suppressed excitement and nervous energy. She waited for Richard to pick up the conversation again, feeling herself going tense with sexy feelings.

'No there isn't any discipline in the course, because there are many who would object to it. But it is here for those who ask for it, Susan.'

'I'm not sure I'm asking,' she confessed suddenly. She twisted her hands nervously round and round in her lap. 'I'm not sure I'm asking but –'

'Why not tell me about it?'

The voice was smooth, persuasive and strong. Susan melted under the authoritative manliness and began to talk.

'I've been interested for a long time, and thought I was peculiar. Then I found a magazine on a bookstall in London; it opened my eyes to a whole new world. I found out I wasn't strange after all, that there are many people like me. I've read lots of magazines since, but there hasn't been anyone I could ask, there hasn't been anyone who has offered –' she trailed off, looking at Richard with pleading eyes, asking silently for him to take the initiative, as she was afraid of asking out loud, of actually putting it into words.

'I have a cane right here in my desk drawer.' He raised a hand to stop her from saying anything. 'There have been other ladies in my office who felt just as you do, Susan. Just as nervous, and just as afraid. I can assure you they enjoyed the experience, some of them actually came back for more before they left Cornfield School, I hope it did them a lot of good. I can also assure you that no one, outside of you, me and Emmy, who saw your magazine, and whom I trust completely, will ever know about it. I wouldn't dream of announcing to the assembled masses that Susan Mintell reported to the owner of Cornfield School and bent over the desk for six of the best whilst she was in residence! Think what the papers would make of that! So, absolute discretion and confidence is assured. Are you willing?'

As he talked Susan felt herself going weak with desire to experience it.

'Yes,' she replied, before she could stop herself. If she had had more time, if Richard had phrased it any other way she might well have chickened out. But the die was now cast, the decision taken from her by the needs of her own body.

Richard was opening the drawer and taking out a long thin cane which he whipped through the air. He smiled.

'I won't promise not to hurt, as that's the whole point, isn't it? Come on then.'

She stood up a little uncertainly, holding on to the edge of the desk, her eyes rivetted to the wicked-looking cane. Richard saw her look and laughed.

'Still worried? Don't be. Relax, enjoy it. When the lines are fading, you can come back for more to take home with you if you want. But for now, come on, there's a good girl. Knickers down, bend over the desk, hold on tight to the other side, that's it.'

This was it, the moment she had dreamed about, fantasised about and read about over and over again. The moment when she would, indeed was, hooking her thumbs into her oh so brief briefs, and lowering them to her knees under Richard's watchful appreciative eyes. There was still the chance to cry off, to say no, and there would be nothing he could do about it, and yet –

She leaned over the desk, feeling the cold wood press against her stomach. Her pubic hair crinkled uncomfortably as she wriggled a little, producing a sigh from Richard.

'My dear Susan, you have the most beautiful bottom.'

Even face down, not having to meet his eyes, she felt herself blushing. Her fingers reached for the other side of the desk and she tried to quell the mounting apprehension.

Immediately there was a sharp whistling sound and a line of pain leapt across her bottom, burning both cheeks. She yelped and held on tight. Richard said, 'one' very quietly and she groaned aloud. She could hear him laugh and at the same time a searing line drew itself across her skin. She cried out.

'Two.' There was amusement in his voice. 'You're doing very well, Susan, I'm not doing it very hard either, I could cane you a lot harder than this!'

Susan didn't believe it, it hurt so much and there were still four to go! Sentences, paragraphs, photographs flashed through her mind as the third stroke landed, and she realised even through the pain that he was doing it very well indeed, that each of the three lines burned separately, not crossing over anywhere.

'Only another three to go, Susan, here's the next one.'

And the fourth line bit into her poor exposed cheeks. Tears began to form in her eyes, but didn't fall. She couldn't cry all over his desk, that would never do! The pain, the fire, the burning of the lines! And two more to go! Could she hold out?

The fifth and sixth strokes landed in quick succession and she leapt up, clutching her burning cheeks in both hands. She turned to look at him, 'Does one say thank you?' She tried to smile, whilst rubbing carefully at the pain. Susan realised suddenly that the embarrassment had disappeared, along with most of her dignity.

It was extremely difficult to be dignified when you have just exposed nearly all of your most private areas to the gaze of a comparative stranger, who has dealt out stinging punishment without so much as an apology, and then to stand in front of the stranger, knickers around stocking tops, rubbing at the wounded area!

'You could say thank you,' he responded, smiling.

'Thank you, kind sir.'

'Now tell me, was it as you anticipated?'

'It hurt more, it burned more than I expected,' she confessed, tugging her knickers back into place carefully.

'Well, when it's all settled down to a nice glow, you can think about it a little better. If you want any more, let me know, next time I'll do it just a little bit harder.' He opened the door for her and took her hand as she went to pass him. 'You were very brave, Susan.' She blushed and hurried away to her room, anxious to look at the damage.

The door safely locked, she walked to the dressing table and for the second time in a comparatively short time, she lowered her knickers and turned round to present herself to the triple mirror.

The weals looked awful against her creamy white skin, and how they hurt! Definitely never again, she told herself tearfully, never again. The books were wrong, there was nothing sexy about it at all!

She grabbed a pile of cushions and sank cautiously into the armchair. Nothing sexy? Well, that was wrong, for the anticipation had been the very height of excitement. Thinking about it, talking about it, preparing for it. It was the actual inflicting of the pain, being dominated by such a strong man, that was sexy.

As Susan relived the vivid experience she became aware that the pain was subsiding into the most unbelievable glow. Cautiously she slipped a finger into her moist secret place and began to move. Sexy? I should think it was!

Holding Richard's memo in one hand, Hazel made her way along the thickly carpeted corridors to his office. She was feeling slightly silly as the day had gone well, and she was really enjoying the heated discussions that occasionally flared up. She had almost felt like an adult in an education centre for a few hours, but now, heading towards what had been the headmaster's study, she felt young and inadequate all over again. She had worried all through lunch whether she would find enough to talk about to justify asking to see him, and her nervousness was mounting the closer she got to his office door.

'Hazel, come in!' The smile was welcoming, the friendliness unmistakable. Hazel sank into the leather armchair in front of the desk, she began to feel slightly more confident. Richard sat down, and steepled his fingers under his chin.

'You wanted to see me; is there anything wrong with the course?'

'No, nothing like that, it's – it's a silly problem really, one I shouldn't be bothering you with, taking up your valuable time.'

'If you hadn't asked to see me before the course was over, I'd have asked to see you, as I like to talk to everyone at least once during the fortnight, so don't let that bother you! There's only you, me and the desk, why not tell me what it is that's bothering you?'

'Well –' Hazel looked down for a moment and then into the friendly eyes that waited so patiently for her to begin. 'I didn't like school, in fact I'd go so far as to say I hated it. Since I left, I've been avoiding anything like school as it makes me feel stupid and useless all over again.'

'Has coming to Cornfield made you feel stupid and useless?'

'Well, it did at the beginning. It looks like a school, although I have to say you've made it really luxurious, but it is still a school!'

Hazel waited for Richard to respond, prepared to defend her argument against anything he might say. He stirred in his chair and then reached for a cigar from the box, silently asking if she minded. She shook her head.

'What was it about school that you hated the most, might I ask?'

The aromatic cigar smoke drifted towards her, tickling her nose.

'Being made to look foolish in front of the class, you know, if you didn't know the answer the teacher would be sarcastic and everyone would laugh. That sort of thing.'

'But that doesn't happen here, does it?'

'No, but you see, the feeling that has been left in me about school has stayed over the years. I know it's silly, and I hoped that talking to you would get it out of my system.'

'One of the unfortunate things about buying a school is that it does have these overtones of sarcastic teachers, gym sessions, changing rooms, maths, chalk and dust, even if I have turned it into a luxury hotel. It might have helped if I'd changed the name, but that is what is on the deeds, and the locals knew it as Cornfield School, so there didn't seem to be much point in changing it.'

'Has anyone else had my peculiar silly worry?' she asked hesitantly.

'No. But you see, Hazel, a lot of people actually like the thought of being in school again.' He leaned forward, lowering his voice to a confidential level. 'When the headmaster left, he left his cane behind, and sometimes, just sometimes you understand, a lady comes along who likes to relive some of her school memories, and we act out a little charade. Were you punished at school?'

'Once or twice. Not like some, they seemed to get the strap all the time!'

'Oh, the strap! Not the cane?'

'It was in Scotland, they're rather keen on that I understand.'

'Yes, I believe so. Well, Hazel, there's a secret for you to think about. I'm sure I can rely on you not to tell anyone, can't I?'

'Yes, of course. What you're saying in effect is, it isn't a particularly bad thing to relive some school memories, am I right?'

'Right first time. And if you have any fantasies you'd like to live out, let me know.'

'I don't think that's very likely.' She stood up and held out her hand. 'Thanks for seeing me, and for listening to me.'

'If there's anything troubling you, then it isn't a silly thing. I hope I've helped.'

'I think you have. Thanks again.'

Hazel walked thoughtfully back to her room, considering the interview. What a charming man! And so honest and open with her too! Surely he hadn't meant the invitation seriously, though. Did people actually go along there to be caned? Are there perhaps others like me who have school memories they can't escape and try working them out instead?

Sitting at her desk, gazing out across fields stretching away from the grounds, Hazel let her mind slip back to her school days for the first time since she had arrived. She relived incurring the teacher's wrath, and being ordered to the headmistress's study. She remembered the seemingly endless walk along the long corridors, the timid knock on the door, the hard voice ordering her in. She remembered handing over the note with hands that shook, the stern look bent upon her quivering body, the strap swinging from the hand, wickedly pliable. She recalled being ordered to bend over the chair and how she wailed and cried as the strap descended with the full force of the adult arm upon thin-knickered cheeks that shrieked their agony through the cloth. Sobbing, she had hidden in the girls' toilets until she could sit properly again before returning to class and the sympathetic gaze of her friends.

If he thinks I'd go through all that again, voluntarily, then he has another thought coming! Hazel laughed at the thought. But I wonder what it would be like, now I'm an adult? Would the feeling be the same? Would a cane hurt like the strap?

Foolish thoughts, almost as foolish as the ones that sent me there in the first place. A caning indeed!

But despite all her protestations, the thought simply refused to go away.

Carole's opportunity to talk to Richard Edwards came at the dinner at the end of the first week of the course. She had seen him a few times before then, walking the corridors, popping his head round the door of lecture rooms, but the opportunity had never been right. This Saturday evening, with sherry flowing smoothly and everyone in an amiable mood, it seemed like a good time to drop some hints and see whether they were picked up.

She saw him standing alone for a moment and went across to him.

'Hello, Mr Edwards.'

'Hello there it's – Carole Davidson, isn't it?'

'It is. Do you remember the faces and names of everyone who comes on your course?'

'I try. Part of the training, you know, goes down well if you remember someone's name.'

'I'll have to remember that,' Carole laughed, still keeping her eyes on Richard. 'Your maid, Emmy, isn't it? was telling me this really was a school, not purpose-built for you.'

'That's right,' Richard looked round. 'Would you care to sit down?'

'Thank you.'

He led the way to a couple of empty seats next to a small table. When they were settled, and he lighted one of his slim cigars, he started to tell Carole how he had acquired the school after the number of pupils had dropped dramatically and it could no longer pay its way.

'It certainly is a beautiful place,' she looked round at the hall. 'It could have been built for you.'

'It did come onto the market at the right time.'

'Emmy said you use the headmaster's old study for your office and you keep it just as it was.'

The comment was innocence personified but Richard knew which way the conversation was going; he was an expert in the art of double-talk with willing ladies.

'Yes, exactly as it was. The desk is huge, solid oak, beautifully made. I couldn't have bought a better one. I've kept all the old books, more out of interest than anything, and added a few of my own. It's a lovely room, you must come and see it some time.'

'That's a new line, isn't it? Come and see my study some time, I've kept it just as the old headmaster did,' she teased, her eyes dancing with suppressed excitement. Richard grinned.

'Not exactly a novel line of approach, is it, but then it is a genuine offer. You can come and see my office any time you like.'

'I think I will,' she replied shyly, looking into her drink.

'Tomorrow, if you like. Sundays are rest days, so you aren't tied to a lecture or anything.'

'Then I'll come tomorrow, after dinner. All right?'

'I look forward to it. Until tomorrow then. I think I'd better circulate a little more before the evening is over.'

Carole watched him walk away, strong and tall and exciting. She felt her excitement reaching the point when she could orgasm there on the spot if she wasn't careful. For all the outward casualness of the conversation, she had made an assignation with the cane, and she knew it as well as he did. Tomorrow, after dinner. Could she wait that long?

The interminable Sunday dragged by. Carole spent most of it in her room, writing a passionate letter to David and looking at his framed photograph for inspiration. Would he understand if she told him? Possibly not. It was one secret she would have to keep. As it was, she had to hope the marks would fade by the time she got back unless she made a game of it, and told David he had acted like a real headmaster, caning naughty ladies who didn't concentrate during lectures. It would be worth trying to find out if anyone else on the course had had the cane as it would affect her own escapade a little.

As the thought crept into her mind, she abandoned the letter. If she could prise a secret or two out of Richard Edwards, it could be mentioned in the letter to prepare David for the revelation when it came. On the other hand, if the marks faded, and she had no idea how hard he would cane, she could boast of others being caned but her concentration had been so good, her contributions so excellent, she hadn't been punished. Not that he would believe that for a moment but it was worth a try.

The dinner gong sounded, breaking her reverie, and she hurried to the dining room. Anticipation had put an edge on her appetite and she was ready for almost anything.

By the time the substantial meal was over, Carole was quivering with excitement. She politely fended off invitations for cups of coffee and chat from the others, and went casually back to her room. There she took a quick shower and changed her undies to the black lace set she had packed 'just in case' not knowing whether they would really be needed.

Richard's door stood slightly ajar, and she tentatively tapped on it with her finger nails and peeped round the edge.

'Do come in. Isn't it a lovely Sunday?'

'Yes, the weather's fine, if that's what you mean!'

Richard laughed. 'You obviously don't need any training in the art of quick conversation!'

'It depends entirely on whom I'm talking to, of course.' She smiled provocatively at him, and walked over to the glass-fronted bookcases. 'This lot should be worth something, you should let a dealer look at them.'

'Mercenary, aren't you?' He stood beside her, looking at the books. 'I just like having them around. I like links with the past, traditions and all that.'

'So I understand.' She endeavoured to put a double meaning into the simple statement.

'Why not? After all, some things that were done here before I came are worth continuing, aren't they?' He looked seriously at her, knowing she understood his meaning as clearly as he had hers.

'I do most certainly agree. Sometimes the old ways are more – interesting.'

Richard sat down in his big chair. 'Come and sit down, Miss Davidson. I think there is something we have to discuss.'

'Certainly sir.' She walked carefully across the thick piled carpet, hoping her heels wouldn't snag.

'Now it has come to my notice that you have been expressing an excessive amount of interest in a certain tradition once maintained by this school, that is, corporal punishment.'

Her stomach muscles contracted so violently that it was all she could do to play along with the charade.

'Yes, sir, it is a subject I am deeply interested in, and have been a student of for some time.'

'Then it would appear that I would be doing you a favour in furthering your studies.'

'It would seem that way.'

Richard leaned back and opened the drawer. He took out the cane and flexed it in his fingers.

'This is the cane, Miss Davidson. Normally I allow students who need such extra curricular – uh – activities to divest themselves of any posterior coverings and lean over my desk. However, on the few, I might say rare, occasions when an avid student of the subject presents herself I do make the exceedingly rare gesture of offering slightly more than the traditional six of the best. You may or may not avail yourself of the extra discipline, as the mood dictates.'

'May I enquire, sir, what this extra discipline consists of, so I can make up my mind?'

'Most certainly. I am offering the added bonus of a thorough bare-bottom spanking, across my knees, before applying the cane to the same part of your anatomy. I understand it adds a certain – something – to the pleasure.'

This was far more than Carole had hoped for, she made up her mind immediately.

'It would be nothing short of churlish of me to refuse such an offer. I accept, willingly.'

'I had hoped very much that you would. Come round this side of the desk.'

Carole kicked off her high-heels and padded softly round the solid oak desk. Without any hesitation she laid herself across Richard's knees, leaving him the pleasure of turning back the red dress and finding nothing more than black lace panties, suspenders and stockings in the way of the promised spanking. He sighed with pleasure as he eased the tiny panties down and left bare, ivory white cheeks.

'It is almost a sin to destroy its purity,' he mused, bringing his hand down hard in the middle of her left cheek and then again on the right. Carole wriggled slightly to make herself more comfortable, and prepared to enjoy, if that was the right word, the regular slapping of his expert hand on her cheeks, bringing a flush to them (and to her face) as erotic feelings surged through her. The spanking was sharp, hard, and professionally done, he was an expert. How much practice had he managed here at the school? Building steadily from tingling to stinging to painful, she wriggled and kicked a bit as the spanking reached a crescendo. At the perfect moment he stopped, just when it verged on unbearable, and helped her to her feet, smiling at her red face and increased rate of breathing. Her breasts moved as she shook herself, adding to his desire as well as her own. Then he picked up the cane.

'Come on, I don't intend to let that beautiful posterior cool off before I cane it!'

She smiled a little ruefully and stretched over the desk, presenting Richard with an unforgettable picture. The red dress tucked up around her waist reflected the redness of her burning cheeks, framed by her black lace suspender belt and lowered panties.

Carole was absolutely aflame with desire, far more intense than anything she had experienced before. This was, after all, a stranger who knew only too well how to spank and was probably about to prove he could cane very effectively too. In that moment she remembered she hadn't asked him about the others –

'One.' And the cane descended with stinging force across the reddened skin. Despite herself, she yelped a little and hung on tightly to the edge of the desk, awaiting the second one which came all too soon.

'Two.' Fractionally lower than the first, but equally as sharp. He *did* know how to cane!

'Three.'

This time she cried out, kicking her feet in agony, knowing she was probably moving her panties even lower, but not caring.

'Come on Carole, only three more. I thought you were a student!'

'I am but – ouch!'

'Four. What were you going to say?'

'I've not been spanked that hard – Ooww!'

'Five. Only one more to go, hold on, six!'

Carole slid gracefully to the floor, rubbing at the lines,

and pulling off the panties which were hindering her movements. She looked up at Richard, aware of the erection pressing at his trousers, aware of his eyes on her exposed body, and held out her arms.

'Finish the lesson,' she whispered, moist and waiting, holding out her arms. A once in a lifetime chance and she was determined to take it. Richard looked down at the picture of erotic beauty before him, unzipped his grey trousers and freed his cock; ready, hard and throbbing with desire. He knelt down and touched her quim gently with both hands, and then, as she reached for him, plunged straight into her. With regular rhythmic strokes, they clung together, moved as one, then came together in a shattering and hasty climax.

Afterwards, with some semblance of dignity restored, clothing in place and a shot of whisky in her hand, Carole returned to the earlier thought she had had.

'I'm asking out of curiosity more than anything, although I do have another reason. Have you, er, chastised anyone else on this course?'

'Now why should I tell you that? It would be breaking confidence.'

'Of course it wouldn't, how many women are there on this course?'

'Ten. Take away you, that only leaves nine. I can't have you asking sensitive questions of the nine others between now and next Sunday can I?'

'No, I don't suppose you can. All right, tell me this. Did you cane anyone on the last course?'

'That's something I can answer without fear of upsetting anyone. Yes. On the last course there were five ladies who condescended to, how shall we phrase it, try out the comforts of my desk.'

'Five!' Carole stared at him in astonishment. 'Did they all like it?'

'No. In fact, none of them did, but it was a sharp lesson

they were well overdue to receive. It helped the concentration no end.'

'Thanks, that's exactly what I hoped you'd say.'

'Are you going to tell me why?'

'In case there are any marks left by the time I go home. I'm planning to drop some hints to my fiancé, you know, discipline is strict here, on the last course five ladies were chastised . . . You know, that sort of thing.'

'I see. Can I take it then that there will be no repeat performance?'

'No, better not.' She rubbed gently at the still burning lines and sighed. 'I shall be sorry not to repeat it, though, it was quite something. Still, I'll have to be satisfied with that, until I get home. Thanks for the drink – and everything.' With a pert smile, she rose from the chair and blew him a kiss. 'See you around, headmaster.' And then she was gone, leaving Richard with a dull ache and a very happy memory.

During the course Hazel had become friendly with Susan Mintell. At times she was exasperated by Susan's dreamy attitude, and at others amazed at the sharpness of her perception. It was to Susan that Hazel turned when she needed help in deciphering the badly-scrawled lecture notes. She tapped lightly on Susan's door and pushed. It opened. Susan looked up from her armchair, hurriedly stuffing a magazine down the side of the cushion.

'Oh Hazel, come in, I didn't hear you knock.'

'The door was open. When I knocked it swung in. I hope I'm not interrupting anything.'

Susan blushed and then laughed.

'If I can't tell a friend, who can I tell? I was reading this.' She drew the magazine from its hiding place and offered it to Hazel who looked at it in disbelief.

'Spanking? You?'

'Well, it depends on what you mean by that. Slip the lock on the door, make sure we're not disturbed.'

Hazel locked the door and sat down, wondering at the strange fluttering feeling she was experiencing.

Susan was excited at being able to share with someone. 'I've been interested for a long time, you know, reading these magazines, but I've never had anyone to give me what I wanted.'

'Don't suppose you have.'

'I brought the magazine with me when I came, I hoped for a quiet read. When I unpacked I foolishly stuffed it under the mattress.'

'Don't tell me, Emmy found it.'

'Right first time. She left a note saying, "If this is what you want, see Mr Edwards", so when I had my chat with him during the first week, we talked about it. And when he offered to cane me, I agreed.'

Hazel was silent, trying to take it all in. She tried to match the story she had just heard with the allusions Richard had made during the interview, and then tried to tie the whole thing in with the persistent nagging thoughts she was having. And of course the strange feeling she was now experiencing.

'What was it like?'

'Painful! More painful than I thought it would be! At first I thought everyone was wrong, that the magazines had exaggerated, but they didn't. When the pain settled down, the glow was fantastic so I went back for some more this week.'

Hazel thought she had reached the point where nothing else would surprise her, but Susan's last comment definitely did. 'You went back for more?'

'Why not? I don't know when I'll get another chance, do I? So I thought I'd make the most of what I can get now. And it was even better the second time, because I knew what to expect.'

'Just as painful?'

'More so because he did it harder. I cried out a few times, but took all six. I had to really, didn't I? If you ask for something, you take it.'

Hazel shook her head in disbelief. 'Unbelievable.' She searched through her notes. 'OK, all secrets told are safe with me. Now about these notes –'

Back in her own room Hazel had a job shaking the images from her mind. The photographs in the magazine conjured up pictures of Susan bending over, over what she hadn't asked. His chair? His desk? What did one use for such an activity, and how did you go about talking about it? She thought back to the strapping she had had, tried to recall whether the pain had settled to any kind of glow, as Susan described it, and gave up. It was all too far back in the deep and distant past to recall such details. She could only remember the terrible humiliation of it all.

Would it be the same with a grown man like Richard Edwards who was undoubtedly one of the most fanciable people she'd met in a long time? Before sleep that night she decided to go and see Richard Edwards, headmaster in disguise, to find out for herself what this whole strange business was like. What did it matter if she hated every moment of it? No one need ever know, and at least she would go home with her curiosity satisfied.

Richard responded immediately to her request for an interview, and at three that afternoon with fluttering stomach and a slightly sick feeling that refused to go away, Hazel walked slowly along the corridor to his office. I've not decided to go ahead with it, she told herself, yet she knew deep inside that she would, which explained all the illness she felt.

Richard was friendliness itself, as he had been before, when she sat in the same chair and confessed to her silly worries about the school feeling that hung over her.

'Well now, Hazel, what is it this time? Another problem I can resolve for you?'

She shook her head, not sure where to begin. Then she recalled the word he had used during their earlier talk.

'I've been thinking about the charade you mentioned.'

'Oh yes. Are you interested?'

'Now this seems even sillier than before, but I've been thinking about it ever since you mentioned it, and then I was talking to Susan and looking at her magazine . . .' she trailed off and looked at him. He smiled knowingly.

'You're curious to know what it's really like, and before you go home you'd like to find out. Is that about it?'

'Yes, I think so.'

'It's Friday, you'll be leaving Sunday morning. You won't have to walk around with your secret for very long. It's a good idea to try everything, you know, while you have the opportunity and the privacy. No, more than that, the complete confidentiality of an extra-curricular activity!'

She smiled at his choice of words, and then stood, determined to go through with it. 'You're right, I would like to find out what it's like, and yes, I have left it until now, just as you guessed. I didn't think I was that transparent!'

'Not transparent, Hazel, not at all.' Richard opened his desk drawer and took out the slim cane. 'I just know ladies very well, that's all. Now if you're sure about this . . .'

'I'm sure.'

'Then if you'd like to lean over my desk?'

'Don't you want to me - to take my knickers down or anything?'

'No, I don't think so. You're not like the true afficionados of the most delightful forms of pain and pleasure known to man. You'll feel better with just a little protection.'

His understanding was complete. Hazel felt some of her nervousness slip away from her. She leaned over the desk as he asked, and felt suddenly cold as he turned back her dress and slip, leaving her covered in only the pale pink nylon panties.

'A very pretty sight indeed if I might say so,' Richard commented. 'I should be able to see what I'm doing through those.'

The cane whistled down and cracked across her cheeks and she cried out in shock. It hurt far more than she had anticipated, but she was determined to find out everything, and stayed where she was, hanging on to the edge of the desk. The second stroke landed, a mere whisper away from the first and she cried out again.

'You can tell me to stop any time you like.' Richard's voice was calm and steady as if this was the most natural thing on earth.

'No, do go on.'

The third whack brought her head up and she gave a sharp cry, but still she held on.

Richard laughed. 'You've got guts, that's for sure.'

There was such a note of admiration in his voice Hazel decided to take the other three, come what may. The thought had crept unbidden into her mind that she might call stop after the fourth stroke.

The next one somehow didn't feel quite so hard, and she was able to stay in place for the last two, although she was anxious to leap up and rub frantically as soon as he told her it was all over, in the same calm voice. He returned the cane to the drawer and looked at her.

'Well, what did you think of the experiment?'

She tried to sort out the conflicting emotions.

'Not as ghastly as I thought but more painful.'

He laughed and walked round the desk to her. 'Believe me when I say all the ladies tell me that in a very short while the glow is quite unbelievable. It should be the same for you. Do you think you'll ever be tempted to repeat the experiment?'

She shook her head, smiling as she let her skirt fall back into place. 'No thanks. Now I know what it's like I don't have to think about it. I don't think I'll be joining the enthusiasts.' She held out her hand and he took it. 'But I'm grateful to you for letting me find out, I really am.'

'I can assure you the pleasure was all mine.'

Richard walked over to the window and stared down the long drive. Shortly there would be an exodus of students, all waving goodbye and promising friendship and lasting memories. Some had more memories to take home than others, he thought, remembering the second time Susan had come to him, desperate for another session, recalling the joy of her delightful body, too. Carole might have a few faint lines left but she was heading for another expert who would soon replace them. And Hazel, her lovely bottom never to be seen again like that by anyone. What a waste, but at least he'd had the opportunity to cane it which was something worth remembering!

Soon another batch of students would arrive; more faces to learn, more problems to solve, and who knew what the next two weeks might hold?

19

Freezeframe

This is a true story, in that here is my history; my slow steps into SM, laid out for you, mixed with a few stories and a few fantasies, but mostly fact. It concludes this book because there is nothing much to say after all this.

'Stand up! Come here!'

I leave my chair to stand in front of the man who has ordered me to do so. His eyes bore into me, his voice demands to know why I have not carried out the order he gave me which was to think of a punishment to fit the crimes I had committed.

What crimes had I committed? Answering back, saying no, not making the appointment he had asked me to make. (Do these sound trivial? If so, put this book back where you found it – it is not for your eyes. If you understand, read on.)

My thoughts are travelling wildly, my excuses falter. They sound weak and pathetic in the light of the calm, quiet, authoritative questions I am asked. I know it and falter even more.

Orders are given. I obey instantly. To do anything else does not even cross my mind. It will only be later that I question my own motives. Why not say no? Why not refuse things which are deeply humiliating?

Because the man dominates, with his voice, his manner, his personality. Because a submissive has no choice but to stand, head down, pleading forgiveness, body shaking with apprehension and love.

Because in the scene there is no alternative.

Part of my penance is to write out the story of my initiation, and details of an earlier relationship. The rest of my penance is for me and my Master to know. Some things cannot be told even to the blank page.

Master, I have obeyed. I can but hope it pleases you.

Let me be honest with you. Let's face it, if I cannot be honest with my reader in the very first pages of my story, when can I be?

Let me set out the scene as I see it and where I stand in relation to it. Then you can follow the remainder of my story with a clear vision of the writer.

The sado-masochistic scene is a strange one. It is also badly named, conjuring up visions to outsiders which do not accurately reflect the scene. True disciples are not sadists or masochists. They are people who enter willingly into a relationship, which conventionally means one becomes dominant the other submissive. At times roles are reversed, giving as well as taking.

Look at it like this. There is a tuning fork on the table. There is a handle; where we stand sexually immature and waiting. Some are sexually aroused by the sense of power, by the giving of punishment to another by the fact of their domination of another. They walk the right-hand prong of the tuning fork.

Some are sexually awakened by responding to that powerful domination, by immediate response to all commands, by instant obedience, by taking punishment when the obedience is not as instant as it should have been. They walk the left-hand prong.

Some are sexually aroused by both aspects of this

strange scene. They are in the centre, the space between the prongs.

Those who are not aroused and awakened by any aspect of this scene stay right where they are, on the handle. They will never bother to read this story, nor attempt to follow the right- or left-hand paths. We can ignore them.

I walk the left-hand path.

The discovery was many years in the making. Are you interested?

Then press REWIND on the VCR remote control. Let us go flying back through the years . . . My years . . . To see how it all began.

STOP. PLAY.

Cue soft music, gentle piano, fingers drifting over the keys. Touch of violins, perhaps, to evoke a mood of nostalgia, of innocence and childhood: days when the sun shone endlessly and people were kind, when friends weren't cruel and dogs did not bite.

You know what I mean.

Zoom in, closer and closer. We are looking at a girl. She is fourteen, with soft brown hair worn in long ringlets, her eyes, hazel and dreamy, are indistinct behind glasses. She is not very tall, about five foot three inches, very slim and has long fingers and nails. She is not attractive, not the pretty calendar girl we expect from someone in a video, she is simply ordinary – and innocent.

A touch of menace in the music – no, not so much menace as a hint that there is an event looming; that slight increase in tempo that warns the viewer things are going to happen.

Our heroine turns the pages of the old western she is reading in the seclusion of her bedroom. A line leaps out, edged in flame, touched by insanity it reaches into secret places, sends a thrill through her that is unexpected,

211

unexplained, unimaginable in its excitement: *'Ma'am, I reckon you need a spanking.'*

She reads the line again: and then reads the remainder of the book as if it were about to self-destruct. But the heroine, the haughty self-centred daughter of the rancher, never does get the spanking.

Does that event warrant a change of tempo, a sense of happening? Yes, for it marks the beginning of her sexual awakening, even though this is a long time in the making, a long time happening. We mustn't rush. Things take time, after all, and adolescence is a long and painful journey we all have to travel, to look back on, grateful we have made it safely to maturity.

One more event and I promise you action to see you through until this story increases its sex quota or, if you prefer, the action for which you began to read in the first place. Or simpler still the M – (masturbation) Factor.

We move to a 'family' magazine, full of stories, funny items, puzzles, crosswords – and find a story about a man baby-sitting a precocious young girl. The detail of the relationship eludes me, is he neighbour, uncle, family friend? Whatever, she sets out to seduce him by trying a cigarette and looking closely into his eyes; but she winds up over his knees being spanked with his slipper.

While the detail escapes, the illustration doesn't, nor does the feeling, reading the story, roused in this immature but rapidly-changing female. Such a story today would not appear in a family magazine, could be found only in a specialist magazine. Such are the changing times in which we live.

From here on out, the girl we are looking at indulges nightly in a strange fantasy in which she is the wife of a film star who is kidnapped and treated abominably by her captors.

We have to FAST FORWARD some years, as I do not

think you will be interested in the details of a fantasy. I am sure you would prefer facts.

In the scene everyone needs to think – to know – people exist who walk the left-hand fork, people who can and do take beatings from those who walk the right-hand fork. (And someone complained of my use of the word 'beatings' but they are, aren't they? However you muffle it up it's a beating. If it isn't, you're in the wrong game, my friend.)

Put the music on HOLD, send the pianist out for a drink, come with me into a different time, a different place.

Press EJECT and take the cassette out of the machine. Choose one of the others stacked by the side, yes the black one without labels.

It is time for some M-Factor to enter this tale.

My Master is displeased with me. I have been arguing with him, by post, over the tights versus stockings issue, preferring tights every time. He has had enough, has decided that I am far too 'bolshie' for a slave, and has ordered me into his presence, telling me to wear a black lace suspender-belt and black, seamed stockings beneath a straight black dress, and finally, high-heeled shoes.

In his presence I quake a little in those high heels; for my list of misdemeanours is lengthy. How easy to argue by letter, and discount the possibility of all sins being one day expiated on my bottom! The lecture is endless, I squirm and wriggle and am ordered to be still.

My Master produces a short chain with which he secures my wrists. My Master has always said that slaves look good in chains, while rendering them helpless. They add to my feelings of submission. Chained, I am totally at his command. I know that punishment is close. I feel it.

Sentence is pronounced, a stinging hand spanking, followed by ten strokes of the tawse which I have brought with me as ordered. Finally six hard strokes with a malacca cane, the last two portions of the punishment to be given while I am secured over a stool unable to escape a single stroke.

My Master sits on the high-backed chair and waits. There is no need for command, I know what I have to do. I walk over to him and lay down over his knees, feeling foolish as always, and clumsy with my chains. It pleases my Master to disrobe me himself, provided I have obeyed his orders (heaven help me if I haven't!), and he raises my skirt and tucks it out of the way, lowers my knickers and pushes them down to my knees; nothing is allowed to get in the way.

My Master has a hard hand, it is applied vigorously to my bum, hard from the very first slap, no gentle warm-up this, but punishment! Chains stop me getting my hands in the way, my legs kick of their own volition, trying to avoid the hard hand. His arm loops around my waist, I am held firmly, I am spanked hard. I struggle and plead for mercy but none is to be found. It is then I wish I had obeyed!

Only when he is satisfied that I am well and truly spanked can I go and stand, sniffling and fighting tears, in the corner.

Ten minutes' respite; it isn't long enough for the burning to disappear, it isn't long enough before I am ordered back, to have my wrists unchained so as to allow me to bend over the stool and be rechained with the addition of a large strap round my waist. There is, and will be, no escape.

The stool is tall, padded thickly for comfort (of a kind) and with chains for my ankles and wrists. The large belt goes round my waist to ensure I cannot even slide sideways off the stool and escape a single part of the punishment. It will be a two or five fingered tawse, it matters not which one. Ten strokes of the tawse, delivered soundly, with pauses between each one, his ears deaf to my pleas and cries. They are all the same, thick lengths of leather cut to the required length, with a firm hand hold; split tails to individually fly apart and land fractionally apart, doubling or tripling the experience. My Master refuses to keep a tawse in the house, I always have to bring my one with me, folded in my bag, afraid I will accidentally pull it out in a shop somewhere before I get here, afraid someone will see and recognise it – would they? – and then I hand it to him to use on me. Oh cruel Master!

Bands of pain shriek at me but I have to stay there. I have to take them, every one. Another ten minutes' respite, standing in the corner holding the cane in trembling fingers, reflecting on the sins which brought me here, vowing aloud never to do it again to obey my Master in all things and in all ways.

It isn't enough to deflect him from the final stage, the caning.

My ten minutes are up, with tear-streaked face I return to the stool and prostrate myself over it. Chained in position again, I await, with fear and apprehension of the stomach-sinking kind, the kiss of the cane. Before that I have to kiss it, the instrument of so much pain.

The stool is still warm from the last time I laid over it. The chains feel comfortable now, I am used to them. They secure me and I give up all responsibility for what will happen. It is a giving up of all will, I am in the hands of someone else. I am still crying a little, tears run down my nose and drip onto the carpet. I don't know what my cheeks look like, but it pleases my Master; I see a gleam in his eye as he looks. He walks around me with the cane, tapping my back, my arms, my calves, stinging, touching, tormenting, for I know it will hurt.

And it does. It begins with a single cut to the centre of my cheeks, across the fullest part where the spanking seems to have hurt most, then creeps upwards and then down; he never crosses over anywhere, he never places one anywhere but where he intends it to be. I think they

215

overlap but I know that when I check the mirror later I will find they don't.

Six cuts of the cane, six screams from me, six screams for mercy which are ignored until the last one.

And then I am unchained, the door is opened, my Master's love slave comes in. She brings cold cream and tender fingers; she brings silky jelly and relief to an aching clit and longing pussy.

It almost makes the punishment worthwhile.

REWIND. EJECT.

Replace original cassette in the machine, recall the pianist from the bar, and resume story.

PLAY! Cue music.

The scene – London: the time, '60s, swinging, love, drugs, freedom, money, adventure.

The fantasy is wearing thin. There are times when it no longer works. There are just so many variations on a theme when it is a mind game.

Since we last looked at this video, our heroine has been through a traumatic marriage and divorce – the whole episode lasting just three years – and she has tried, without success, to coax different boyfriends into spanking her by saying: 'I had a dream last night, I dreamed you spanked me', and waiting for their response. Nil response.

One boyfriend irritated her to screaming point by saying, without prompting, 'I think you need a spanking to knock some sense into you but I think you'd like it so I won't.' The relationship collapsed shortly after that.

Increase music tempo just a little – a hint of something. Pan camera along Fleet Street to The Strand. See crowds of people, mini-skirts and 60s hairdos, men in long jackets. Close in on a stall selling newspapers and magazines. In the top right hand corner is a magazine with the lovely, basic, evocative title: SPANKING. It is a whole pound. Before you laugh, remember our heroine is earning only around £10 a week right now. But the cover, a lady kneeling on a chair, bottom bare and waiting, overcomes the twin reservations of spending a whole pound on a magazine and asking a man for it. Close camera in on the knowing, lustful look he gives her as he hands over the magazine without a word passing between them.

It isn't easy being a female and wanting to buy a spanking magazine. It isn't easy at all. Even men who aren't interested in the scene are capable of looking with lust at someone who obviously is.

Today, in the 90s, it is all right to walk into a Private Shop and spend £10 or more on a CP magazine; it is all right to come out with a brown paper bag covering your purchase. It is hard to remember in detail the feeling at that time, buying a magazine with such an erotic title and cover from a newspaper stand in Fleet Street, with half of London walking by.

Yet the memory remains, after all these years; the memory of buying the magazine, the man's look, the one pound note that brought erotic dreams that night.

There weren't many magazines. Memories recalled of reading the headlines in someone's newspaper on the tube; a spanking case brought to court. Buying the paper on leaving the underground, savouring it over lunch – what a lunch! – being grateful my parents had the *News of the World* delivered on a Sunday and only now asking why, and what they got from reading such salacious stuff.

We have moved on. Our heroine is older, wiser and about to become involved in a relationship that will change her life.

Before then, we need a little more of the M-Factor.

Press STOP, remove video, replace with another of the black unlabelled videos.

PLAY.

* * *

217

There are times when my rebellious nature seems to take over and determine that I will end up in trouble, whether it is my intention to do so or not.

My Master asked me in a letter for my neck size so he could acquire the appropriate collar.

I didn't send it.

He asked again, adding that I would be punished for inattention.

I sent it, but asked in a subsequent letter if he had the collar for me.

'Did I ask you to return the subject?' came the swift response. And new orders are given to punish me for my insolence.

I stand before my Master, my skirt pegged firmly to my collar, knickers lowered to my knees, hands chained before me. My Master walks around me, lecturing me non-stop on the stupidity of slaves who forget to do something and then argue about it later. Each walk around me is accompanied by a sharp, stinging stroke of the cane – not hard, but surely marking me – and preparing me for the punishment to come.

I am shaking inside, wet, biting my lips to stop myself crying out, for a protest will result in a further dozen added to the sentence, it is every time. And, having experienced being chained to the stool and punished, thinking the punishment is over only to have my Master say, 'there's the small matter of –' and receiving a further dozen, I dare not protest now.

It is a sunny day. Hobbled by chains, I am led into the garden, blindfolded and secured to a large tree, my arms firmly fastened around the trunk, the rough bark pressing against my stomach and thighs. No words are spoken. I have no way of knowing where my Master is, what he is thinking, what is he doing. There is virtually no human sound, only the birds and insects and the occasional plane flying overhead. Would that the pilot could look down and see me, bottom bare, helpless, waiting. For what? And why should I want someone to see me?

Because what is on display is fit for viewing; large, round, shapely (I quote my Master not my mirror) and it is a pleasure, if not a real thrill, to be on display.

Time goes by, time eternal, time which seems as if it will never end; this waiting, this apprehension – it ends suddenly – with a switch across the cheeks, hard, cutting. I cry out and am rewarded with three sharp strokes in succession, each hurting more than the one before. Pause, a respite, then twelve sharp strokes, bringing tears.

'Useless slave! Argumentative slave! You will not argue with me again!'

The switch changes to something larger, heavier, wider. The paddle? The three-fingered tawse? After the switching it is hard to tell. All that is certain is that the pain leaps through me with every stroke. I am longing to be free; the rough bark scratches and chafes, the wetness trickles. It is over and I am allowed my freedom, only to be swung over a knee and spanked over the top of the weals already there.

Then I am ordered to kneel on hard flagstones and beg for forgiveness.

Which I do.

REWIND. EJECT.

It is time the pianist earned some of the money we are going to pay him (aren't we?) for providing the tinkling background music to lull the senses, increase the sensations, touch the parts my words might not reach.

On the other hand, if I am not reaching you, you're not reading it, so why am I paying this pianist?

I always was a soft touch when it comes to a good little piano man. And you can take that any way you wish.

Replace original cassette, yes, the one labelled 'Life

Story of Josephine Scott'. I think it's becoming familiar by now, isn't it?

PLAY.

Working in a solicitor's office gives you the opportunity to meet all manner of people – including private investigators. The one our heroine is to meet is a short, dark, stocky man with an engaging smile and a winning way. She confesses to wishing to learn the basics of photography, he invites her to his office and a darkroom to learn.

She goes.

Here, with bows sweeping across strings, bringing heart-rending beautiful music to the background, our heroine stands in the cluttered, untidy darkroom, adjusting her eyes to the infra-red light, taking in nothing of what he is saying, knowing only she has been overwhelmed with a desire to have this man. It must be telepathy, he stops his talk of developers and paper to say: 'I could sleep with you. Could you sleep with me?' And she hears herself say 'yes' to the accompaniment of crashing cymbals and a roll on the drums.

But he is married, dear viewer, he is married.

'Don't let that stop you,' he says, smiling the smile that gets deep into her.

And then, when his wife is out visiting, they are on the settee, he is half-naked, she is totally naked; eight stone two pounds of not very much; frigid, scared, in love.

Frigid, it hurts, the penetration hurts, she cries out in genuine fear and pain. He stops, rests on her, looks deep into her hazel-flecked eyes and says, 'There's a big stick coming it's coming now, it's going to hurt, it's coming!'

And with a rush and surge of feeling such as she has never known, ever, she does come.

'How did you know?' she asked in a tiny whispery voice afterward, sitting together, holding hands, exploring new feelings.

'I didn't, but I guessed.'

And a whole new world opens up . . .

EJECT.

Put to one side, replace with another cassette. More M-Factor on the way.

Ready? PLAY.

Wearing a silky black knee-length dress, buttoned to the neck, with long sleeves over which I am wearing a white apron to symbolise my maid/slave status, I stand before my Master. I wear a lacy white slip and black seamed-stockings which are tautly suspendered to a corselette. A chain falls from my neck to the chain linking my ankles, and my wrists are chained behind my back.

This is the moment to dread.

This is the moment when my Master spends time relating my sins, my crimes, and a lengthy list they make too! Why do I do it? Naturally rebellious, naturally wishing to argue at every given moment. I suppose I will never learn.

(Do I *want* to?)

My Master doesn't really think a punishment has taken place unless it starts with a prolonged and stinging hand spanking. The chains are unlocked, I am put across his knee and I wait.

The spanking begins. Oh how I long to be able to remain still, not to twist and writhe, not to try and kick, but the chains prevent me. And not to put my hand in the way. Fatal mistake!

Nothing is said, but my hand is put firmly to one side. I know I will suffer for that later!

I am allowed a rest, allowed a moment to sniffle and plead, ignored as always, and then I am prepared over the padded stool which I love and hate at the same time – love when I remember the session when I am home and safe – hate while I have to lie across it and take what is given to me. The paddle is applied steadily and firmly, reddening further the already red and burning cheeks. I am then allowed a further rest but not for long, for the cane (he says) has to be applied when the bottom is red and sore for maximum impact. Pain over pain. I have been asked which hurts most, spanking over a caning or caning over a spanking? There's nothing to choose!

Do *you* have a favourite instrument?

What am I doing? This is *my* story. Your favourites are for your mind and your slave.

When I think back on it I love the cane, long for the sting, the cutting sharp edge of pain, the weals, the bruises. At the time I am in agony longing for it to be over. Afterwards it lives in my memory and I am driven to insolence and cheek; driven to disobedience and misbehaviour just so I can feel its sting all over again.

I wish I hadn't put my hand in the way.

Have you got the original cassette in the machine again?

Then let's press PLAY and carry on from where we left off.

Oh, just a moment. Does anyone know where the pianist went? Come on, piano man, I need a tinkling piano around here for this bit. I am about to confess a serious mistake.

We went to the cinema, my friend, her husband and me. We went to see *The Taming of the Shrew*. When we got home my friend said, 'What did you think of it?'

I said, without thinking, 'I thought she should have been spanked.'

'She was, in the original story,' said my friend with the strangest of looks. 'Is that what you'd like?'

Too late for lies, for cover-ups, for any kind of deceit. I said yes. And I asked where I could buy something. No, I asked what I could buy for games.

We had been to Spain, my lover and I, we went there

to take someone who was going there to live for a while. We had a car loaded down with baggage all the way there, but on the way back there was room for another kind of luggage - green bamboo.

I can assure all you SM people that unless you've been thrashed with green bamboo you don't know what it's all about. It is flexible in a way only something recently living can be; it beats a malacca or rattan cane every time and cuts like nothing else. But it dried out and became useless, he said. Not enough sting, not enough punishment. And a garden cane isn't flexible.

So, I asked.

'A riding crop,' my friend answered. 'Safe to buy and to carry about if you have to.'

Another confession coming up here. I hate horses. I hate the largeness of their teeth, their great hooves, their legs.

The fact is, I know nothing about them or their harness and their other accessories.

I bought a riding crop in a local shop. I bought what I thought was a riding crop. And for a horse no doubt it is. What I got was not what I now see on CP videos; a leather thing with a small square of leather on the end, an item that punishes without cutting. What I got was a length of fibreglass bound with nylon and with a tiny loop on the end which he cut off. What I got was a vicious weapon indeed.

My friend had visitors when I went back, carrying this long, thin thing wrapped in brown paper. She asked me later how I felt, walking in with my riding whip, hoping no one would notice. I said I felt stupid. I also felt very excited, but I never told her that.

It was time to move out, to leave my friend, to depart for a new life. I had intruded on their home and hospitality long enough. I went to share a flat with someone I met at work, a startling blonde with dazzling looks and an ice

223

cold heart (see 'Fire and Ice'). Newly divorced, she preferred to keep men at arm's length. Me, I'd welcome anyone in.

My lover and I tried the crop a few times, a few light smacks, not dangerous. We didn't try it seriously until I offended him one day and he ordered me to bend over the back of the kitchen chair, then he whacked me three times with it, causing pain so deep I could hardly breathe. And bruises which outshone any others I'd had. It was truly vicious.

And he said, 'I have a plan' – which I'll tell you about later.

Before the thing I have to tell you we went through strange and terrible times. He seemed to go off me at intervals, we almost broke up but he would come back as if nothing had happened.

One night he sat calmly and quietly in our lounge and destroyed me completely. He told me I had no looks, no personality, no dress-sense, no ambition, I wasn't clean enough or sexy enough or anything that suited him. I was completely and utterly shattered. After he did it, he walked out and left me there. Alone.

This hurts – this telling hurts. But I have to, because 'Freezeframe' is to be an *honest* account of my time with him. I am using you as a psychiatrist's chair, I am unburdening myself of things which have troubled me for so long. Perhaps putting it down I can rid myself of the guilt, the recriminations, the self-hate I have nurtured over it all. What I do know is that this story could not be told anywhere else but in England. Only an English reader will understand. This is particularly English, much of what I have written here only you will understand.

The story continues. It gets worse.

Three long, lonely weeks later he came around as if nothing had happened and demanded I go with him to my friend's house. He told me he had been having an affair with her as well as me, that he wanted to corner her with it in front of her husband, and that I had to be there to back him up. He said if I didn't, he'd never speak to me again.

In all the circumstances I wish I hadn't agreed. God, how I wish I hadn't agreed! It would have been worth the pain of his leaving me not to live with the pain that came later!

Hindsight is a valuable asset, isn't it?

I was to confirm that he had told me earlier (which he hadn't) that my friend had a long stretch mark into which you could put a finger. The fact he knew that told me that he had slept with her.

We duly arrived, we duly argued, and I confirmed his story.

I heard my friend say, 'After we gave her a home too.'

That, more than anything, broke me for weeks.

You are the first people to know this. It's a betrayal I have kept close to my heart for years. For 23 years. I've regretted it time out of mind. I've wished I could turn back the clock and that I had refused him.

But love, that blind, all-encompassing, obsessive love which drives out all reason before it, does not allow you to think straight. And I loved him with that kind of an obsessive love that doesn't allow any thinking at all.

And he knew it. But an added factor was that I was working for him, part-time, serving papers, tracing people when I could, making visits to take statements from witnesses. In short, earning money which was much needed. A secretary didn't really earn enough to support a car, half an expensive flat with a spendthrift flatmate, and have something left over to live on.

But that isn't a good enough reason and I know it.

And I'm so sorry.

* * *

Remove that oh so heavy cassette with its oh so heavy burden of misery and guilt, let's have some M-Factor to lighten the proceedings. In the next section I'll tell you about the magazines I had, the caning I got, and finally, no, I'll save that one for later. I think.

An M-Factor to lighten the mood.

The pianist gave up after that last lot, he went out for some heavy drinking. All too much for him.

This time we'll have some light pop music, I think, just by way of change. You don't like pop music? Just whose story is this, anyway? Pop music this time. I said so. We might get around to the music I really love later.

My Master isn't happy with the last slave letter I sent him, it didn't fulfil all his requirements, there were no details of my imagined fantasy. My Master says, 'could do better', and to impress the lesson he has brought along a hairbrush to add to my misery.

My Master stands no nonsense. I go across his lap as always, dressed, letting him have the pleasure of revealing what is beneath the clothes. A large, well-rounded bottom, charming enough for any discerning Master, I believe. Or so I have been told. I am modest, after all.

A spanking follows, and my Master as always surprises me. His hands look soft, they look as if they would not hurt but when applied to a bare bottom, they do hurt! I am wriggling and squirming and pleading but to no avail. And then, horror of horrors, a hairbrush comes smacking down on tenderised flesh! Screams of dismay follow but the hairbrush comes down again and again and again. Hard wood on soft flesh.

Pleasing for a master – hell for a slave.

I am allowed ten minutes in the corner, hands on my head, before the cane is administered. Six stinging cuts.

I will do better next time. My Master says so.

* * *

The pianist got well and truly drunk last time (do you blame him?) so I got in a blues band instead. Not much. A four-piece: guitar, bass, drums, a vocalist who is also capable of handling a superb tin sandwich (or gob-iron or simply harmonica to the uninitiated). Since the untimely death of Stevie Ray Vaughan, I've been searching for a blues sound that is cool enough to chill the heart, the soul, and bring tears tumbling as I –

I'll settle for the band I have here for now. I have forgiven the piano man, by the way, he'll be back next time. I still need his gentle touch.

You've got the original guilt-laden cassette in the machine?

Press PLAY. Let's take the story forward.

I moved out of the flat.

My flatmate was, in all probability still is, a raving beauty. Blonde, elegant, chic to the point of perfection. But cold, ice cold. Her husband divorced her because he said it felt like rape every time, she was so unresponsive, so cold, so hard. She was obsessed with money, spent it as if it was going out of fashion; lied, stole and cheated to get it. I'm telling you this in the strictest confidence, but knowing with certainty that she won't read it anyway, she isn't into this scene. By the way, everything in the main story cassette is absolutely one hundred and ten percent true. I think you'd realised that, anyway, no one could invent what I'm writing here. And I feel much better for telling you.

Some of this is being told for the first time ever. Some has been mentioned in correspondence with people I trust and care for, but the whole story from beginning to end has never been told before.

Where was I? Proof? You want proof? Letters daily with shop names on the back, callers, a convenient bonfire of something that looked remarkably like files – and people who work in solicitor's offices DO NOT burn files.

I moved out of luxury – my own room, a nice lounge, tiniest bathroom ever invented but it was clean – into a tiny caravan. Lounge with bed that came down from the wall (damp), coal fire (not very efficient), tiny kitchen (cold), bedroom (cold), outside loo.

I owed some money to the tax-man for the earnings I'd made with the investigation business. I owed money for the car. My lover took my finances in hand, divided up my resources, paid the rent, took fifteen shillings (75p) a week for his wife to cook me a meal every day, left me twelve shillings and sixpence (62p) to live on.

And then he took my car keys from me one day and refused to let me leave his house until I'd showered.

It wasn't easy living in that place. The Calor gas ran out in the middle of meals, I had to carry bags of coal to the caravan myself, the car got snowed in once and the owner of the park had to pull me out with a tractor, I was commuting to London from Essex, and life was, overall, tough.

I had a job which lasted six weeks, the woman was a newly made-up partner, had bugger-all to do, and I got bored out of my skull. A new secretary started, spent the entire morning typing out the standard form for the letters as this firm wanted them done, then walked out at lunchtime and never came back. I walked out after six weeks and never went back. I had my skills as legal secretary to market, and I marketed them. I found a job setting up a practice for two young solicitors, right there in Temple, in Chambers!

Slowly the debts got paid off, I was clear of everything and had some money for myself.

And I bought CP magazines. American ones, with delightful photographs and outrageous stories.

And my lover used to visit. He would look at the magazines too, sometimes if he was in a good mood I'd be caned with a bamboo garden cane. I remember once he caned me twelve times and wondered why I'd not cried out, flinched, moved or anything. I confessed the thick pleated skirt I wore absorbed it all; he removed the skirt, caned me three times really hard and left me crying.

More often than not he would get up and walk out, saying he didn't feel well enough to cope with making love to me.

'Sorry, I know how worked up you get over the magazines.' Then he would leave me frustrated, angry and tormented.

Sadism at its most unpleasant.

At this time I was experiencing hardly any CP at all. The longing was unbelievable! Contact magazines gave me fantasies and ideas, but he wouldn't allow me to answer any ads, so I never did. Life was cold, hard and still very unpleasant.

That's why I wanted the blues band in. It's the only music that fits that time. I was working with two young men who were great fun but married, I went home to an empty, lonely caravan, where I would type my letters and get on with the fund raising (we were both involved in Leukaemia Research and raised a lot of money).

And then, out of the blue, he raised the idea of the game. Again. The crop was not used, it was gathering dust somewhere in my caravan, he wanted to use it.

And that's for later too.

In the meantime, have some more M-Factor.

Have you decided yet whether the M-Factors were true or not?

PLAY.

An orchestra, sweeping strings, with just the hint of the piano overlaid or underlaid depending on your point of view.

Autumn. Autumn verging on winter, a sharp chill in the air, trees dripping dead leaves and moisture. Underneath a thick carpet of dampness, moss, leaves, grasses turned brown by frost and rain. My Master is muffled in a thick, warm coat, I have on a light, summer dress and raincoat, all I have been allowed. Underneath that, just as the leaves and mosses are beneath our feet, I am wearing a black bra, black suspender belt and black stockings, seamed of course. Heels are inappropriate, but he has insisted.

He finds a large tree stump and sits down. I have no need for orders, I know what I must do: remove my raincoat and dress and stand before him in bra and suspender belt. They are brief, so brief they will get in the way of nothing.

Shivering, both with cold and apprehension. For in his pocket is a martinet, the thongs long and eager. Also in his pocket is a plastic ruler. I have just paid for that, walked into a shop, approached a young man, asked for a ruler and then asked – as ordered – whether it will stand up to a spanking. He grinned, looking embarrassed, looked away, then back at me again. Then he said 'yes', so I bought it and pray it will.

I also pray my Master saw the man because I will be in double trouble if he doesn't believe I carried out his orders.

He stands up, slowly, carefully, removing the martinet from his pocket and swinging the thongs.

'Hands on head.'

I obey and wait, cold, goosepimply, scared of passers-by (would there be any on such a grim day? You can never tell, there's no accounting for ramblers). As he walks around and around me, using the martinet, the thongs are everywhere. He uses it rapidly, I am being systematically whipped from neck to knees, front and back, my breasts sting, my back hurts, the thongs bite and bite over and over; the warmth builds.

He stops, sits down on the stump, gestures to me.

'Over.'

And I walk carefully over, afraid of my heels, afraid of what is to come, the lines hurting, the cold biting as much as the thongs. He pulls the slipper from his pocket, the one I was ordered to bring with me, and spanks, hard. I can yell, there is no one around, and yell I do, as the slipper finds me again and again, over the lines, over the coldness.

'Now we'll see.' And he pulls out the ruler. Don't let it break! I'll be double punished if it doesn't stand up to the spanking! Hard, cold, it does the job I bought it for.

And finally it is time to bend over the stump; the wood slimy, cold and hard, the edge cutting into my stomach, my breasts crushed against the coldness, legs outstretched, hands gripping roots to hold on, not to move, while he slowly and deliberately canes me, twelve times. Over the redness, over the whipping, over the slipper and ruler spanking, twelve times.

A lady wrote to a CP magazine and said caning a woman six times was enough – if properly laid on. I wish someone would tell my Master that.

I wish sometimes I could tell whether the dampness I feel is the day – or me.

Insert cassette, press PLAY and sit back.

This is the part you've been waiting for if you've followed the hints I've dropped as we've gone through 'Freezeframe'. Well, all is about to be revealed. I hope it's been worth waiting for.

I repeat, we planned a game.

Remember I told you the riding crop was fibreglass bound in nylon and a particularly vicious thing.

OK. The accumulator game, as he named it, was this.

Fully dressed, I was to bend over the back of a chair and take six with the crop. If at any time I got up during that six, I was to remove a layer of clothing and take another six, plus whatever amount was left from the first. And if I moved again, another layer would be removed, another six would be inflicted, plus the accumulated totals of the first two and ever onward.

For three weeks we planned and talked; for three weeks I lived in an agony and ecstasy of anticipation and desire, of apprehension and downright fear, for I remembered (just) what the crop could inflict.

But it is a well known fact that women cannot remember pain. We go back for more each time because we can't remember, when it's over, what it was like. I didn't remember it clearly enough to say no to the game.

Summer time. A hot summer – and that isn't just in my memory – the day we played the game. The house was empty and stinking hot. I went, wearing minimum clothing because to wear anything else, tweeds or thermal knickers, would have aroused suspicion. And he wouldn't have accepted it anyway, for with those layers of clothing on I would have been able to take all six. So I went wearing a summer dress, slip and panties and not much else.

Where's the piano man? I need him now, I need him to tinkle his fingers gently over the keys as we sit and talk and I see the crop lying casually on the hearth-rug.

Thank you, that's just what I need.

'Right.' And my heart and stomach flip over in tune with another. Synchronicity going on here.

Remove glasses. Put them carefully to one side. Move to the back of the chair and lean over, gripping the arms with fingers that are knuckle white.

'Start. One.' And the crop comes down with shocking speed and impact.

'Two.' And it is all I can do to hold on.

'Three.' And I'm backing away holding my bottom in both hands, tears beginning. God, it hurts!

'You agreed. Dress off.' And I take it off and fold it and put it to one side and I lay over the settee arm and take another four (I'll never know how) and jump up. He is immovable.

232

'Slip off.' And I do it, flooding the settee with tears. There are another five still due and I cannot take them.

I run for the door, run upstairs, throw myself in the bedroom. He pursues me holds me over the bed and beats me until I am screaming. Only the noise I am making stops him.

Later, I creep downstairs to recover my clothing, to find him sitting with a beer and a satisfied smile.

'I calculate you had nineteen in all.' It's hard to walk properly, the pain is intense, I am in agony.

'Go home.'

Going home means driving, it means sitting, moving my feet and legs, but I do it somehow. I dare not look in the mirror. I crawl into my bed and cry.

The next morning I am yellow and black and sore. And sexy.

I drive back to his house and find him alone.

'I want you.'

'You're addicted to pain.'

'I want to play the game again but with the cane this time.'

He breaks the crop to pieces in front of me. 'It isn't healthy, I shan't beat you ever again.'

He isn't listening, never has listened. The beating has left me frustrated and unhappy, I need satisfying, which never happens.

There are those who object to the word 'beating' preferring any other word instead. That was a beating. It was a whipping with a cruel implement designed – as my friend put it – to hurt a horse who has a thicker hide than I have. I marked easily then, I still do. A five-minute spanking leaves me with bruises which last a week. It was a beating.

But I would have given anything to have repeated the game. Only finished off with sex, as every game should be. If not immediately then the next day, when the pain has settled and all you have left is the vivid and overwhelming erotic feelings which were there, underneath the pain. If they weren't underneath the pain you had no right being there in the first place.

This is why I object to models starring in CP videos, models who are there for the money, not for the lovely erotic feelings the spanking or whatever will give them. They go home with bruises and cash, vowing, probably, never to do it again. We – submissive women – would go home with bruises, cash and a happy smile. There's a difference.

But what difference did my protests make at that time? None. He never touched me again, nor did he ever make love to me again.

But when I left him for someone else, as was inevitable he spent an hour – a whole, long, drawn-out, tortuous sixty minutes, on the phone to me at work, begging, pleading with me to go back to him; telling me he would give up his wife and the other women for me and me alone. And he would commit suicide if I didn't. I held out, and he never took the pills.

Instead he left a note under my windscreen wiper telling me secret, dark and evil things about the man I had found – he had gone straight out and investigated him. What he didn't know was that my new man was borrowing my car that night, he found the note and destroyed it.

When we booked a wedding date he said he would give it a year. If it lasted that long he would buy us the biggest wedding present we ever had.

Piano man, I thank you for your busy, merry fingers during the long drawn-out session we've had here. I'm sorry about the guilt and the blues band. Oh, and the orchestra too, but you did get drunk, after all, and I needed someone.

But thanks anyway – the cheque will be in the post.

Here's where the words go rolling up the screen to the trailing sound of strings.

Josephine Scott has been married to her "new" man for over twenty years. They have a teenager, she has a satisfying career and a lifelong companion. She only saw her ex-lover once, when he called one night after the baby was born, three years after the wedding. He didn't bring a wedding present, and she has never seen or heard of him since.

Afterglow

If you've read this far through my book, well, thank you! But you may be wondering where the 'Fantasies of Josephine Scott' bit comes in, as most of the stories appear designed to please all the dominants among you.

The fantasy comes in my remembering the things which really happened or wishing some of the things could happen; life, partners and family permitting. The fun has been in the copying out of the stories, wet knickers all over the place here . . .

Now, I'll go write some more books for you.

Josephine Scott

NEW BOOKS

Coming up from Nexus and Black Lace

Fallen Angels by Kendal Grahame
July 1994   Price: £4.99   ISBN: 0 352 32934 3
A mysterious stranger sets two young ladies the ultimate lascivious challenge: to engage in as many sexual acts with as many people as possible. Rich rewards await them if they succeed – but the task proves to be its own reward!

The Teaching of Faith by Elizabeth Bruce
July 1994   Price: £4.99   ISBN: 0 352 32936 X
Until she met Alex, Faith had never experienced the full range of pleasures that sex can bring. But after her initiation into his exclusive set of libertines, a whole new realm of prurient possibilities is opened up for her.

The Training Grounds by Sarah Veitch
August 1994   Price: £4.99   ISBN: 0 352 32940 8
Charlotte was expecting to spend her time on the island relaxing and enjoying the sun. But now, having been handed over to the Master, she has discovered the island to be a vast correction centre. She'll soon have a healthy glow anyway . . .

Memoirs of a Cornish Governess by Yolanda Celbridge
August 1994   Price: £4.99   ISBN: 0 352 32941 6
As Governess to a Lord and Lady, Miss Constance's chief task is to educate their son Freddie. But word soon gets about of her unusual techniques, and before long, most of the village is popping in for some good old-fashioned correction.

The Gift of Shame by Sarah Hope-Walker
July 1994   Price: £4.99   ISBN: 0 352 32935 1
Helen had always thought that her fantasies would remain just
that – wild and deviant whimsies with no place in everyday
life. But Jeffrey soon changes that, helping her overcome her
reservations to enjoy their decadent games to the full.

Summer of Enlightenment by Cheryl Mildenhall
July 1994   Price: £4.99   ISBN: 0 352 32937 8
Karin's love life takes a turn for the better when she is introduced to the charming Nicolai. She is drawn to him in spite of
his womanising – and the fact that he is married to her friend.
As their flirting escalates, further temptations place themselves
in her path.

Juliet Rising by Cleo Cordell
August 1994   Price: £4.99   ISBN: 0 352 32938 6
At Madame Nicol's strict academy for young ladies, 18th-
century values are by turns enforced with severity and
flagrantly scorned. Juliet joins in her lessons enthusiastically;
but whether she has learnt them well enough to resist the
charms of the devious Reynard is another question.

A Bouquet of Black Orchids by Roxanne Carr
August 1994   Price: £4.99   ISBN: 0 352 32939 4
The luxurious Black Orchid Club once more provides the
setting for a modern tale of decadence. Maggie's lustful adven-
tures at the exclusive health spa take an intriguing turn when
a charismatic man makes her a tempting offer.

NEXUS BACKLIST

Where a month is marked on the right, this book will not be
published until that month in 1994. All books are priced £4.99
unless another price is given.

CONTEMPORARY EROTICA

CONTOURS OF DARKNESS	Marco Vassi		
THE DEVIL'S ADVOCATE	Anonymous		
THE DOMINO TATTOO	Cyrian Amberlake	£4.50	
THE DOMINO ENIGMA	Cyrian Amberlake		
THE DOMINO QUEEN	Cyrian Amberlake		
ELAINE	Stephen Ferris		
EMMA'S SECRET WORLD	Hilary James		
EMMA ENSLAVED	Hilary James		
FALLEN ANGELS	Kendal Grahame		
THE FANTASIES OF JOSEPHINE SCOTT	Josephine Scott		
THE GENTLE DEGENERATES	Marco Vassi		
HEART OF DESIRE	Maria del Rey		
HELEN – A MODERN ODALISQUE	Larry Stern		
HIS MISTRESS'S VOICE	G. C. Scott		Nov
THE HOUSE OF MALDONA	Yolanda Celbridge		Dec
THE INSTITUTE	Maria del Rey		
SISTERHOOD OF THE INSTITUTE	Maria del Rey		Sep
JENNIFER'S INSTRUCTION	Cyrian Amberlake		
MELINDA AND THE MASTER	Susanna Hughes		
MELINDA AND ESMERALDA	Susanna Hughes		
MELINDA AND THE COUNTESS	Susanna Hughes		Dec
MIND BLOWER	Marco Vassi		

MS DEEDES AT HOME	Carole Andrews	£4.50	
MS DEEDES ON PARADISE ISLAND	Carole Andrews		
THE NEW STORY OF O	Anonymous		
OBSESSION	Maria del Rey		
ONE WEEK IN THE PRIVATE HOUSE	Esme Ombreux		
THE PALACE OF FANTASIES	Delver Maddingley		
THE PALACE OF HONEYMOONS	Delver Maddingley		
THE PALACE OF EROS	Delver Maddingley		
PARADISE BAY	Maria del Rey		
THE PASSIVE VOICE	G. C. Scott		
THE SALINE SOLUTION	Marco Vassi		
STEPHANIE	Susanna Hughes		
STEPHANIE'S CASTLE	Susanna Hughes		
STEPHANIE'S REVENGE	Susanna Hughes		
STEPHANIE'S DOMAIN	Susanna Hughes		
STEPHANIE'S TRIAL	Susanna Hughes		
STEPHANIE'S PLEASURE	Susanna Hughes		Sep
THE TEACHING OF FAITH	Elizabeth Bruce		
THE TRAINING GROUNDS	Sarah Veitch		

EROTIC SCIENCE FICTION

ADVENTURES IN THE PLEASUREZONE	Delaney Silver	
RETURN TO THE PLEASUREZONE	Delaney Silver	
FANTASYWORLD	Larry Stern	Oct
WANTON	Andrea Arven	

ANCIENT & FANTASY SETTINGS

CHAMPIONS OF LOVE	Anonymous		
CHAMPIONS OF PLEASURE	Anonymous		
CHAMPIONS OF DESIRE	Anonymous		
THE CLOAK OF APHRODITE	Kendal Grahame		Nov
SLAVE OF LIDIR	Aran Ashe	£4.50	
DUNGEONS OF LIDIR	Aran Ashe		
THE FOREST OF BONDAGE	Aran Ashe	£4.50	
PLEASURE ISLAND	Aran Ashe		
WITCH QUEEN OF VIXANIA	Morgana Baron		

EDWARDIAN, VICTORIAN & OLDER EROTICA

ANNIE	Evelyn Culber	
ANNIE AND THE SOCIETY	Evelyn Culber	Oct
BEATRICE	Anonymous	
CHOOSING LOVERS FOR JUSTINE	Aran Ashe	
GARDENS OF DESIRE	Roger Rougiere	
THE LASCIVIOUS MONK	Anonymous	
LURE OF THE MANOR	Barbra Baron	
MAN WITH A MAID 1	Anonymous	
MAN WITH A MAID 2	Anonymous	
MAN WITH A MAID 3	Anonymous	
MEMOIRS OF A CORNISH GOVERNESS	Yolanda Celbridge	
TIME OF HER LIFE	Josephine Scott	
VIOLETTE	Anonymous	

THE JAZZ AGE

BLUE ANGEL DAYS	Margarete von Falkensee	
BLUE ANGEL NIGHTS	Margarete von Falkensee	
BLUE ANGEL SECRETS	Margarete von Falkensee	
CONFESSIONS OF AN ENGLISH MAID	Anonymous	
PLAISIR D'AMOUR	Anne-Marie Villefranche	
FOLIES D'AMOUR	Anne-Marie Villefranche	
JOIE D'AMOUR	Anne-Marie Villefranche	
MYSTERE D'AMOUR	Anne-Marie Villefranche	
SECRETS D'AMOUR	Anne-Marie Villefranche	
SOUVENIR D'AMOUR	Anne-Marie Villefranche	
WAR IN HIGH HEELS	Piers Falconer	

SAMPLERS & COLLECTIONS

EROTICON 1	ed. J-P Spencer	
EROTICON 2	ed. J-P Spencer	
EROTICON 3	ed. J-P Spencer	
EROTICON 4	ed. J-P Spencer	
NEW EROTICA 1	ed. Esme Ombreux	
NEW EROTICA 2	ed. Esme Ombreux	
THE FIESTA LETTERS	ed. Chris Lloyd	£4.50

NON-FICTION

FEMALE SEXUAL AWARENESS	B & E McCarthy	£5.99	
HOW TO DRIVE YOUR MAN WILD IN BED	Graham Masterton		
HOW TO DRIVE YOUR WOMAN WILD IN BED	Graham Masterton		
LETTERS TO LINZI	Linzi Drew		
LINZI DREW'S PLEASURE GUIDE	Linzi Drew		

Please send me the books I have ticked above.

Name ....

Address ....

....

.... Post code ....

Send to: **Cash Sales, Nexus Books, 332 Ladbroke Grove, London W10 5AH**

Please enclose a cheque or postal order, made payable to **Nexus Books**, to the value of the books you have ordered plus postage and packing costs as follows:

UK and BFPO – £1.00 for the first book, 50p for the second book, and 30p for each subsequent book to a maximum of £3.00;

Overseas (including Republic of Ireland) – £2.00 for the first book, £1.00 for the second book, and 50p for each subsequent book.

If you would prefer to pay by VISA or ACCESS/MASTERCARD, please write your card number here:

Please allow up to 28 days for delivery

— — — —   — — — —   — — — —   — — — —

Signature: _____